THRESHOLD

THRESHOLD

ROB DOYLE

B L O O M S B U R Y   P U B L I S H I N G
NEW YORK • LONDON • OXFORD • NEW DELHI • SYDNEY

BLOOMSBURY PUBLISHING
Bloomsbury Publishing Inc.
1385 Broadway, New York, NY 10018, USA

BLOOMSBURY, BLOOMSBURY PUBLISHING, and the Diana logo are trademarks of
Bloomsbury Publishing Plc

First published in 2020 in Great Britain
First published in the United States 2020

Extracts from the following used with kind permission:
True Hallucinations by Terence McKenna. Copyright © 1993 by Terence McKenna. Courtesy of
HarperCollins Publishers.
The Archaic Revival by Terence McKenna. Copyright © 1991 by Terence McKenna. Courtesy of
HarperCollins Publishers.
Visions of Excess: Selected Writings 1927–1939 by Georges Bataille. English translation copyright ©
1985 by the University of Minnesota. Originally published in George Bataille's *Oeuvres complètes*;
copyright © 1970 by Editions Gallimard.
DMT: The Spirit Molecule by Rick Strassman, M.D. published by Inner Traditions International
and Bear & Company, © 2000. All rights reserved. http://www.Innertraditions.com Reprinted with
permission of publisher.
Nadja by André Breton, translated by Richard Howard. English translation copyright © 1960 by
Grove Press. Original publication copyright © 1928 by Librarie Gallimard. Used by permission of
Grove Atlantic.
I Love Dick by Chris Kraus. Copyright © 1997, 2006 by Chris Kraus. Used by permission of
Serpent's Tail (UK) and Semiotext(e) (US and Canada).
"Mirror in February" by Thomas Kinsella. Originally published by Dolmen Press in *Downstream*;
copyright © 1962 by Thomas Kinsella. Used by permission of the author.
Georges Bataille: Essential Writings by Michael Richardson. Copyright © 1998 by Michael
Richardson. All rights reserved. Used by permission of Sage Publishing and Grasset.
Robert Bolaño: The Last Interview and Other Conversations compiled and translated by Melville
House Publishing. "The Last Interview" originally published by *Playboy* Mexico; copyright © 2003
by Monica Maristain. Used by permission of Melville House Publishing.
The Crying of Lot 49 by Thomas Pynchon. Copyright © 1965, 1966 by Thomas Pynchon. Used by
permission of Melanie Jackson Agency.
Tres by Roberto Bolaño, translated by Laura Healy, copyright © 2000 by the Heirs of Roberto
Bolaño, translation copyright © 2011 by Laura Healy. Reprinted by permission of New Directions
Publishing Corp. *Tres* by Roberto Bolaño. Copyright © The Estate of Roberto Bolaño, 2000, used
by permission of the Wylie Agency (UK) Limited.
"The Sea Close By" in "Summer," 1954 by Albert Camus, translated by Ellen Conroy Kennedy
© 1970, used by permission of Penguin Random House LLC (US) and the Wylie Agency (UK)
Limited on behalf of the Camus estate. *Lyrical and Critical Essays* copyright © 1950, 1951, 1954,
1956, 1958, 1959, 1963 by Editions Gallimard.

Bloomsbury Publishing Plc does not have any control over, or responsibility for, any third-party
websites referred to or in this book. All internet addresses given in this book were correct at the
time of going to press. The author and publisher regret any inconvenience caused if addresses have
changed or sites have ceased to exist, but can accept no responsibility for any such changes.

ISBN: HB: 978-1-63557-414-2; EBOOK: 978-1-63557-415-9
Library of Congress Cataloging-in-Publication Data is available.

2 4 6 8 10 9 7 5 3 1

Typeset by Newgen KnowledgeWorks Pvt. Ltd., Chennai, India
Printed and bound in the U.S.A. by Berryville Graphics Inc., Berryville, Virginia

To find out more about our authors and books visit www.bloomsbury.com and
sign up for our newsletters

Bloomsbury books may be purchased for business or promotional use. For information on bulk
purchases please contact Macmillan Corporate and Premium Sales Department at specialmarkets@
macmillan.com.

To Simon Kelly, to Róisín Kiberd, and to Paul Maguire

Even if it's often a question of getting high, it's not a work about getting high, but about the idea of existence as a drifting boat with no port of arrival. The main subject of the film is rather the sentimentality of mammals and the shimmering vacuity of the human experience.

Gaspar Noé, *interview*

So you should view this fleeting world.

The Diamond Sutra

I'm staying on the top floor of a tower block on the edge of Zagreb. I've never been to Eastern Europe before. I got here on Friday. It's now Sunday afternoon. I have beside me an opened 500 ml bottle of Tomislav dark beer 7.3%. I've eaten today a banana and a handful of blueberries, and drunk a cup of instant coffee. I watched the end of a horror film I had started streaming on Friday night but was too scared or distracted to watch until the end in a dark room. I also watched several porn clips, mostly of women pissing, which never particularly interested me before.

Last night Ana, the representative of the publishing house, took me to see a punk gig with her friends. This turned into a binge that went on until 4 a.m. I drank a bottle of Westmalle Tripel 9.5% beer, then a shot of rakia, then a bottle of Tomislav, then several bottles of a beer called Budweiser Dark, and more shots of honey-flavoured rakia. I took the tram back to my flat at 4:50 a.m. I went to bed at 6 a.m. after streaming an anime video.

On Friday morning, on the plane from Dublin, my nerves were frayed from too much coffee and my thoughts were horribly obsessive. To relieve the nervous tension I filled some pages in my notebook which is marked 'Anything'. I wrote about how a few people would have to die if I'm ever to be happy. I wrote about how civilisation forbids me from acting on my violent urges (I smile, shake hands), so my instincts wither inside me, making me unhealthy. I had a changeover at Munich and when I got to Zagreb I was informed that my luggage had never left Dublin. A listless woman in a drab lost-and-found office took my number

1

and gave me an overnight emergency pack, which contained the following items: folding pocket comb and mirror; small tube of Colgate toothpaste; toothbrush; T-shirt in XXL size; razor; tube of shaving cream; tube of shampoo; small packet of detergent.

You told me you are burned out and hate books, hate writers, hate the reasons why books are written and the reasons they seem to be read, hate even your own work. Incidentally, I used to live for hate but now I am often frightened of it. Some say it is self-indulgent to write about oneself but there is nothing more self-indulgent than writing. I consider myself cowardly in some ways and brave in others. Outside my room there is a steel balcony, and clusters of what I like to imagine are communist-era high-rises in the middle distance. The blue tram shuttles in and out of the city centre. The Croatian women are shockingly beautiful – as beautiful as the French but vivacious, game. Some of them have deep, masculine voices. Many of them are strikingly tall, as are the men. In a world without consequence I would like to have sex with a different woman every day of my life. I am angry almost all of the time, arguably without justification. Some of my friends have started having children, many of them have not. On Tuesday I turned 34. A friend emailed and said, 'What age are you, 34?' Seeing the figure on the screen was disturbing. But this also happened at 19, 28, 30. It's all relative. I turned 30 in San Francisco when my life was carnage and failure. For years I have worried that I drink too much. For years I have been drinking too much. After I send this I will head out to the city. The birds that landed on the balcony have flown away. Write to me about shame. Or puzzlement. Or hate. Tell me something that nobody knows.

Mushroom

Some time ago I lived for a year in Stoneybatter, the pleasantly self-contained neighbourhood of brick terraces just north of the Liffey. My back garden, as I soon came to think of it, was the Phoenix Park – its seven hundred hectares began just a five-minute walk from my door. A couple of weeks after I moved in, I arranged with my friend Fran to go picking magic mushrooms in the park. It was mid-October, the height of the season.

Even if we hadn't found any mushrooms, it would have been a well-spent evening. Phoenix Park is resplendent at that time of year, ablaze with golds, mauves, browns and greens under vast skies. I'd been going out there a lot since moving to the area, to wander in the open spaces and the cold invigorating air. Fran is in his forties and has been taking magic mushrooms since his teens. He has been coming to the park during picking season for several years now, after chancing upon a batch during a walk with a friend. I had only ever been out foraging for mushrooms a couple of times in my life, with moderate success – once at the Sugar Loaf, in County Wicklow, and later on the hills along Dublin's southern coast. While I might be liable to confuse the 'magic', psilocybin-containing mushroom with similar but non-hallucinogenic varieties, Fran knows exactly what to pick. The target variety – *Psilocybe semilanceata*, commonly known as the liberty cap – is quite small, and smooth, with brownish-white stems; Fran advised me to look for 'the little nipple on top'. We found about fifty liberty caps that evening, most of them near the trail of the herd of deer that roams through the park: magic mushrooms tend to grow in fields fertilised by the faeces of certain herbivores, such as deer, cattle and sheep.

We split the mushrooms evenly, and dried them out in our respective homes, pressed between sheets of newspaper. When they were dried, the mushrooms shrivelled into stringy, dark-brown, faintly sinister-looking versions of their handsome former selves. A week later, Fran and I made an infusion by boiling them up in a pot at my house. Some users of Irish magic mushrooms prefer to bake them into a cake, or spread them on a pizza. The mushrooms can also be eaten directly: for a nice hit, you roll about twenty of them into a ball and gobble it down. The only drawback to the direct method is the possibility of stomach cramps caused by bacteria that the boiling process kills off.

It was a Wednesday afternoon: Fran had got off work early for the occasion. We drank the mushroom tea, hung around the house till the effects began to be felt, and then wrapped up in scarves and beanie hats and walked out to the park. It was a mild trip and, for me, undercut with anxiety. We had not taken a strong enough dose to have full-on hallucinations, only an intensification of the visual field, with heightened colours and vivid, shifting surfaces, together with a quickening of the intellect, a capacity to reflect on memories, ideas and phenomena from novel perspectives. I later wondered if the anxiety the excursion brought out in me had been triggered by a few stray mushrooms of a malign variety we had inadvertently cooked up in our brew. Likelier, though, it was a manifestation of the latent anxiety I carry around with me at all times, a free-floating dread that seizes on to whatever object presents itself.

After a couple of hours, the anxiety passed. It was another beautiful, slow-burning autumn evening, another limitless sky. We came upon the herd of deer. As the sun set, we watched them retreat into a copse at the end of the elevated plains, the antlered males stationed around the perimeter as sentries, the does and fawns calmly blinking at us as they ambled among the foliage. By the time night had fallen, the only other people in the park were joggers, mostly in clusters, with flashlights fixed to their heads. Without having to make much of an effort, we picked another small batch of mushrooms as we wandered. One more heavy rainfall, said Fran, and the park would be full of them.

It rained the next day. The day after that, a Friday, while most of the city was at work, I set out alone on my bike with an empty salt-and-vinegar Pringles tube. I cycled past the Wellington Monument, that towering imperialistic monolith proclaiming battles won and enemies vanquished, with the listed names of faraway cities up each side – a phallic Ozymandias declaring the grandeur of a dissolved empire as children played and students strummed guitars around its base. Fran had told me that the metal used in the engravings that adorned the monument had been stripped from captured enemy cannons. I recorded in my notebook the vainglorious paean etched on one of the monument's sides, presumably to the Duke of Wellington:

ASIA AND EUROPE, SAVED BY THEE,
PROCLAIM INVINCIBLE IN WAR THY
DEATHLESS NAME, NOW ROUND THY
BROW THE CIVIC OAK WE TWINE, THAT
EVERY EARTHLY GLORY MAY BE THINE

I too had played at the foot of the monument as a child, with no understanding of its significance, nor its curious poignancy, its sense of having been left behind, an erratic, far from home.

I cycled up the hill, from where there are views over the quaint, tree-lined village of Chapelizod and the Liffey valley, the city, and the mountains in the distance. I passed the old arsenal, now a well-fortified concrete shell, from where the British used to keep watch over the city, poised to quell any insurrection and enforce the ominous motto emblazoned on the city's coat of arms: *An obedient populace is a happy populace.* Then

I was out on to the plains, with the looming white cross on the far side, erected in 1979 to commemorate the papal visit. More than a million people attended that visit, one of whom was a seven-year-old Fran, despite his parents being determinedly secular. The papal visit took place in late September, so it is likely that a great many magic mushrooms were trampled under the feet of the multitudes. A series of well-tended football pitches stretched along the length of this raised section of the park, ending with the copse where we had watched the deer, fringed by a road dropping into a valley.

I stayed out there for three or four hours, and picked about three hundred mushrooms. I didn't really want the mushrooms for myself and thought I would give most or all of them away. It's something about being in my thirties: the appeal of psychedelics has receded, and the unease I associate with drug usage in general has increased. Maybe it is natural, a self-preservative mechanism that kicks in at a certain age, or maybe I just have more to be apprehensive about. But even if I didn't really want them, I thought it good that others have them. The magic mushroom is among a handful of psychotropic substances that I have, with certain qualifications, actively encouraged others to try, whose wonders it seems to me a shame to get through a human life without encountering. The psychedelic experience, I have long felt, is so astonishing, opens up such startling vistas of beauty and otherness, that to live and die without knowing it is comparable to never having encountered literature, or travelled to another continent, or attempted to communicate in a foreign language.

I first tried magic mushrooms in my early twenties. I can't remember the precise occasion, nor much about the trip, but it must have been pretty good or I wouldn't have taken to them so enthusiastically afterwards. Before trying mushrooms, I had felt towards psychedelic substances the same sort of curiosity that drew me to philosophy, art and literature, particularly those varieties that trafficked in the mysterious, the sublime, the fantastical and the shocking. At the root of my interest in both drugs and art was the longing for an encounter with otherness, a seeking-out of astonishment for its own sake. The craving for fascination that I slaked with the work of, say, Borges, or the more colourfully speculative branches of philosophy – the Presocratics, Nietzsche, the Hindu metaphysicians – also motivated me to investigate the mind-altering effects of plant hallucinogens, and drugs in general. The counterpoint to this hunger for the strange and the sublime was the profound boredom I felt for the world I had grown up in, the revulsion for what seemed to me a crushingly drab, incurious, cultureless environment.

Down the years, I have had many wildly enjoyable, sometimes awesome trips on magic mushrooms, and a few bad ones. Most of the latter have been largely my own fault: I took the mushrooms irresponsibly, wilfully so, in the wrong circumstances and frames of mind. Thelonious Monk had a line about how he would start his improvisations by striking the *wrong* chord: the music would flow as he tried to make his way back to the right one. For a while, I told myself that my attitude to taking magic mushrooms was in a similar vein, but really it had more to do with impatience and recklessness, and the results sometimes were terrifying, though they never lasted more than a few hours, and usually resolved in a plateau of insight, serenity and euphoria.

A decade before I foraged in the Phoenix Park, Ireland had gone through a period, lasting a couple of years and now legendary among aficionados, during which magic mushrooms from around the world were legally available for over-the-counter purchase. The most commonly propagated version of how this golden age came about is that a Trinity College law student discovered a loophole in Irish legislation: while it was illegal to process or prepare magic mushrooms, it was lawful to possess and sell them in their natural state. When knowledge of the loophole became general, around 2004, outlets across Ireland began selling mushrooms legally, importing potent varieties from Thailand, Mexico, Indonesia and elsewhere. The mushrooms were kept in refrigeration and could therefore be sold and consumed fresh, circumventing the law. My friends and I, enthusiastic about drugs in general (with some exceptions – I never really knew anyone who had taken heroin, for instance), greeted the new-found availability of these exotic mushrooms with an exploratory zeal. There was one summer when we bought and ate mushrooms pretty much every weekend, usually to ecstatic effect. As summer faded into autumn, we realised we needed to lay off them for a while: perhaps as a somatic braking mechanism against an accumulation of psilocybin in our systems, our trips became harrowing and unpleasant, despite our efforts to take the mushrooms in congenial moods and settings (often in the flat of one of our group, with music and musical instruments on hand).

Before that, there were some memorable occasions. There was the birthday of a friend of mine who lived in a shared house in Bayside along with my then girlfriend. It was a sunny evening; we had erected a marquee and spent the day drinking beer and having a laugh. As the sun set, five or six of us ate the Thai *cubensis* mushrooms we had bought from a head shop in Temple Bar. The effects lasted for hours, were blissful and intellectually stimulating, and inspired us to retreat into the garage, which my friend had converted into a music studio. There, we performed and recorded a chaotic, instrument-swapping, genuinely psychedelic sonic extravaganza that, when we listened to it soberly the following day, really was what it had seemed to be in the moment of creation: the weirdest music we had ever made, in youths devoted to making weird music. A friend mastered the live mix and we put out a few DIY copies under the band name Heads Will Roll.

That same summer, a ginger-haired friend we'd met in college invited us out to camp and surf with him on a deserted beach in his native Mayo. I had little interest in surfing but, like my friends, I reckoned that the raw Atlantic coast, with its dramatic skies, was an ideal venue for yet another mushroom trip. The first night was a disaster: my friends and I, city-dwellers all, had made no real preparations for a night in the screaming wind and cruel cold of a remote Mayo beach. We took some mushrooms (*Psilocybe tampanensis*, also known as philosophers' stones or, to us, truffles) then sat there for hours, shivering in misery and darkness. The effects of the mushrooms conspired with our physical discomfort to provoke relentless, brutal introspection – a long dark night of grim self-confrontation. In the morning, though, we found we once more had a huge, golden stretch of beach, crashing sea, plunging dunes and revivifying sun all to ourselves. The others put on wetsuits and got ready to surf, while I decided to eat the remainder of the mushrooms and wander off alone.

I was gone maybe four hours. I followed the beach out to where there was no trace of anyone. I climbed dunes and walked along the crest of the sea. As I moved, the psilocybin flooded my system, nurtured by the warm sun, the stretching of my limbs, and the beauty and expansiveness of my surroundings. There are certain experiences that are impossible to describe satisfactorily, which you can only know by having them yourself. So I'll keep it relatively brief: alone on the beach, which felt endless, I lay down in the warm sand, sheltered by a towering dune, and watched the sky. It would have been magnificent even without psilocybin; with it, the vastness of swirling, voluptuous clouds framed by bottomless blue became an immense mosaic, depicting a cosmic drama of copulation, birth, transformation and unlimited eroticism. All boundaries were erased – women, men, children and beasts fused in amorous plenitude, a shifting, simultaneous fulfilment of every carnal yearning and sensuous whim. I drank it all in, smiling helplessly at times, powerfully aroused yet deeply serene. As ever, there was a faint sadness to the experience: I knew, even as I was undergoing it, that I could never possibly express the richness of it to anyone else, neither through art nor conversation. Having no skill for painting and being a mediocre musician, the best I could hope for was a few inadequate sentences in a book such as this one. Some hours later, sated with wonder, bliss and insight, I got up and walked slowly back along the empty miles of the beach, to my friends, who were cooking sausages on the stove.

In October of 2005, a thirty-three-year-old businessman named Colm Hodkinson bought a carton of mushrooms for twenty-five euro from a shop on Capel Street. He ate three of the mushrooms at a party in a friend's apartment the evening before Halloween. Having vomited and alarmed his friends by exhibiting signs of panic and confusion, he rushed to the top of the building and went over the edge, falling to his death. In the days following his funeral, Hodkinson's family campaigned to have magic mushrooms criminalised. This led to a meeting with the then Tánaiste and Minister for Health and Children, Mary Harney. At the end of the meeting, Harney, moved to tears, promised the Hodkinsons that legislation criminalising magic mushrooms would be enacted without delay, and so it was. 'It was a bit of an anticlimax when we heard the news,' said Sean Hodkinson, Colm's brother, after the new law had been put in place. 'We were surprised that it happened so quickly. Mary Harney said it would happen within three weeks and it did. But there was no elation, just a kind of emptiness.'

Since 31 January 2006, it has been illegal to possess or sell magic mushrooms in Ireland, including the kind that grow wild in the country. I left Ireland in the spring of that year, and would not properly return for another seven years, during which time I made it my business to see as much of the world as possible. The next time I took magic mushrooms was in Thailand, in a wooden hut that served as a bar and cafe perched atop a hill in the centre of the paradisal island of Ko Pha-Ngan. I rode up there on a rented motorbike along with French and German friends. We bought the mushrooms at the bar – it wasn't legal, but it was tolerated (payments had probably been made). We had fun, and mild hallucinations, but not the deep psychedelia and startling insights I had experienced on stronger doses. A year or so later, I was travelling and living in South America. There, I had several marvellous encounters with the hallucinogenic cactus San Pedro, which grows on the Altiplano of Bolivia and Peru. Later, first in Peru and then in Colombia, I had many even more intense experiences with the hybrid hallucinogen ayahuasca (or yagé), generally considered among the most potent psychoactive substances in the world. Ayahuasca is a central part of the cultural and religious life of some indigenous tribespeople of Amazonia. The friends with whom I gathered to drink ayahuasca every weekend at an artist's house in the hills outside Bogotá were professors, writers, artists and scholars, mostly in middle age, who had been deeply involved with the experiential, scientific and philosophical study of yagé for many years. The ceremonies were always overseen by their friend Crispin, a young, softly spoken shaman (or *taita*, in his own dialect) from the Amazonian south. Crispin travelled up to the capital each weekend bearing several flasks of the foul-tasting concoction. His entire life revolved around ayahuasca. Throughout the imbibing ceremonies, during which fragrant woods were burned, smoke wafted and incantations uttered, Crispin referred to the yagé with the affectionate, diminutive form *yagécito* – as if the spirit that he believed animated the brew was his otherworldly little friend. Ayahuasca exerted such fascination on me that I made plans to return home and begin a PhD on the affinities between the atheistic mysticism of Georges Bataille, Nietzsche and other Western philosophers and the psychedelic shamanism of the Amazon basin.

It was in South America too that I first came upon the writings of the ethnobotanist Terence McKenna, a brilliant advocate of the consciousness-expanding effects of hallucinogenic plants. Even if the often jaw-dropping ideas suggested in books of McKenna's like *The Archaic Revival* and *Food of the Gods* turned out not to be true, they could still be read with great pleasure, and to wildly stimulating effect, as an outré breed of speculative or science fiction. Throughout his work, McKenna puts forward the claim that it was plant hallucinogens, particularly psilocybin mushrooms, sprouting in various parts of the world and offering consciousness-enhancing evolutionary advantages which enabled the great leaps forward in human culture that, among other things, provided the ur-experience of religion.

McKenna sometimes deploys a sober, professorial voice while putting forward arguments that, if true, would hurl into disarray all that our orthodox philosophies hold to be the case. In an essay entitled 'Mushrooms and Evolution', he writes: 'For tens of millennia human beings have been utilising hallucinogenic mushrooms to divine and induce shamanic ecstasy. I propose to show that the human–mushroom interaction is not a static symbiotic relationship, but rather a dynamic one through which at least one of the parties has been bootstrapped to higher and higher cultural levels.' Here we glimpse one of the strange notions about magic mushrooms that find fuller expression elsewhere in McKenna's work, namely that the mushrooms may constitute an intentional, conscious species – that they, in some sense, have an agenda.

McKenna insists that 'the mushroom religion is actually the generic religion of human beings', and that 'all later adumbrations of religion stem from the cult of ritual ingestion of mushrooms to induce ecstasy'. Elsewhere he makes even more vehement claims for the ontological implications of the experiences offered by other plant hallucinogens, in particular ayahuasca and its psychoactive component, DMT (N,N-dimethyltryptamine). The numinous and profoundly weird experiences produced by these substances, in which one will frequently have a compelling sense of coming into contact with entities, landscapes and intelligences external to the self, and even to broader human experience, are *religio* mainlined – not prayers, art, texts and rituals gesturing towards the ineffable, the transcendent Other, but the thing itself. The shamanic imbibing ceremonies of the *ayahuasceros* of the Amazonian region offer immediate access to a 'hyperdimensional' and 'hyperspatial' zone that McKenna claims is teeming with non-human entities. Perhaps it is futile to voice McKenna's more outlandish claims to those who have never experienced the effects of the plant hallucinogens at high doses ('heroic doses', in McKenna's exhortative phrase), but to those who do have first-hand experience of the deeply alien, sometimes shocking vistas they open up, his ideas may not seem so far-fetched.

The next time I ingested magic mushrooms was a number of years later, in San Francisco, where I lived for a few months. My then girlfriend, not a drug user, had been given a bag of mushrooms by a friend. There were enough for two or three people to enjoy a strong trip, but I persuaded myself otherwise and consumed the entirety of the contents one thickly overcast early afternoon. I then left our apartment to wander around Haight-Ashbury, one-time mecca of the hippy dream and now a sordid, dismal zone of wrecked aspiration. Soon realising that I had consumed a formidable dosage, I retreated to the top of Buena Vista Park, a steep, forested hill from where one can see the bay, the Golden Gate Bridge, the skyscrapers of downtown San Francisco, Ocean Beach and the Pacific. As fog swarmed in to engulf the hill, I plunged into dread. All of my semi-repressed anxieties – the full awareness of the catastrophe I was then living – rose to the surface. Growing desperate, I felt the only hope I had was to adopt a meditative posture and marshal all my psychic and emotional resources in order not to become swallowed up in the black hole of my own terror. The hallucinations were so strong that, at the height of it, it made little difference whether my eyes were open or closed. As I gradually grew calmer and gained a hold on my fears, intense but more benign emotions flooded me. I had a vision of twenty-first-century America as a wasteland of broken, defeated people, a sorrowing mass of human wreckage and unanswered prayers – I knew then that I could not live there permanently, a possibility I had been strongly considering. By the time I finally came down from the hill, it felt like a very long time had passed. In reality, it was about six hours. The trip was distressing, yet not one I regretted having. The next morning I began writing a short story that delved deep into sorrow and trauma and emerged, I thought, with some glinting shard of truth.

In the Phoenix Park, the sun was setting as I continued filling my Pringles container with liberty caps. As I stooped by the white paint markings of a soccer pitch, a man who was walking his dog along the pathway greeted me and enquired if I was picking magic mushrooms. I said I was and we began to chat. He was in late middle age, with grey hair, and was amiable and respectable. He told me that he and his friends had picked and consumed magic mushrooms for years in their youth. They used to go out to the Curragh, he said, and fill up cornflakes boxes with enough mushrooms to last the entire year, until it was time to go picking again. 'We'd just sit there, in one of the lads' places, and laugh all night,' he said. He tentatively warned me about being seen picking mushrooms by the police. 'To them it's probably the same as if you had a box full of LSD,' he said, but admitted he wasn't entirely sure of what the law stated. He was thoughtful for a moment, watching his dog as it scampered by a goalpost. 'It's a bit silly, when you think of it,' he said. 'People were picking these things long before there were Guards. The mushrooms were growing here before there was any legislation at all. Can something be illegal that grows in the ground?'

He said he had picked up a few of the mushrooms earlier, noticing that they did indeed look like the hallucinogenic variety, but a friend had warned him that these were a 'mimicking' kind, not the real thing. He was wary about picking the wrong ones because of a bad trip he'd once had, at the twilight of his psychedelic youth, when one or two 'bad shrooms' must have gone into the mushroom cake he and his friends had baked. 'I totally freaked out. Took me about two weeks to get back to normal.' He wished me well and hoped I had a good time.

I remember telling a friend, when I was twenty or so, that I took drugs so that one day I wouldn't have to take drugs. The idea was that, by gaining access to the weirder potentialities of consciousness, my basic stance towards existence would be altered: shorn of the tedium and banality that oppressed me in those years, I hoped I could come to experience consciousness itself, and the bare fact of being in the world, as ineffable, awesome, impregnably mysterious. The funny thing is that this really did happen. The occasional mushroom excursion aside, I rarely bother with drugs any more. The drugs I took in my youth – along with the art, literature and philosophy I imbibed with equal enthusiasm – helped to reconfigure the lineaments of my consciousness so that, nowadays, the mere fact of being here at all, the fact that something exists, consistently astonishes me. I don't mean to suggest that one needs drugs, or even art or philosophy, to connect with the mystery of being, the supreme unlikeliness of finding oneself alive in an unaccountable universe. I mean only that I spent part of my youth oppressed by a boredom I now consider to have been a delusion, born of the depressive belief that the world around me was mundane, paltry, comprehensible. Bitterly at odds with my surroundings, I needed certain jolts to get me back in touch with my own capacity for wonder, which I now happily find to be a self-replenishing source.

A week after I had spent my Friday in the Phoenix Park, my girlfriend Alice was visiting from France, and my friend Sam came up from Wexford for the night. It was Halloween – the old pagan feast of Samhain, as Sam reminded me. The three of us had dinner at my place, in candlelight, with the fireplace blazing and music from Spotify streaming through the speakers. After dinner, I boiled up a brew. The anxieties I had attached to the mushrooms a week earlier had dissolved. The mood was ideal; I knew we would have a lovely time. Neither Alice nor Sam had ever taken magic mushrooms before, so I kept it mild. There was no anxiety, no unwelcome intensity, only joy, laughter and keen, open conversation. Later we wrapped up warm and walked to the Cobblestone pub, where a cluster of traditional musicians were playing in a corner, and some of the clientele were dressed as pirates, ghouls and zombies. Before going to bed that night, I swallowed the mushrooms I had boiled earlier, so that whatever residual psilocybin remained in them would animate my sleep. And so it did: I slept deeply, with strange, otherworldly dreams. I wandered through ancient hallways, encountering gods and sculpted sages who were immeasurably older than me, and who regarded me with solemn, unfathomable gazes before looking away towards unseen horizons, bearing intentions I would never understand.

I expected Zagreb and its inhabitants to be war-scarred, mistrustful, hardened, but it's relaxed and pleasant. Ana seems happy to show me around, which means the solitude is not freighted with the awareness, familiar from other cities, of having to fill each hour of every empty day. Today I slept till noon. I've been dreaming well here – brilliant, vivid dreams. Then I wake up and check my phone, and any connection I have to that world is lost.

The photographs I sent are from a day spent walking in the residential areas beyond the centre. I relish overcast days in foreign cities, in the afternoon when no one is around. The playgrounds are empty, the breeze rustles the trees. It's good to be hungover on such days: it opens you out, makes you receptive. I imagine that my human life is a mission from some other universe: the purpose of writing is to record my impressions of this earth-world, and send them back there – an audience of aliens. Yesterday I saw an exhibition by a Norwegian photographer who lived in Tokyo. She wrote: 'Skyscrapers and gaming arcades help me construct a holographic city in images and memory, a fictitious city that is based on an actual place.'

If I am 'either writing myself into a novel or writing myself out of one', as you too seem to be doing (will these visions overlap?), a question arises: how much effort should I put into rendering myself as a 'sympathetic character'? Am I one of those? To you, say? While we're on the subject, let's define our terms. For my purposes, a novel is simply a long chunk of prose in which whatever is said to have happened may or may not have actually happened, even if the author *doesn't bother to change his own name, but changes the names of others, or invents these others wholesale. In short, a novel is anything I tell it to be. By the same token, whatever I point at and call novel, is novel – even if it looks like memoir, travelogue or naked confession. This is an old argument, endlessly renewed. It doesn't matter – it's something to read. The idea, like I told you in that weird cafe in Hackney, is to write a book whose binding tissue is not overt narrative but obsessions, fascinations, places I can't move on from till I've written them out, visions of my life as it is or might have been. The narrative is what becomes of the consciousness that passes through all this experience and through which all this experience passes.*

I started writing a column for a right-wing newspaper. They suggested the topics, which were of no interest to me. I wrote it and it was published the next day. (One friend advised: 'You should use your position for evil.') It amused me to write the column because I knew it would be mildly disgraceful among my peers to write for a conservative newspaper. As soon as you're liked you've been tamed, co-opted. I don't know if I believe that. I sometimes fantasise about being a hate figure, a Shylock, but I don't have the constitution for it.

Anyway, opinions are the sewage of the world, aren't they. 'Think pieces', tweets, columns. Have you stopped writing that kind of stuff? I hope you have. I wouldn't have seen it – I'm in retreat from the internet.

You're what, ten years older than me? You've had children, been married, owned property. You chose x wherever I chose y. But we're not so far apart in how we live now: the moving around, the hustling, the laughable loves.

Where are you now? Who do you sleep with?

Sicily

At a time in my life when I was entirely without direction and aware of having achieved little beyond consuming psychedelics and drifting through far-off countries, I moved to Sicily for a few months. I had found a language school online advertising teaching vacancies in the town of Alcamo, an hour outside of Palermo, perched on a hill overlooking the Gulf of Castellammare. I did an interview over the phone with the Scottish woman who managed the school, knowing as she chattered away that I would treat the job as I've treated every other job I've had: with contempt, as a means to pursue my private ends. I assured her I had a passion for teaching, worked well in groups, was basically a people person, all the while sounding her out for any corners I might cut, gauging the absolute minimum of work I could get away with so as to direct my energies elsewhere.

I intended to spend my time in Sicily writing a novel, which I had tentatively begun that winter while living in my parents' house in Dublin and claiming the dole, after the school where I'd been teaching went bust.

I liked being on the dole, found that the arrangement suited me well, but I also found it humiliating to live with my parents at that age (I was twenty-six). What was more, I didn't believe I could produce a work of literature in my childhood bedroom.

It was raining hard on the night I flew into Palermo airport – the night after Barack Obama's inauguration – and it did not let up for days. For my first week in Alcamo, the narrow streets and alleys were torrents that flooded my shoes whenever I ventured out to get the measure of my new home. I lived on the top floor of a building in the centre of town that was deserted but for me and my flatmate, Coby, who was also my colleague at the language school. There were no prospects in Alcamo: most of the young people moved north to mainland Italy, or emigrated. On my first night, Coby and I went out for a beer, sitting under a tarpaulin watching the rain hammer down on the piazza.

The following morning we walked to the language school's premises, a minute from our door. Along with Coby and me, the school currently employed a blonde English girl named Georgina, who had arrived a few days earlier. Our boss – the Scottish woman I'd spoken to on the phone – explained that the lessons had not quite started up yet after the Christmas holidays, so there would be little work for two or three weeks at least.

Unable to see much of the island because of the bad weather, I settled into a routine of writing and studying

Italian. Coby was a Miles Davis devotee – he boasted that he had on his hard drive not only every album but every *version* of every album, and every bootleg, live recording, demo and outtake known to exist – and as I worked, music drifted in from the living room and kitchen, where Coby cooked aromatic pasta dishes I always hoped (in vain) he would share. When the rain held off I took walks around the town. Alcamo was enclosed by the old town walls, with the gulf and the seaside town of Castellammare laid out below on one side, and hills on the other that led towards the island's interior. The sea was the Tyrrhenian – it thrilled me to live in sight of the Tyrrhenian, to be able to say 'I live in sight of the Tyrrhenian' in the few emails I managed to send (we had no internet at home and a temperamental connection at the school). Our flat had no central heating, only a pair of rickety electric heaters, one of which I had to pull close to my bed every night as I lay gazing at the damp patches on the ceiling.

At the weekends, Coby, Georgina and I drank in Alcamo's five or six bars. Georgina had instantly become a celebrity among the town's young men (and envious young women), who were in a frenzy of competition to win the attentions of this glamorous new arrival. One night, as I watched her being encircled by shiny leather jackets, white T-shirts and predatory grins, an unemployed architect – everyone in Sicily was an unemployed architect, apart from those who were unemployed lawyers – described to me the Sicilian tradition of *la mattanza*. Each year at the start of summer, the island's fishermen would link their boats in a huge ring just off shore, and trap hundreds of the enormous tuna that teemed in Sicily's waters in a vast net. As the net was raised, the fishermen would hack the thrashing tuna with swords and knives, till the sea ran deep crimson.

Another Saturday night, while Georgina was being driven around on the scooter of an admirer, Coby and I sat drinking bottles of strong Belgian beer in a bar named Jack the Ripper. Women came and went in small groups, glancing at us with fleeting curiosity before resuming the detached, bored expressions that seemed to be a requirement of young Sicilian femininity.

'So why Sicily?' I asked Coby when we were on our second beers. The DJ was playing the insipid house music that was dismayingly popular across the island. The track that came on now, which I had heard many times before, featured the refrain 'Love, sex, American Express'.

'Had to go somewhere, I guess,' said Coby. 'I have a buddy here too. Ricardo. He lives on the other side of the island, in Messina. Before I came here I figured Sicily was just like this little island and we could hang out. But it's huge. I haven't even been to visit him yet.'

Coby had little interest in studying Italian, content to get by on whatever he picked up on nights out, bantering with locals. He was a few years older than me, in his early thirties, and had been teaching English as a foreign language on and off since he'd finished college. Every now and then he returned to his hometown in Northern Ontario to 'get fucked up' with his friends who still lived there, but his life had fallen into a rhythm of moving from city to city.

'Bangkok was the best,' he said. 'I wish I didn't screw it up.'

I bought us two more bottles of Chimay and he told the story. He had moved to Bangkok for three years after travelling around South-East Asia. The money was good and the lifestyle pleased him greatly. 'It's not a myth,' he said. 'You can sleep with a different woman every night. Dude, the white man still holds some sway out there. And those girls … Seriously, I thought I'd never be attracted to occidental women again. It's the way a Western guy and an Asian chick's bodies fit together. I call it the Asian Contagion. And the psychology too. Just like how a white woman and a black guy works so well. Miscegenation – man, that is the *future*.'

In Bangkok he hung around with expats, mostly teachers, went out to bars and clubs four or five nights a week. After he'd been there a while, tired of paying too much for drugs, he had a friend back in Canada post some over. First it was just enough for personal use – acid, cocaine, MDMA – but soon he realised he could supplement his teaching wages by selling to friends.

'I wasn't looking to get rich,' he said. 'It was mostly, like, altruistic purposes. Just shit for my friends to get high with. I liked the sort of reputation.'

One afternoon he was coming home from work. As he got off the bus and turned on to the block in downtown Bangkok where he lived, his phone rang. It was an American woman who lived in the same building. She warned him not to come back: the cops were all over his apartment; they had knocked the door down. Now Coby could see the police cars parked around the front of the building, some cops with walkie-talkies stationed outside. He walked away and boarded the first bus he saw. After withdrawing as much as he could from an ATM, he took a taxi to the bus station and boarded a coach out of the city more or less at random. For days he hid in the countryside, even sleeping some nights in a cave.

He finally worked up the nerve to cross the border into Cambodia. From there he flew to India and spent a month in Goa, getting stoned and drunk and 'having a nervous breakdown'. Even now he would wake up in seizures of anxiety, convinced that the Thai police were about to come barging through the door.

'Dude, there was *so much* LSD in that apartment. They would have put me away for life. It's possible I would have been executed.'

'So I take it that was the end of your career as a drug dealer?'

'Hell, no. I've had shit posted here. The Italian cops are dumb. I've got some mescaline I've been saving for a rainy day. As in, a day that isn't rainy.'

Most of our work involved travelling out to nearby towns, some of which were not so near at all – Castellammare, Castelvetrano, Sasi. I didn't have a driving licence, which meant either I was at the mercy of the Sicilian public transport system or I had to be driven by Coby, sometimes Georgina. For the first time in my life I regretted not having learned to drive. Back in Dublin, it hadn't seemed necessary. In Sicily, people were appalled when I told them I didn't have a licence. Sometimes they would stammer embarrassedly, as if I'd confessed some bizarre sexual proclivity.

'*Ma* ... how do you go around?' asked my friend Marco one afternoon on a cafe terrace off the main street. (We met there twice a week so he could practise his English and I my Italian. Marco had a lot of free time on his hands, being an unemployed architect, or perhaps an unemployed lawyer – I've forgotten which.) How *did* I go around? It was a fair question. No more than two or three buses left Alcamo every weekend, at sadistically early hours. The Sicilians' contempt for public transport was almost as great as their contempt for the police. Driving offered them the chance to marry their scorn for the law with their individualistic automotive pride: they weren't happy unless they were going twenty miles an hour over the limit, accelerating into corners, overtaking blindly and generally being so reckless it was a wonder more of them didn't die in fiery smash-ups. But then, many of them *did* die in fiery smash-ups – the sight of wrecked cars by the side of the *autostrade*, with drivers holding their heads in their hands and sirens blaring, became unremarkable. Drunk-driving wasn't just tolerated in Sicily, it was fashionable, almost obligatory. On weekends, we *stranieri* would pile into the car of some local playboy keen to impress Georgina, and race from nightclub to nightclub, a trail of them specked across the north-western coast and inland hills, with the driver pounding back as many vodka and Cokes as the rest of us.

Each Tuesday and Thursday afternoon, Coby and I drove out to teach at a secondary school in Castelvetrano. The town was inland, unrelieved by the sparkling sea that took the edge off the economic depression and social torpor elsewhere. Matteo Messina Denaro, the Sicilian mafia's current *capo dei capi* – the boss of bosses – was born in Castelvetrano. For nearly two decades he had been in hiding, allegedly moving between safe houses scattered across the island. In the last known photograph of him, which the FBI used on their Ten Most Wanted posters (he was in third place then, below Osama bin Laden and 'El Chapo'), Denaro is young and dangerously handsome in shades and a dapper suit.

My students in Castelvetrano were in their final year. There were around thirty pupils, ranging from those with a genuine interest in learning English to those with no interest in anything at all. Among the former was Angelica, smart, lively, eighteen and, I realised within moments of stepping into the classroom for the first time, tormentingly attractive. Seeing her quickly became the only thing that alleviated the tedium of driving out there to teach those suckers in that grim town. As I sat at my desk or slouched by the whiteboard, watching Angelica was even more tempting than watching the clock, though it was tricky to watch either the clock or Angelica with thirty pairs of eyes on me, ready to pounce at any sign of weakness. After going through some grammar and vocabulary, I would give the class a written exercise and sink behind my desk to surreptitiously tinker with printed chapters of my novel. I was frequently caught gazing at Angelica, on one occasion by the school's own *capo dei capi* (the principal), who had been standing in the doorway for Christ knows how long.

I couldn't help it. There is no way to avoid saying this: the period I spent living in Sicily was marked by the most acute sexual frustration. The beauty of the Italians will come as a surprise to nobody – they run neck and neck with the French in a two-horse race to be Europe's most gorgeous people. As the spring arrived and the first glimpses of tanned bare flesh appeared, I was entranced by the beauties that paraded the alleys and streets of Alcamo, or idled on the piazza, or licked ice cream with lascivious abandon outside a 'bar' (that is to say, an Italian bar, namely one that mainly sold coffee and ice cream, therefore not a bar at all). Italy's was a culture devoted to beauty, to sex and its flaunting, a purely visual culture of labels and lingerie, of sexy fascist uniforms and fascistic catwalk modelling. And yet it was also highly conservative, traditional, Catholic. Or maybe that was just Sicily – perhaps it was this conservatism, and not the dearth of jobs and prospects, that compelled the young to emigrate or head north. Perhaps they were not economic migrants but horndog migrants, lust migrants. A superabundance of beauty and sex was everywhere on display, yet it could not be touched – or not by me, at any rate. In my heart I knew that the Sicilians were as actively eroticised as they appeared to be, and the ostensible conservatism was really just a facade, a sort of ideological lingerie to heighten the dizzy pleasures it – just about – concealed. The Sicilians were fucking like rabbits. But I was a foreign teacher in a small town: it would be disastrous if I were to earn a reputation for myself as a fiend, a womaniser, a pervert. I couldn't go for a walk in Alcamo without students waving to me, or having to bid *buongiorno* to a teacher from a local school. Everyone knew who we were, the three *stranieri*. Boiling over with frustration, every night I would jerk off to visions of Angelica – of fucking her over her desk after her classmates had filed out; of pulling aside the flimsy knickers she did or didn't wear under those tight jeans and lapping at her like a dog; of having her straddle me in the toilet stalls amid the stench of shit and the graffiti cocks while the rest of the class hunched over some bullshit exercise, awaiting my return.

Three months in, my sexual confidence had utterly withered. I wondered what the hell I'd been thinking, coming to this shitty island full of untouchable women; I considered getting back in touch with the woman I'd been seeing (and touching) before moving to Sicily – an Italian, just to rub my nose in it. I badly needed to get laid, but the very need made getting laid at all at first unlikely and then utterly impossible. I exuded desperation and the most unattractive thing in the world is desperation. Women instinctively rejected me before I'd even made a move, and so I would jerk off before going to sleep only to wake up half an hour later to jerk off again, my mind polluted with imagery that grew more and more questionable, more and more desperate, by the day. I would have given anything to spend myself inside her, to perish while ejaculating torrentially inside Angelica with one final howl of joy and rage, but I had to make do with pulling myself off while thinking about her. I found myself blushing and stammering whenever I saw her in real life, unable to meet her eye or answer her questions, even such questions as 'Can I go to the toilet?' or 'Do you have my homework from Tuesday?' (I did not: I had jerked off all over it and then burned it, overcome by shame.) I knew that she knew – *everyone* knew. In short, it was a desperate situation and it was going to end badly if I didn't find a girlfriend, one who wasn't my teenage student.

One morning, after a night of jerking off, I awoke to the sound of my alarm clock. I stood under the shower, intending to cleanse myself of the night's encrusted semen and sweat, only to find that no water flowed from the showerhead. Not a drop. Irritated rather than alarmed, I turned the tap on the sink: there was a choked gurgling noise followed by a violent spurt of brown water, and then nothing. It was the same in the kitchen. Coby came slumping out of his bedroom, muttering dazedly to himself as he reached for the cafetière.

'There's no water,' I said.

'What?'

'I've tried all the taps.'

'There's no …?'

'There's no water.'

'Then how am I gonna … make coffee?'

'You're not going to make coffee, Coby. There's no water with which to make it.'

'Dude, there's no water?'

'No.'

'Fuck.'

The lack of water was a real problem, because I was due to teach four lessons that day and I stank of dried semen, of desperation. It was already an uncommonly warm day (this was the beginning of April) and I felt like I was steaming. I hadn't even brushed my teeth.

'Fuck this shit,' said Coby.

'Yes.'

We called our boss, the Scottish woman, because it was she and her school who had sourced the accommodation for us.

'Oh yes, that happens sometimes,' she said chirpily.

I waited for more.

'See you in twenty?' she said.

'But I haven't washed. We can't even flush the toilet.'

She sighed down the phone. 'If it's really urgent, you can probably use Georgina's bathroom.'

I made a point of being late that morning, showering long and leisurely at Georgina's, who sympathised but was a little taken aback to have the two of us in her apartment, taking turns to wash ourselves. When Coby and I returned from work that evening, tired and stressed, the water still hadn't come back on.

It is said that any populace is only three missed meals away from revolution, but not enough has been made of the insurrectionary potential of a water supply that unexpectedly dries up. The discomforts accumulate: you can't wash your hands after you've eaten something sticky; you can't make a cup of tea; you can't clean the dishes that pile up smeared and encrusted, beacons to flies; you can't flush the fucking toilet. Whenever I feel decentred and agitated I like to take a shower, but now I was unable to take a shower, could only dwell on how decentred and agitated I was feeling. Two, three, four days passed and still there was no water. It was a full-blown drought. Had there been any plants in our flat, they would have wilted. At this time the *sirocco*, the hot dry wind that blows in from North Africa, gusted up so that the streets outside were dusty and stinging, no refuge from the aridity of our apartment. The world was a grimy, wind-whipped desert.

Coby and I continued to shower in Georgina's flat, to shit in public toilets and to clean our teeth and make tea from big plastic vats of water we filled at a public fountain. Every day I told myself that enough was enough, we had to stop working until this issue was resolved. I wanted to stage a dirty protest but we were already dirty. My mood was likewise foul. At school I snapped and roared at students, belittled teenagers who couldn't conjugate, made six-year-olds cry by mocking their grammatical errors with acid sarcasm.

One morning, before Coby, Georgina and I set out for our classes, I went to see our Scottish boss and told her that this was the last, absolutely the last, day I would work until she got our water running again. I could not, I said, continue to teach under these Third World conditions.

'Well, if you don't work, you won't get paid,' she said.

It took a monumental act of self-control, an appeal to the Buddhist principles I had studied years earlier, not to lunge at her, to throttle her, to hurl her out the window on to the street below. In the book on Italian history I was reading, defenestration was a common method of political murder, and now I was close to committing an act of defenestration myself.

'Fix it,' I said.

'It's being fixed.'

'Fix it now.'

'It is being fixed now. It's being fixed as fast as it can.'

'It's been six days. We've been living without running water for six days.'

'That's Sicily,' she said with her ghastly grin.

'I'll teach my lessons today, but I'm not coming into work tomorrow if the water hasn't come back on.'

'If you don't work, you won't get paid.'

'You barely pay us anyway.'

I didn't say this last line, but I wanted to, and I wanted to say so much more, so much worse. I barked at my students for the next eight hours. One little boy confused the present perfect with the preterite: I made him stand on his own in the centre of the classroom and rotate slowly on the spot while we all pointed at him and jeered loudly.

And then, on the seventh day, as in some biblical tale, the water came back as suddenly and inexplicably as it had ceased. 'Let there be water,' decreed some unseen bureaucrat, and water there was. In giddy bafflement, Coby and I stood watching the tap in the kitchen sink gushing forth, a heavenly vision in the Dust Bowl of our parched apartment. There was some unfathomable parable in all this about Sicilian ways, redolent of *omertà*, enigmatic glances that passed between old women in sun-baked villages, whisperings amid lemon groves. One day your water was running normally, then it ceased for a week, and then it came back on again. No explanation would ever be offered. We were strangers here, *stranieri* in a strange land. There was no point trying to understand.

At weekends I took trips: to Messina; Mount Etna, which was veiled in fog as I ascended it on a rickety train; San Vito Lo Capo, where the sky filled with thousands of kites during a festival; the theatres and street markets of Palermo. To get anywhere, I had to wake up at five or six in the morning, exercising all my willpower not to stay in bed. My days off were thus notable in that they began in exactly the same manner as my days on, just even earlier. One of the less remarked-upon barbarities of the five-day working week is how it imposes on the weekend a manic, anxiety-ridden quality: workers are so desperate to enjoy themselves that they can only fail to do so; they run around like convicts on day release, finally drinking themselves into a stupor because at least alcohol makes it seem that time is not passing, it is present, that we are not elsewhere, we are here and now. The worker's grim determination to enjoy his two days off has the effect of ruining those two days, filling them with worry and the bitter knowledge that soon it will be Monday again, and he will spend five dreary shifts anticipating the next weekend, which, like all the others, will be a disappointment.

Usually I took my trips around Sicily alone, being a firm adherent to the maxim that no company is better than bad company. In those days I prided myself on my high standards. I viewed them and the solitude they entailed as signs of a Nietzschean 'aristocracy of spirit', but it's possible I was just an arsehole. Whenever I had previously gone on excursions with people I wasn't close to, I had suffered from not being able to do exactly what I wanted when I wanted, which usually meant burying my head in a book. Often I spent my trips to renowned historical sites ignoring the renowned historical sites in favour of reading in a nearby cafe, or writing in my notebook, or getting quietly fucked up and enjoying the drift of my thoughts.

As the days grew warmer, I felt less inclined to stay indoors working on my novel. Our flat had a balcony looking along a street that ran away from the piazza; instead of writing I would sit out there, eating incredibly succulent olives I bought from peasant farmers at the monthly street market. No one likes a traveller who lectures his compatriots on how much better things are elsewhere. And yet I had the sense, eating those olives that were so plump and juicy that the eating of them was a rapturous, almost a sexual, experience, that I had never really eaten olives before, that the puny, meagre, olive-shaped things I'd bought in jars in Ireland were not olives so much as insults to olives, shameful betrayals of the olive experience. I'd had a similar revelation eating fruit in Asia. None of the fruits I'd previously eaten – dutifully, as part of my five-a-day – had prepared me for the ravishing, implausible, juicy sweetness of the mangoes in Thailand, the pineapples in

Vietnam, the watermelons in Laos. Even the banana – dullest of fruits, whose consumption had hitherto been a chore – pulsated with flavour. So delicious and juicy were the fruits of Asia, I was amazed such things could occur naturally, that such a congruence could exist between the produce of nature and the human capacity for sensual delight. It was almost an argument in favour of intelligent design – more compelling than the march of the penguins or whatever – for a benign Creator who liked us and wanted us to have lovely things, at least whenever we could afford the plane fare to Thailand.

From my balcony vantage I would watch the young Sicilians on Vespas clattering by, the girls in Prada and Dolce & Gabbana who texted while they talked, and the old men having long conversations that consisted exclusively of hand gestures (in the bookshop off the Corso VI Aprile there was an illustrated dictionary of Sicilian sign language, which I perused to decipher these exchanges). One afternoon there was a crash directly beneath the balcony: it was not too serious, but for an hour or so the young motorcyclist lay on the ground crying, while his friends and the paramedics who arrived on scene shouted and gesticulated at one another, ignoring the injured party (eventually he was taken on to a stretcher while his friends wheeled his twisted scooter away).

It was far more entertaining to sit on the balcony eating olives and watching the life of the street than it was to write. It wasn't just idleness. Living in what the sunny weather increasingly revealed to be a gorgeous town populated by beautiful people, I was beginning to feel that it was wrong – sinful might even be the apt word, with its Catholic and therefore Sicilian connotations – to stay cooped up in a dim flat, typing away at a lightly fictionalised account of a prior period of my life, a period when I had been really *living*, in the sense of doing things that were worth writing about, even if doing them led to heartbreak and misery, to bitter remorse that I had done them at all.

My friends Matt and Sophie came to visit in late May. They rented a car, which Sophie drove (like many Irish males of my generation, Matt and I were used to being driven around by women, who had earned their licences while we were smoking bongs and playing in go-nowhere bands).

One Saturday morning we drove down to Castellammare to rent a speedboat. By eight o'clock it was already as warm as the nicest day of the year in Ireland. The four of us bundled into the shiny white boat (Georgina had come along, relieved to get away from Alcamo, where two hot-headed rivals for her favours were squaring off in what looked like the initiation of a mafia blood feud). After a brief piloting lesson and some safety advice, we were off. We bounced across the waves, heading west along the coastline, whooping every time a spray of foam washed over us. We dropped anchor off the coast at Scopello, in view of the *faraglioni* – dramatic rock formations that rose out of the water, fringed by moss. The sea was a ravishing blue, deep and inviting. We stripped to our trunks and bikinis and, standing around the rim of our bobbing vessel, dived into the ultramarine depths. Matt and I vied to outdo each other with the daring and technical prowess of our dives and jumps, incited by the presence of the onlooking women. Georgina was magnificent in her white bikini. To my surprise, I had never felt attracted to her over the time we'd spent working together, even though she was desired by seemingly every male in Sicily. Now the sunlight glinted in shifting watery ovals on her midriff, shoulders and long slender legs as she sat back laughing; I wondered how I could have spent months alongside this woman without taking an interest – all the while jerking off to visions of too-young, too-wrong Angelica. I found myself saddened by this sudden desire: it had come to frustrate me that I couldn't seem to stay friends with a woman without desiring her, and that this desire invariably ruined the friendship, either through its consummation, or through the jealousy and frustration that developed if there was none.

I dived again, dissolving my confusions in the blue. There are few experiences more exhilarating, more conducive to the simple feeling of joy, than swimming in the sea in a part of the world where it is warm enough to do so without discomfort. Growing up in Ireland, I had assumed that swimming outdoors was essentially an ordeal. It always had to it a punitive, masochistic, ceremonial quality: you did it to prove that you could do it, to have done it. It was basically something to be gotten over with. On a wind-lashed shore on the furthermost rock in Western Europe, you stood before the hissing surf in grim resolve, psyching yourself up to take a plunge. Seconds later you were out again, shivering violently, craving a hot whiskey. Was it perhaps the coldness of the sea that gave life in Ireland its harsh and sullen quality, produced such coarse, tormented, lumpen people? 'Is possible,' as my friend Marco would have said.

A few days before Matt and Sophie reached the end of their stay, Coby knocked on my bedroom door.

'Check out what the mailman brought.'

It was a rather basic food hamper: a jar of honey, a bar of chocolate, some type of sandwich spread and a packet of crisps.

I looked at the hamper and then at Coby. 'Very nice,' I said.

'Try the chips.'

I opened the packet and tried one. They were salt and vinegar.

'Not bad,' I said politely.

'Dude, look deeper. Find yourself.'

I fished around with my fingers and pulled out … a little plastic bag. Inside was a square of translucent paper, divided into faintly coloured sections.

'Ten tabs of acid, motherfucker!' said Coby.

The following day Georgina drove us out to Segesta, to see the Greek temple I'd been telling everyone about since visiting it on a rainy Saturday in February. On the drive, Matt, Sophie, Coby and I dropped acid. It was coming on just as the temple appeared on the horizon – majestic, serene and proudly aloof from the landscape around it. It was as if a vast starship had alighted in that remote place, or indeed as if a solitary god had made his home in the lushness of the Sicilian countryside – but which god? I knew nothing about the temple's history, only that it had been there for a very long time, since the sixth century before Christ.

'Which god is it for?' I asked no one in particular.

'Apollo … Creed?' suggested Coby, who had double-dosed.

'Dionysus,' said Matt. 'I don't know if that's true, but let's assume it is. That way, our coming here and getting fucked up becomes an act of worship.'

'We should have an orgy,' said Sophie.

The temple was perfectly preserved – deathless and splendorous, immune to the centuries. We were not visiting the ruins of an ancient temple, we were visiting a temple, one that had stood its ground and would be there when the Sicilian countryside was arid and withered, when humankind itself had fallen into dereliction amid carcinogenic skies and poisoned seas. As when I'd come here first, there was no one else around, the landscape silent for miles in every direction, intensifying the aura of what can fairly be called Olympian detachment emanating from the colossal structure. 'Dude …' said Coby. He was able to draw an impressive range of emotion from that word and today it was awed and reverent. The broad pillars were pink-hued as they basked in the afternoon light. The pristine sky framing the temple was supernaturally blue. We stood before it, our necks craned. There was no noise, no breeze, no motion in the countryside around us. A lone bird soared high overhead, perhaps on migration to Africa. In the trance of psychedelia, the temple's millennial stillness appeared not as an absence of change but as a positive force, an energy. The temple was both a mirror to our evanescence – our youth, the glow of our skin – and a doorway on to the eternal, an emission from some changeless substratum from which we had emerged, and into which we would soon resolve.

And then Matt and Sophie were gone, everyone was gone. Blasted by a cumulative hangover, I walked through the shaded streets of Alcamo, past the churches, across the sunny piazza, in an agreeable daze – the result of the Valium that Matt had left me as a parting gift 'to soften the blow'. It was a midweek morning and the town seemed empty. Coby had left to visit his friend in Messina, and Georgina was staying with her lover Filippo – the man she would later marry – in his family's summer house on Lake Como. Our teaching duties were all but fulfilled, the school closing for summer. I wandered into the gated courtyard behind the piazza, where I sat for a spell on a bench by a lone tree that

I imagined was a palm. The church bells struck noon. Having no thoughts in my head, my senses heightened by fatigue, I heard with pellucid clarity their chiming and resounding, each nuance of tone and oscillation, as if the bells were ringing inside my mind, as if I were the campanile. The bells rang on and on, bounding through the alleys and across the piazza, over the rooftops and the sea air. I thought of the words from Plato that Matt had quoted as we stood before the temple in Segesta, stunned by sky and magnificence and hallucination: 'All in all, nothing human is worth taking very seriously; nevertheless …' Three weeks later I would leave Sicily on a train that set out from Palermo, crossed the Strait of Messina on the deck of a ferry, and traversed the spine of Italy all the way to Milan. I would make no effort to stay in touch with the people I had met on the island, the friends and colleagues, the students and drinking buddies. For now, I sat in the courtyard in what I remember as total contentment. After a while I stood up and made my way out through the gate that creaked on its hinges, across the piazza in the shadow of the old church. As I stepped on to the Corso VI Aprile, I passed an old man who hobbled slowly through the shade, bolstered by a walking stick, his legs trembling with the effort.

———

I leave Croatia in the morning. The last time I lived in France I came to pieces: grinding, distorted, obsessional thoughts; relentless paranoia. But circumstances were different then. I was living on my own after a break-up, and there were problems in my life that felt so severe I couldn't see a way out. You get spooked; you stop trusting yourself. Your brain becomes an enemy. But I think you know what I mean. I too used to have dreams of being swept away by the incoming tide, when I was a child. Some of the dreams were sketched as in pencil; in some of them my mother stood on the shore, helpless or impassive. Later there were nightmares of a flood: black waters rising up to drown the world.

The newspaper dropped me after that single column, and rightly so. I don't care about whatever they required me to care about. They want someone with social concern, chronic indignation, a feel for the fluctuations of mob hysteria. Essentially I accept the world as it is. This is where you and I are different. You exert yourself in making some small change for the better, even though you suspect that it's 'closing time in the gardens of the West'. You believe that writing should concern itself with political action, a dutiful inching towards utopia, whereas I feel insufficient loyalty or vigour, and too much bitterness, to align myself with any of these movements. Politics engages me purely as an aesthetic phenomenon, as something interesting. I know this incenses you, yet here we are, still friends, sort of. Despite our differences, I imagine us as symptoms of the same drive towards oblivion. You, as a woman, admit you feel no dismay at the prospect of a civilisation you say oppresses you being swept away. I feel no *dismay either — the spectacle of the catastrophe exhilarates me, at least insofar as it doesn't impinge on me too directly. I used to feel appalled at myself for this; now I feel absolutely normal.*

This afternoon I took the tram to the Mirogoj Cemetery, on a hillside just out of town. It was serene there, among the dead: autumn sun and fallen leaves; monuments to the soldiers of both world wars; the tombs of famous Croatians I'd never heard of. I sat on a bench by a war memorial to write and read, till there was no longer enough light. While I was there I came up with a possible title: European Graveyards. *But I soon dismissed it.*

Grave

In January of 2015, half a decade after I had left Italy and two weeks after the *Charlie Hebdo* terrorist attacks, I took a trip to Paris with the vague intention of researching an essay on the Romanian writer E. M. Cioran, who lived in the city from 1937 until his death in 1995. What this research would consist of was not really clear. Cioran's life in Paris was notable for the fact that, other than write books, he had done absolutely nothing of interest there. He had simply lived out year after year in the flat on Rue de l'Odéon that he shared with his long-term partner, Simone Boué, where he finally became senile, fell ill and died, inadvertently backing out of the suicide pact that he and Boué had made together. It seemed likely that my 'research' would be confined to loitering around Cioran's grave at the Montparnasse Cemetery, and staring up at his inaccessible apartment from the street below. Nonetheless, I had persuaded myself that spending time in Paris was the only way the essay would ever get off the ground.

On the morning of my trip, I woke at 4 a.m. and made it to the airport in good time to catch my 6:25

flight. When I showed my boarding pass at the gate, however, I was informed that I'd been queuing for the *wrong* 6:25 flight to Paris. This was Air France and I was Ryanair. I ran back the way I'd come, and for reasons unclear was instructed to pass through security all over again. Hurrying towards the Ryanair gate, I told myself that somehow it would all work out. I had never missed a plane, regardless of hangovers, stoned muddles and misfiring alarm clocks: it followed that I would not miss this one. When I reached the gate, sweating extravagantly, the airport worker in his high-vis jacket told me that the plane had been delayed – that was it out there on the taxiway – but the doors were all closed up and there was no way of getting on. I would have to book another flight and check in all over again. And no, there wouldn't be any refund from Ryanair.

I ended up flying with Aer Lingus a couple of hours later, at a cost I'd rather not think about. The one consolation in all this was that Aer Lingus actually flew me to Paris, rather than to what Ryanair calls 'Paris', in reality a remote zone called Beauvais, which on previous visits seemed to me even further from Paris than Dublin itself. Looking out the window of the train that brought me from Charles de Gaulle to the Gare du Nord, I ruminated on how I had always prided myself on never having missed a plane, and now I had missed one. It seemed to me that, as I grew older, the stock of personal traits I could pride myself on was steadily diminishing – I had managed to slip up in almost every category. Perhaps I had no option but to start taking pride in things I *had* done – accomplishments – rather than in things I had refrained from doing, such as missing a plane.

At Gare du Nord, I boarded the Métro. As the crowded train was pulling out of the station, I looked out the window and saw four soldiers with machine guns descending the stairs on the platform. The sight triggered a momentary panic: had the soldiers arrived because they knew something? Were they moments too late to board the train and shoot dead the jihadists who were now about to blow us up or flood the carriage with poisonous gas? The panic receded as I reminded myself that the chances of actually being caught up in a terrorist attack, in Paris or anywhere else, were slim. On the other hand, the very fact that I was thinking like this – having to remind myself that I was probably safe – demonstrated the efficacy of terrorism: I felt terrorised, therefore terrorism had achieved its goal. I recalled the five years I had spent living in London. Not once had I managed to take the Tube in that city without imagining, as we hurtled through narrow tunnels deep underground, the horror that would ensue if a bomb went off or a gas attack was perpetrated – the airless panic as bodies pressed against one another, everyone desperate to get out but knowing there was nowhere to go. I used to wonder how much my nervous system could take before the agony caused me to pass out: I told myself that it wouldn't be so bad, that the body would automatically shut itself down to avoid intolerable pain, but I never really believed it.

As the train approached my stop, I noticed the unusual typography of the book being read by the young black guy sitting next to me. It looked very much like a book of aphorisms, and when I leaned over to check the title I was delighted to see that it was Cioran's *De l'inconvénient d'être né*. Zoé, the friend in whose flat I would be staying, had told me that Cioran was not really taken seriously in France: his extreme pessimism and insistence on the wretchedness of life, humanity and everything else were considered a bit of a posture. 'If that was really how he saw things, why didn't he just kill himself?' she asked in paraphrasis of the widespread French attitude.

The guy with the Cioran book was reading it bareback, as I thought of it, meaning without a pen in his hand. My own copy of *The Trouble With Being Born* back in Dublin was very heavily underlined, perhaps the most heavily underlined of all my books. I had read it numerous times, on each occasion happening to use a different-coloured pen to highlight the passages I considered particularly remarkable. The problem was, the whole book seemed particularly remarkable: the prose (in Richard Howard's wonderful translation) was so consistently striking, its mode of attack so viscerally elegant, that, after the third or fourth reading, almost the entirety of the book had been underlined. These rampant, multicoloured underlinings (which gave the impression of graffitied subway walls, like those we were now hurtling past) negated the very purpose of underlining in the first place. When a given text is uniformly excellent, it is futile to make out the strong passages because one will end up, as I had done, underlining the entire thing.

I disembarked at Corentin Cariou, just inside the north-eastern rim of the Boulevard Périphérique, which marks off central Paris from its surrounding suburbs. Directly outside the station was the building where Zoé was renting a sixth-floor flat. I let myself in and, exhausted, went straight to bed. When I woke a couple of hours later, I read the note Zoé had left explaining how to get to the theatre on the far side of the city where she was directing one of her plays (she was already there, rehearsing what would be the final performance in the run). Dazed from my nap, I wandered the quiet streets near the canal to find a bistro where I could eat steak tartare. As I walked, I asked myself what the difference was between a bistro, a brasserie and indeed a restaurant. This part of the nineteenth arrondissement was home to a sizeable Jewish community, and soldiers had been deployed here after the killing of four people in a Jewish supermarket during the terror attacks. The soldiers I saw, with their machine guns and cocked pistols – when jihadists come, they come fast – looked to me like kids. They say that as you age, policemen seem to get younger all the time. The same was evidently true of soldiers; I wondered if it might be so with jihadists.

After my steak tartare, still groggy from sleeping through the afternoon, I boarded the Métro. Embarrassed at having missed my flight that morning, I was determined not to arrive late for Zoé's play. To make sure of being on time, I peered intently at her note, reading over and over the name of the final Métro stop, checking it against the listed stations on the map above my head. When we reached the stop, I disembarked and followed the directions to the venue. Having done so, I found I was standing not outside a theatre but on a weed-strewn traffic island between two screamingly busy motorways. All I could see was edge-of-the-city wasteland, massive hotels and business parks. I called Zoé.

Having gone over the directions she had written, she said: 'Are you sure you got out at the right station?'

Of course I was sure! Had I not checked it a dozen times? Of course I was sure. I glanced down at the piece of paper. Zoé waited silently on the other end. Finally, in a quiet and sheepish voice, I told her I would be there in twenty minutes.

When I finally made it, very late, to the theatre, I glanced at my ticket to see what the play was called: *L'Homme est la seule erreur de la création – Man is Creation's Only Mistake*. In the darkened hall I took my seat amidst tuts of disapproval, feeling like a man capable only of making mistakes. I reached out and apologetically squeezed Zoé's hand – we had the kind of friendship in which these gestures would not be misinterpreted – then settled down to watch the play.

It was a decidedly avant-garde production, and my French was too weak to grasp much of the slang-heavy dialogue. I had no idea what was going on. A talking coffee table spoke into a handheld camera, its image projected on to a screen on the other side of the stage. The Hindu god Vishnu appeared, or maybe it was just a boy painted blue. Lovers had arguments while perched atop a bed that wheeled around the set like a raft on a choppy sea. Attractive actors took off their shirts, pulled down their trousers or lay on couches, howling and vomiting.

Afterwards there was a party to celebrate the culmination of the run. Zoé's parents, Marie-Claire and Hassan, had come down from Normandy to see the play. Stupefied with fatigue, the result of the insomnia that had been assailing me in recent weeks, I chatted with them in French that was not so much broken as completely shattered. To endure situations like this, I had formulated an emergency plan: whenever the appropriate French words eluded me, I would simply speak Italian instead. The similarities between the two languages were such that my interlocutor would generally have at least a vague idea of what I was talking about, or so I hoped. As I was now discovering, though, my Italian, once so fluent, was itself betraying signs of severe deterioration. It occurred to me that, by learning French, I was in fact burying my Italian – just as, by learning Italian, I had buried the Spanish I had spoken with equal fluency at an earlier time in my life. My French not yet being very good, I found myself in a situation whereby the new language – French – had succeeded in significantly erasing its precursor – Italian – without having properly installed itself in its place. Exiled from Italian, not yet at home in French, I was stranded in a linguistic no-man's-land, like some partisan hiding out in the hills around the French–Italian border. I restricted myself to nodding and saying 'Oui' or, if it seemed more appropriate, 'Non'.

Zoé told me that the theatre's director, a grey-bearded spirit-of-'68 type, was upstairs in his office, taking 'lots of cocaine' with some of the actors and production staff. Keeping up the non-conversation with Marie-Claire and Hassan, I found myself gazing longingly towards the stairs, tempted to excuse myself and pay a visit to the unfolding drug binge, but knowing it wouldn't do if Zoé's parents discovered me to be a coke snorter. When they finally left, I hurried upstairs, knocked on the door of the office, and was invited to take a place at the round wooden table, where everyone was talking animatedly about Michel Houellebecq. ('One morning we'll turn on our televisions and see him on his knees, getting beheaded in a basement somewhere.') A tray full of neatly cut lines was being passed around. It was a wholly civilised affair, as if we were back in the days of Freud or in Victorian England, when cocaine was a fashionable and legal after-dinner pick-me-up among the chattering classes. The office was strewn with magazines, books and posters for plays and films.

Mellow jazz issued from speakers buried under the clutter. Richard, the ageing theatre director, made sure I got a couple of lines into me, but quickly gave up on the limited conversation I was able to offer in favour of more stimulating dialogue.

Zoé and I took a taxi sometime after four, watching the meter in grim fascination all the way home.

The following afternoon, after some reviving coffee and croissants, we took the Métro to the Rue de l'Odéon, to see the apartment where the Romanian upstart Emil Cioran had transformed himself into the great French writer E. M. Cioran. On the way, I told Zoé about Cioran's strange relationship with Simone Boué. Afraid to tell her rural-dwelling parents that she was living out of wedlock with a man, and a Romanian at that, Boué kept their relationship a secret for many years, claiming that she was living with a friend, and hiding Cioran whenever her family came to visit. Zoé's own parents, I knew, had lived out almost exactly the same scenario: Marie-Claire could not bring herself to tell her father that she was living with an Algerian, one who had, indeed, spent his first years in France in an internment camp. For a time the couple considered eloping, but Hassan decided he could not ask Marie-Claire to abandon her family for him. The dilemma was solved by way of an unexpected visit from Marie-Claire's father. After his initial anger, the father eventually accepted that his daughter was in love, and gave them his blessing.

At 21 Rue de l'Odéon, we stood on the footpath and gazed up at the row of garret-level windows, wondering which one was Cioran's, and whether we could get up there to see inside. A year earlier, I had come here and done exactly the same thing with my then girlfriend. Was I destined to return annually to the flat of a deceased Romanian nihilist and reflect upon yet another failed relationship? There were a lot of them, failed relationships, like burned-out tanks on the battlefield of my life.

In the summer, Zoé and I had visited Gdansk and Frankfurt together, to see the houses where Arthur Schopenhauer had lived in his childhood and his maturity respectively. There too we had been frustrated in our desire to enter the houses – in Gdansk it had been unclear if we were at the right house at all. Nonetheless, I'd found it exciting to see the same streets and buildings that the young Schopenhauer had possibly seen, and those that the older Schopenhauer certainly had.

Zoé had been a good sport in Germany, accompanying me to these (for me) heightened, ultramundane places, and doing her best to console me when the novella I tried to write, narrated by the succession of poodles that were Schopenhauer's only companions in his embittered later years, came to nothing. She was being a good sport here in Paris too. In truth, though, none of it meant a great deal to her. She was as passionate about literature as I was, but she never felt the urge to seek out the sites where the great writers whose books she loved had lived and worked, nor felt any great frisson whenever she happened upon them.

'For me, it's all in the work,' she said, picking up an old conversational thread as we stood there in the street, looking up at Cioran's former home. 'The only way I get the same excitement is if I read about certain streets in a novel by Zola or Huysmans or whoever, and then I find myself in that same street. Then the world does feel a bit magical. But the effect emanates from the work, not from the life of the author. It's only the literature that is magical. The authors are just the vessels. Even their lives are not that interesting to me. I mean, I never really read biographies.'

She was silent for a moment as I took a couple of photos on my phone.

'You're more of a Catholic than you imagine,' she said.

'How do you mean?'

'I mean this: you coming out here to look at Cioran's apartment, visiting Kafka's house or whatever. It's not so different from what you told me about your mother, how she queued up for three hours to look at the relics of St Anthony or whoever it was when they came to Dublin. You've just switched mythologies.'

I took a couple more photographs, glancing up and down the street.

'Taylor Swift culture,' Zoé said vaguely, though I probably misheard her.

The building where Cioran had lived also housed the offices of the publishing house Flammarion. I took a few photos of those too, feeling like a member of an Al Qaeda sleeper cell on a reconnaissance mission. The offices had been evacuated on the day of the *Charlie Hebdo* attack out of a fear that, as the publisher of Michel Houellebecq, Flammarion might be a target. In what was presumably an astonishing coincidence, Houellebecq's novel *Soumission*, which imagines a near-future France under Islamic rule, was published on that same day, while the author's caricature adorned the front page of the then current issue of the magazine. Houellebecq himself left the city under armed escort that afternoon.

We walked across the road and into the Luxembourg Gardens, where for many years Cioran took his daily walk. The sky was pleasingly grey and it was the kind of cold I loved: an invigorating cold on just the right side of severity. All my visits to Paris had taken place in wintertime: for me, Paris existed under permanently grey skies, and always should. The idea of the city in spring or summer did not appeal to me. One of the reasons I loved Paris was that I associated it with grey skies, just as I associated San Francisco with constant blue skies, which in turn I associated with depressed spirits. A couple of years earlier, while spending a few months in San Francisco – where I endured the shattering mushroom trip in Buena Vista Park – I had come to the realisation that I could never live for very long outside of Europe, because nowhere else was grey to the same degree or in the same comforting way.

It was already late afternoon and soon it would be dark. We made our way out of the gardens and to the Montparnasse Cemetery, where Cioran was buried. Soon the cemetery would be closing for the evening. We took a map from the kiosk at the gates, which showed the locations of the cemetery's famous inhabitants. Montparnasse was evidently a fashionable place to be buried for a certain type of French intellectual, even if they weren't French. Susan Sontag was buried here; Samuel Beckett too. We stepped between the rows of headstones and found Cioran's diminutive grave. It was tempting to read the stone's modesty as a classic Cioranesque provocation, scornfully dismissive of even death itself. Simone Boué was buried alongside him: she had been found drowned on the beach at Dieppe, in Normandy, two years after Cioran's death; it was unclear whether her death had been accidental or not. On the day we visited, someone had placed a Romanian tricolour over Cioran's grave. The tricolour was held in place by what initially appeared to be two pieces of shit, one on either side. On closer inspection, the shit turned out to be broken-off segments from a rusted metal wreath. Even if they had been pieces of shit, it is debatable which insult would have been graver to the memory of Cioran – the shit or the flag. After all, here lay a man who had left Romania as soon as he came of age, settled in Paris after some years of roaming and there exerted a great deal of energy purging himself of the stigmata of his birthplace, including its language, which he rarely deigned to speak even when among Romanian expats. Cioran felt humiliated by the fact of being Romanian. In his early, notoriously fascistic book *The Transfiguration of Romania* (which was written in Romanian), and in letters to friends, the twenty-three-year-old Cioran called for three quarters of the nation's population to be exterminated, and for all Romanians to be dragged into police cells and beaten to a pulp. Perhaps that, he fumed, would rouse his compatriots from their congenital mediocrity and goad them towards a higher destiny.

I could understand it, this yearning of Cioran's to cleanse himself of all traces of a despised motherland. Never, even as a child, had I felt proud of my country, or even that I really belonged to it. I had spent most of my adult life in flight from Ireland, yet I always went back, if only because it was there that, if the shit hit the fan, I was able to draw the dole, or stop in at my parents' place for a bowl of soup, and where I still had a few friends I had not yet become estranged from. I had always imagined I would live in exile but now I knew I didn't have the stomach for it. People of other nationalities romanticised Ireland but to me it was an uninteresting place, a backwater of banal, misshapen people. It had produced a certain number of interesting writers, but most of those writers had got out of the country.

Beckett's grave in Montparnasse was even more modest than Cioran's – it was aggressively, even flamboyantly, modest. In fact, the grave was so faint it seemed to flicker on the verge of non-being. If the grave were a poem, it would have been one of those that are made up almost entirely of white space, a scattering of stray words on the surface, poised to vanish into its purity like melting snowflakes. I imagined Cioran and Beckett vying to outdo one another with the exaggerated modesty of their graves, competing in nothingness and scorn. They were like two suburban neighbours, this pair of graveyard nihilists – curtain-twitchers anxious not to be outshone by the glamorous misery of the other. I recalled an article I'd read concerning a peer of the Norwegian pessimist Peter Wessel Zapffe, who 'argued, against Zapffe's view that life is meaningless, that life is *not even meaningless*'.

I took a photo of the grave; my phone offered me the option of instantly tweeting it, which I declined, reflecting on the unsurpassable vulgarity of that, tweeting from someone's grave. I began to laugh. I wondered whether Cioran would be on Twitter if he were around now. What were his later, aphoristic books but collections of tweets, proto-tweets, capsules of provocation hurled out at a despised universe, or at least at Cioran's followers, by which I mean his readers? The aphorism, or rather the collection of aphorisms, was obsolete in the age of Twitter. The aphorism had migrated from the notebook to the laptop and the phone. I contemplated the notion of writing a book of aphorisms myself, and how retrograde that would be, but I liked the idea anyway. And in fact I had started such a book, or at least I had started writing aphorisms, which were simply tweets that, when they came to me, I did not tweet but instead wrote down in my notebook, just like in the old days, the days of Shestov and La Rochefoucauld. One reason why those writers found the aphorism such an amenable literary form, and why I too was drawn to it, is that it is distinctly suited to provocation. Its brevity encourages startling and outrageous insights. But why always seek to provoke, I wondered, standing over Cioran's grave as Zoé hugged herself against the cold. Simple, I thought: because when you provoke you can experience the glee of being hated, which is a subset of the joy of being loved. But there was more to it than that. The venting of aggression was necessary to prevent one imploding with fury, a constant danger if one were inclined to view the world as ugly, dangerous and swarming with horrible morons. For a time, I had used Twitter as a kind of pressure valve by which I could release my pent-up fury on an unsuspecting public, all the bile and hatred I had accumulated over a lifetime, much as Cioran had done with his books. Back then, I had set myself a sort of Oulipian constraint whereby, on my nightly Twitter forays, I would be as aggressive, offensive and hateful as possible, baldly hostile to the fashionable ideologies of the day and the sanctimonious cunts who trumpeted them, but I would do it in a way that would not cause me to lose followers in droves. This tricky game, which I kept up for a month or two before succumbing to a profound self-loathing, involved sugaring the pill, coating my slander and vituperation with just enough charm or panache that people would stick around for more, perhaps in spite of themselves. The game – for that is what it was – afforded me a not inconsiderable pleasure. How awful could I be? How cruelly could I mock the trendy sentiments and masturbatory indignations that cascaded so risibly down my screen? Could I resist this ocean of bollocks without perishing in convulsions of hatred? This game of mine was totally pointless, from one perspective; but writing, it seemed to me, had always been that way, a dubious and malign thinking-in-public – a game played in deadly earnest, but a game nonetheless.

The day after our visit to Montparnasse, Zoé left early for work and I brought my various notebooks to a nearby cafe. My hope was to construct some kind of cohesive theoretical statement from the notes I had been taking over the past year or so on Cioran's books. I had convinced myself that I needed to wait till I was in Paris to begin the essay, and now here I was in the city, with conditions as favourable as they would ever be; yet as I sat down at a small, darkly varnished table with a view on to the street outside, I found myself fighting the temptation to put off working until I was back in Dublin. There, I imagined, I would be able to sit at the comfort of my own desk, without distractions, and work for sustained periods without having to worry about whether I was in anyone's way, or if I should order a slice of cake I didn't want so as not to incite the resentment of the cafe's proprietors. The problem was, I had no energy for writing. I sat there with my laptop open in front of me, a couple of notebooks placed on either side, and could not for the life of me rouse myself to begin. I wanted to get started but on the other hand I didn't want to get started at all, I didn't want to do anything. I was more than happy to sit there drinking my coffee, looking out the window at the pair of twelve-year-old soldiers with assault rifles who were walking past. Such troughs of fatigue, a factor in my life for as long as I could remember, seemed to be growing deeper and more frequent as I got older. I was hardly into my thirties but already I felt the diminishment of vitality associated with middle age – in fact, I had always felt it, even when I was twenty-one, or seventeen. Perhaps I was born middle-aged, I thought. I wondered, not for the first time, whether I suffered from an undiagnosed case of chronic fatigue syndrome – or whether, more simply, I was a lazy bastard.

But fuck this shit, I said to myself, sitting in the cafe – I had work to do and I was going to get it done. I drank an espresso to fire myself up, then began to put some shape on my notes. Just as I was making progress, it began to seem to me that, since I was in Paris after all, I ought to get out of the nineteenth arrondissement and do my writing in a livelier, more *Parisian* cafe in central Paris, where I would find greater inspiration than I would here. I paid for my coffee, packed away the notebooks and laptop, and walked to the Métro station.

Sitting opposite me on the Métro was an impossibly chic woman who was reading a book by Félix Guattari. In Paris, you could have been forgiven for reaching the conclusion that the printed word and literature as we know it were not issuing their death rattle. People read, often in public, on the Métro or alone in cafes. And their choice of reading material was generally not the bloodbath bestsellers and child-wizard fuckery to be seen on the metros of other capitals, but books by authors whose very emblem of authority was their unreadability. I had already spotted a pretty teenager burying her face in Levinas's *Totality and Infinity* as her boyfriend tried to plant kisses on her neck, and a tiny woman who looked to be pushing one hundred thumbing through Derrida's *The Archaeology of the Frivolous* while wearing an expression of indulgent scepticism. An indelibly glamorous race, the French even managed to make reading seem cool again. In Paris, you didn't need to feel obsolescent every time you took out a book in a public place, rather than a phone, tablet or e-reader. Books were still fashion accessories in a way they had ceased to be elsewhere.

The Parisians were also, of course, exceptionally beautiful people. Even the staff at the McDonald's outside the Métro station at Saint-Michel were stunning. Like anyone else, I had noted the gorgeousness of the Parisians on my previous visits to the city. The quantity of not just highly attractive but outstandingly beautiful women had at first been a torment. Back then, I had made it my business, felt it was my duty, to desire every beautiful woman I saw. To do less, I imagined, would have been to dishonour the miracle of it, this implausible concentration of exquisite human specimens. Consequently, those prior visits to Paris had had the character of a long, melancholy sigh. This time around, though, a change had occurred. The women (and the men) were as gorgeous as ever, but a profound inner shift had taken place in me: I found I could no longer be bothered to do all that desiring. It was completely exhausting, and so obviously futile. It would be an exaggeration to say I stopped noticing the million beautiful girls of Paris, any more than I'd stopped noticing those of Sicily when I'd lived there: I just stopped actively wanting them, in both the bluntly carnal and the more yearningly romantic ways. This idea – that I was not beholden to a state of constant, acute and frustrated longing – came as a revelation to me. The process by which I had made this breakthrough – fatigued surrender after years spent cracking my head against the brick wall of desire – seemed to herald a broader fate, possibly a salvation: as I grew older, I would gradually find I no longer had the vigour to desire anything at all, and then I would be free, as serene as a mountain peak, and then I would die.

Here lies Rob. He couldn't be fucked, not even to
be fucked.

However, as I sat in a cafe on Rue des Écoles, at a
table looking on to the busy shopping street, the place
became so preposterously crowded with knockout
women that I quickly gave up hope of getting any work
done whatsoever and resigned myself to gazing about,
lovesick as a schoolgirl and horny as a seminarian.
After an hour and a half, having withstood the serious
temptation to go and wank myself off in the gents,
I packed up my notebooks again and took the Métro
back to Zoé's flat.

It was that same evening, while reading aloud for Zoé
excerpts from Cioran's massive *Cahiers*, the journals he
kept from 1957 to 1972, that I realised why I had, so
far, been unable to get started on the essay. It wasn't
my lack of energy, which seemed now like an illusion: I
was actually feeling quite perky, as I often did in the
evenings. It wasn't even the distractingly beautiful
women of Paris. No. The real reason I was finding it
difficult to write about Cioran was that Cioran did
not want to be written about. At least, the work of the
Parisian Cioran – E. M. rather than Emil – the mature,
aphoristic books that I considered the jewels of his
oeuvre, resisted being written about. The whole point
of his crystalline, perfectly weighted aphorisms is that
they are just what they are: they neither require nor
permit extrapolation or even counter-argument. Each

aphorism is the singular, unimprovable expression of itself. As such, it was pointless to add to them, through criticism or commentary. Cioran never cared to defend his arguments: he simply recorded the explosions of his temperament, artfully vented his inexhaustible bile while taking glee in his outrages, paradoxes and contradictions. Just as his work repelled attempts to expound critically upon it, so too was Cioran's life in Paris deflective to biographical writing – and not only because, anxious to conceal the fascist dalliances of his youth, he shunned publicity during his years in Paris, refusing to be interviewed by French journalists. Little wonder that the only two biographies available in English, Ilinca Zarifopol-Johnston's *Searching for Cioran* and Marta Petreu's *An Infamous Past*, both focused on Cioran's early life, probing the extent and significance of his involvement with fascism: after he settled in Paris, Cioran gave his biographers nothing more to write about. Just as I would never enter Cioran's former flat on the Rue de l'Odéon, I would never know more than I knew now about the decades he spent in Paris: there was nothing else *to* know. Cioran had had the last laugh: he had erased himself in his writing, left nothing behind but his insults.

One of the constraints I had set for myself when I decided to write about Cioran was that I would not quote his work, the reason being that it was too quotable. If I quoted one passage, I would want to quote another, then another, and many more, until I was not so much writing about Cioran as presenting the reader with his entire body of work (as Gallimard had done when they published his single-volume *Œuvres*). To quote Cioran would only underscore the inadequacy of writing about him, just as underlining passages in his work had brought to light its own futility. Having already decided that I would write about Cioran without quoting him, it now seemed I would have to write about him without even writing about him. An essay on Cioran in which both his life and his work were almost completely absent: this is what I was blundering into.

And yet, Cioran had managed to get inside *me*. His unremitting scepticism, his bitterness raised to the status of a cosmic principle, now felt like my own, whether I wanted them or not. Cioran was like the Cheshire Cat who vanished leaving not a grin but a sneer, a malicious sneer from beyond the grave. As I sat with Zoé in her flat, light-headed from the day's exertions, it began to seem to me that all I could see now was Cioran's sneer, the sneer that had burrowed deep into my being, that tainted everything I saw, ridiculed everything, everyone. I felt that if I were to stand up and look out the window, over the brooding skies of Paris, I would see Cioran's sneer, vast and malevolent, gaping across the heavens, and the noise of his laughter would thunder all around. I imagined sinking my teeth into the flesh of Cioran's face and tearing it off. What had Cioran ever given to my life, other than pessimism and discouragement? He had exacerbated the very tendencies in myself I had spent my whole adult life trying to curb: withdrawal, cynicism, nihilism, despair, spleen, derision, scowling, indifference, resentment, defeatism, contrarianism, torpor, detachment, provocation, rage, arrogance, insolence, bitterness, hostility. He had urged me to cultivate my antipathies, finally to turn away from the world, like the Buddhas and naysayer sages down the millennia, Cioran's ancestors and inspirations. I thought of the year I had spent living in solitude in Rosslare Harbour, County Wexford, where I had gone to recover from a devastating break-up: all I'd had down there for company, in a silent house on a half-deserted estate, was a stack of Cioran's books. Heartbroken and drinking too much, cut off from all culture, all social and political life, I had too readily embraced Cioran's insistence that the one honourable response to the world was to turn away from it, to ignore its noise and simply fade back into non-existence. All engagement, enthusiasm and commitment had seemed to me contemptible and delusional states, to be disdained in others and snuffed out in myself. But I was so fucking depressed down there! In Rosslare Harbour I was so depressed, my depression was so total, that I thought I was fucking happy! Or not happy, exactly, but I was unaware of just how miserable I was, sitting alone day after day, night after night, on a windswept beach where I was invariably the only human being, or in the silent house in a transit town where I knew no one, where I didn't even have a car to take me into Wexford town.

What did I expect, when the only company I had was this sneering bastard?

And yet, behind Cioran's sneer, there was a point he tirelessly made that still seemed to me worth heeding. The most cursory survey of the global situation confirmed that, yes, it really was the worst who were full of passionate intensity – the ones to be feared and resisted were not the preachers of decline, the diviners of our civilisation's exhaustion, but all those wild-eyed zealots who strove to create a heaven on earth, refusing to see that, in so doing, they would inevitably unleash hell. Absolutists, zealots, demagogues, jihadists, messianic utopians – all manner of fanatics thrived in the contemporary chaos, exploiting the frightening complexity of the age to hawk their simplistic narratives, their archaic binaries that brooked no ambiguity and sanctioned bottomless bloodshed. It was not only the elegance and philosophical extremism that I found so gratifying in Cioran, it was his hostility to all fanaticism, the lucid insistence that every mania we indulged in, whether political or metaphysical, would only mire us deeper in agony.

Suddenly weary of the back-and-forth of my thoughts, I sighed and closed the *Cahiers*. Through the window, the Paris skyline was slowly lighting up the late-winter dusk. I said to Zoé, 'It's funny. The writers who mean the very most to me, often there's a part of me that wishes I'd never read them at all.'

'You mean like Cioran?'

I nodded.

'But why? You're free to take or leave any ideas you come across. That's responsibility, that's what it means. Nobody forces you.'

'But there are tendencies that writers like Cioran or Schopenhauer can encourage. Despair, withdrawal. In the religions, in Christianity, despair is a sin. That's interesting.'

She considered this, then shook her head. 'I find it very easy to step out of that tunnel when I close the book. I'm not going to reject the universe just because Schopenhauer or anybody else said so.'

'Of course not. But you don't have those inclinations waiting to be triggered. What I mean is, it's a choice. This withdrawal. I feel that it's dangerous, the danger is real. Burning down the world. Despairing. I feel I'm already hanging on with the tips of my fingers. Seriously, it seems very easy sometimes to just stop engaging, turn away from everything. But that's a kind of suicide, a spiritual suicide. That's acedia.' I cleared my throat, hesitant. 'And it would finish me as a writer,' I added.

We heard the young German couple next door leave their flat, their footsteps echoing in the stairwell. The room fell silent. Zoé went to the attached kitchen and poured two glasses of wine. When she returned she handed one to me. She picked up the *Cahiers* and sat back down in her chair, facing the window. She leafed slowly through the pages.

'It is very beautiful, though,' she said.

'I know.'

'And addictive, if you go in for this kind of thing.'

'That's the problem.'

She sipped her wine, then she said, 'Imagine this. Even if the most extreme pessimism accords with how things are, and existence is a nightmare, and consciousness is a chamber of hell, and Western civilisation is awaiting its *coup de grâce*, and we're all adrift in the Unbreathable, or the Irreparable, or the Incurable, or all these things he writes about; what if, in spite of all this, the very articulation of this pessimism was so exquisite, so profound, that it redeemed our moments here in the nightmare? What if the writing itself, the beauty of it, not only pointed towards but *provided* reason enough to stick around a while longer? Wouldn't that be strange?'

I took this in, tried to connect with her meaning. A week later, after I returned from France, the world would watch, or feel as if it had watched, the burning to death of a young man locked in a steel cage, out in some dusty wasteland in a territory resembling hell. Life on earth had perhaps always been this terrible, had offered no less validation to those who thought it better it had never existed at all. But it *seemed* worse, in the new proximity of things.

'Listen to this,' Zoé said, holding up the *Cahiers*.

'Don't quote him …'

'Just once.'

Before I could object further, she read: 'Nous sommes tous au fond d'un enfer dont chaque instant est un miracle.'

I watched her in profile, across the space between us. Still holding the book, she was gazing out the window, over the roof of the Jewish slaughterhouse below, towards the hazed peripheral high-rises in the distance.

She said: 'We are all deep in a hell, each moment of which is a miracle.'

———

Maybe the afterlife is like this, like Paris in the autumn. The last time I met Ellie – in a bar at the top of the Parc de Belleville overlooking the city – I admitted to her how intoxicated I was with Paris. She, having lived here for ten years, replied that it was her mission to disenchant people like me, and point out all that is stifling and regressive in Paris and in French culture generally. No doubt she was right, and what I'm enamoured of is superficial – but only in the way that the initial months of falling in love with somebody are superficial. The experience doesn't show you what isn't there, but rather what you might never again see so vividly, as it gets muddied beneath layers of habit and ambivalence.

You are wrong about drug culture. I've known women with an attraction to drugs equal to my own. I don't take drugs anywhere near as frequently as I used to, though there are periods when this is not true. Last summer in Dublin, I got locked into a prolonged binge involving psychedelics and modafinil. I used the modafinil to work: when it wore off in the evenings it triggered fits of anxiety that necessitated alcohol. It fucked with my sleeping too (remember we kept chatting late into the night and I couldn't wind down?), so that I was stuck in a frazzled, eye-twitching state that required increasing quantities of modafinil if I was to keep working: a vicious circle. I was staying in my friend Matt's flat in East Wall. There was a balcony, and an Indian takeaway downstairs. Friends stayed over for days on end and the flat became spectral and sordid, no one sleeping, dishes piling up in the sink, lines being snorted off all surfaces. There were incense sticks and Buddha statues, and a huge clothbound edition of Carl Jung's The Red Book. *There seemed to be a terror attack every day somewhere in the world: France, Germany, America. We would go down in the morning to buy alcohol and tobacco, and read headlines announcing new atrocities. When the fog lifted I found I had a different girlfriend.*

In the midst of all that I had a panic attack when I started wondering: What if death is no oblivion and we are locked into existence, round after round of anguish and bewilderment? But maybe I'm repeating myself. I slept terribly last night. I worked too late and drank too much coffee and was unable to turn off the awful thoughts even with a tumbler of vodka. I masturbated, twice, in the manner of torture victims who wish to wear themselves out before their next ordeal.

The Valium helped, before it ran out – I owe you. It would be fun if you were here. Although, if you were, who could I write to? It would be nice to drink red wine until everything was a blur, then wander the streets at dawn. I read your story, by the way, and thought I recognised the man, which made me feel I should keep my distance.

Most days I hang around by the canal, the cafes. I'm spending more money than is coming in, as usual. Often I feel I'm not writing or reading enough, that work proceeds too slowly. But then something clears and I realise it's going at exactly the pace it needs to. Says the Tao Te Ching: *nature never hurries, yet everything gets done.*

Hotel

During my final year at college, I took an evening course in meditation at the Buddhist Centre in Dublin. The classes were held in a room below street level, so that you could look up and see the polished shoes and high heels of office workers hurrying past on their way home. Before taking the course, I'd had a vague understanding of what meditation was, coupled with a sense that I was the kind of person who needed it most. My knowledge of Buddhism was likewise vague. I thought of it as something exotic and reputable, a cultural practice of people in distant lands who weren't as screwed up as I was.

On the first evening we were instructed in the two core practices of Buddhist meditation: the one that continually reverts attention to the breath, and the one that cultivates feelings of compassion for self and others. The effect meditation had on me was dramatic and immediate. My psyche was like a virus-clogged laptop that had been defragged and rebooted. Meditating for around half an hour every day, I was amazed at how clear and focused I felt, how in control of my habitually racing thoughts.

I decided that, in order to explore this new-found source of clarity, I would quit all the stimulants I'd been greedily consuming since my teenage years. This had never really struck me as a serious possibility before: drugs and alcohol, coffee and cigarettes were, I imagined, entwined with my very identity. I knew that these substances were not without blame for my ruinous inner state – the depression and exhaustion and anxiety and paranoia – but because they also seemed to offer *relief* from that inner state, I had rejected out of hand any suggestion that I give them up, even when it was put to me by my psychoanalyst. Now it seemed feasible to forego the endless pursuit of a high, because I had discovered something to replace it with.

I began hanging out more at the Buddhist Centre, where I took further courses (yoga turned out not to be my thing – it required effort, whereas meditation involved literally sitting there doing nothing) and bought books on Buddhism. I found the literature luminous and nourishing, a balm after the Gothic explorations of deviance I'd read as a student of psychoanalysis (I was studying for a master's in the subject, impelled by the revelations of my own therapy) and the nihilistic art that was my usual fix. The later Buddhist schools in particular – Mahayana and Vajrayana – were seductively psychedelic and enigmatically metaphysical. (From the *Heart Sutra*: 'The world is the same as the Void. The Void is the same as the world.') It impressed me that Buddhism offered a blueprint for living that was not moralistic but rational – Buddhists rarely spoke of good or evil, only of skilful or unskilful actions. It did not require the abdication of reason but rather reason's full application, though with the ultimate aim of transcending rationality. Buddhism as a whole was sunny and fresh; delving into it was like discovering Bach, or Brian Eno's ambient albums, after years of listening to abrasive punk.

For a period – the phase of my life I want to imagine here – I was fanatically interested in Buddhism and hoped it might offer a way out of the predicament I was trapped in, if I could only exert enough vigour in aligning myself with its teachings. I wondered why everyone was not as passionately engaged with Buddhism – the body of wisdom I learned to call the dharma – as I was.

Time rushes past. We become swept up in life's tumult. Years go by, full of drama and event. We roam the world. And then, during moments of calm, we see that time hasn't really gone anywhere, just as we ourselves are right where we were ten years earlier, though our skin is tougher and lines are etched in our faces. It dawns on us that time does not progress along a line, as we supposed, but expands outwards, and deepens.

The Buddhists tell us, famously, that there is no self (the doctrine of *anattā*) and no abiding substance to the phenomena that make up the world in its flux. That can sound appealing. At least, it sounded appealing to the younger me, for whom the self was, as Nietzsche put it in his loopy idea of eternal recurrence, *the heaviest burden*. I still find it comforting to believe that there is no self – but only on those days when the self throbs like a toothache. Other times – when I get a rave review in a major newspaper, say – I'm quite into my self. I check my self out, admiring its reflection in the world's mirrors. Then a hatchet job appears and I'm all for *anattā* again. The same oscillation runs through my feelings around impermanence, another big theme for Buddhists (*anicca*, they call it). All is transient; therefore do not cling, take life easy, roll with it. None of what arises and falls in phenomenal existence – the rave reviews or the hatchet jobs – is worth being swayed by, because none of it was ever really there. Again, it's a nice theory – in theory. I alternate between taking comfort in the doctrine of *anicca* – nothing that hurts me can last – and being discouraged by it: if nothing lasts, what does anything matter? Why write books, if they and the beings who read them are destined to vanish utterly? It was precisely such runaway trains of thought that had led me into the depression from which I looked to Buddhism for solace. And here I am, years older and none the wiser. When it comes to the doctrines of *anattā* and *anicca*, I still want to have my cake (even though it isn't there) and eat it (even though there's no *I* to do the eating).

When I finished my studies in 2005, I had no sense of what I wanted to do with my life, other than that I ought eventually to become famous – my suffering seemed to merit it – and that I wanted to travel. I had a fair bit of money saved up, having worked part-time and lived at home throughout college. My friend Matt and I booked one-way flights to Bangkok, with the aim of spending a year travelling in South-East Asia. We would have done this anyway, but my recent interests provided an additional motive for exploring a region where Buddhism flourished.

I have been high with Matt in numerous time zones, and drunk with him on more occasions than either of us would wish to remember. When we flew to Thailand, though, it was the newly sober me who accompanied him. After touching down in the Bangkok night, we made for the Khao San Road, where we checked in to a cheap room with a huge, ominously wobbling ceiling fan. We lay on parallel beds as thumping music from the adjacent nightclub rattled the walls and epileptic neon flashed on the window.

After a few days of acclimatising in Bangkok, we set out along the backpacker route. While Matt endured hangovers and chased girls, I visited temples and looked at Buddhist art in museums, aware that if I had been born here, all of this would seem as dull to me as Catholicism did back in Ireland. Each morning, in the hostel rooms we shared to cut costs, I perched on the purple hard-foam blocks I'd bought in Dublin and meditated. While it sometimes felt like a chore, more often I relished sitting in the morning quiet, tuning in to the body, observing the drift of my thoughts. The technique of meditation is simplicity itself. The idea is that by gently insisting on a direct perception of the meditative object – traditionally, the sensation of the breath, considered as it flows through the lungs and abdomen, then through the nostrils, and finally in its entirety – the mental constructions that come between us and reality get cleaned away. It was no surprise that meditation worked so powerfully in my case: I really did need it more than others. If you put five plates into the dishwasher, four of them slightly dirty and one of them filthy, it's the latter that will benefit most. When we arrived in Asia I had been meditating for several months, and the simple truth is that everything in my life had improved: I read better, slept better, wrote better, thought better. I was more present to the people I encountered, less grindingly cerebral and abstracted. I no longer suffered from the social awkwardness that made me avoid eye contact and extricate myself from conversations at the earliest possible opportunity. Before I began meditating, I'd felt I was skimming the surface of life; now I was learning to sink to the depths.

Keen to see what would emerge from a period of intensive meditation, I persuaded Matt to join me on a retreat. Scattered around Thailand are monasteries that welcome Westerners who are willing to meditate for long hours and obey the monastic rules. The first retreat we signed up for was at Wat Pah Nanachat, a forest monastery in northern Thailand. We spent a month there, during which time we pledged to maintain the Buddhist noble silence.

Meditation should make you saner, but at Wat Pah Nanachat I meditated myself crazy. My grievances with the conditions at the monastery were many, and here is just one: the jackhammers that clanged and roared all day *right outside the meditation hall*. Monks in saffron robes wandered hither and yon, but the place felt more like a building site – it *was* a building site – than a realm of tranquil contemplation. My mind began to gnaw on itself with weird fixations and vicious self-critique. Eventually I broke. One evening, a couple of weeks in, I knocked on Matt's cabin door. He let me in casually, as if this were normal and not a violation of our vow of silence. He sat on the wooden floor with his legs crossed, emanating ease, and asked me how it was going. When I tried to reply, tears came to my eyes. Matt looked away, embarrassed. We were not the kind of friends who cried in front of one another. After an awkward moment I pulled it together enough to unburden myself: I explained that I had grown terrified of my own mind. Inside me was a malevolent entity whose intention was to torture and annihilate me, and now this presence had the upper hand – I was at the edge of catastrophe.

Matt asked me, reasonably enough, what I was on about.

I tried to explain. Several hours of each day were devoted to walking meditation – you pace from one end of the hall to the other, bringing awareness to the soles of the feet. When you reach the wall, you turn around, then set out for the opposite wall. Simple enough, or so it would seem. But whenever I approached the wall, a feeling of disquiet would arise, as if the wall were a looming menace. Initially this feeling was mild, but soon it became unignorable. That was the problem: I tried to ignore the dread, with the result that it was all I could think about. I knew I ought to observe these obsessions as transient phenomena that arise and fall like any other, void of substance. But this knowledge was useless because now I worried *about* my worrying, and for all I knew this vortex of anxiety and meta-anxiety would expand to destroy everything good in my life. Any man who has been through the fiasco of sexual dysfunction will recognise the mechanism: first you get spooked by some mishap that would be fleeting and insignificant if you did not fixate on it; but you *do* fixate on it, and soon it is the worry itself – rather than the worry's object – that blocks what ought to happen from happening. Worry *manifests* its object – we ourselves erect the gallows we swing from. Once again I had fucked things up spectacularly, allowed my lunatic obsessions to wreck what might have helped me.

Matt took all this in with calm interest. He himself, it transpired, was having a pleasant time – he would be happy to stay on for an extra couple of weeks, although he was looking forward to getting drunk in Chiang Mai. The evidence of Matt's sanity reassured me – maybe

I could be sane again too – and I managed to stay on for the remainder of the retreat.

We travelled to Laos, then to Vietnam, before swerving into Cambodia and back into Thailand. Our respective experiences in Asia ran in a neat parallel: Matt's was nocturnal and hedonistic, whereas mine remained sober and largely solitary. Without drinking, I found it hard to be around people; I just wanted to get back to my books. Although I had forsworn partying, I got a vicarious kick out of Matt's debauches. Often he would be getting back from his nights out as I arose to meditate. He would recount his drunken, lovelorn misadventures while I set up my meditation space, lighting incense sticks.

We attended another retreat, in the south of Thailand. I was still rattled by the previous ordeal, but this retreat came with strong recommendations and lasted only ten days. Sure enough, it was all that the northern boot camp was not, conducive to insight rather than implosion. Afterwards, Matt returned to Ireland, having exhausted his savings. The night before he flew out, I suspended my year-long abstinence and we whizzed through Bangkok's bars, downing Long Island iced teas. Then he was gone and I was alone in Asia, with no real reason to be there other than an aversion to what other Westerners I met called *real life*, which seemed to mean doing what you did not want to be doing.

One evening, feeling that if I returned to my hotel room I might hang myself, I wandered through

Patpong, Bangkok's red-light district. I had avoided such situations as antithetical to my meditative focus, but tonight, depressed and lucid, I saw that I was free to do as I liked, in this unreal life on the far side of the planet from anyone who knew me. I watched a strip show in a dark venue where I was the only customer. A dozen girls crowded on a platform with a lit-up floor, all in white lingerie. They were like children, giggling and chattering, making no effort towards eroticism. I drank a beer, and left when I felt tempted by the smiling girl who sat beside me and placed a hand on my thigh, saying there was a room upstairs where we could go. Out on the shimmering pedestrian strip, I looked up to see a white girl in a red dress, as alone as I was, walking towards me. Our eyes met in a glance of abashed, charged acknowledgement that neither of us should have been there. A few days later we travelled together to Ko Pha-Ngan, an island in the Gulf of Thailand. At the gaudy tourist enclave of Haad Rin, we rented a motorbike and scouted the island till we found a secluded beach on the north-western coast. Wooden fishing boats drifted in and out from a jetty. A bamboo cafe served pad thai, coconut shakes, mango with sticky rice. We rented a beach hut, paying for three weeks up front. During the days, we lazed in hammocks and read, and rode to the island's hilly interior, and had sex in our cabin with sand on the floor. Afterwards, as our breathing slowed, I could hear the swelling hiss of the surf, the cries of birds, the rhythmic dunk of a fisherman's oar. Once, as I was phasing in and out of sleep, she read me lines from Camus:

> We swim ashore to an empty beach, all day
> plunging into the water and drying off on the sand.
> When evening comes, under a sky that turns green
> and fades into the distance, the sea, already calm,
> grows more peaceful still ... Knowing that certain
> nights whose sweetness lingers will keep returning
> to the earth and sea after we are gone, yes, this helps
> us die.

At night we got drunk on buckets of whiskey mixed with ice and Red Bull, and danced at psy-trance parties in the jungle, where *om* symbols and luminous Hindu deities hung above the dance area. In the mornings I would step down from our cabin and plunge into the gulf to wash away my hangover.

The first cracks appeared in my meditation practice. I'd been scrupulous about not missing a single day, suspecting that, if I did, it would be that bit easier to miss another, until soon I would not be meditating at all. Now, enervated from drinking, dancing, sex and the island sun, I tried to at least go through the motions – the non-motions – however sluggish and dull I felt. Some days, though, I was just too worn out. Looking back, it seems appropriate that my commitment began to waver during that hazy, dreamlike island spell. Perhaps the loveliness of it all – lingering in paradise with an attractive woman, given over to pleasure – showed me that I would never become any kind of Buddhist. The dharma was a refuge where I could alight for a while, recover vital energies lost to terrible times, and then move on. The Buddhists insist that sensual delight is fleeting, can only lead to attachment and misery and therefore must be renounced, but in my cells I knew that the earth housed no higher good. Denying myself would be like declining to swim in the blue waters of the gulf to avoid getting wet. Of course, when you flipped the perspective it was no less clear that *they* were right and I was wrong. All of this would be my ruin. I was hooking myself on a drug that would one day run out, and when it did my anguish would be final and absolute. You fucked until you could fuck no more, at which point you were really fucked. There was nothing out there, nothing beyond – this was it.

Isolde flew home to Marseilles. I stayed on the island for a while, riding the motorbike and getting drunk alone. I left and spent a month trailing listlessly across Malaysia, then flew across the South China Sea to Borneo, too lonely to want to meet anyone. I was meditating every day again, heeding the Buddhist counsel and *sitting with it* – the sadness, the torpor. In the drag of depleted serotonin I boarded a boat that kept going upriver, through the rainforest, from one village to the next, till there was no further village to reach. The tribespeople lived in longhouses, and entertained themselves with illegal cockfighting and drunkenness.

Former headhunters, they had modernised and were now more interested in tattoos. I got a tattoo, covering a prior tattoo I'd grown tired of. I took a picture and emailed it to Isolde. *If you get bored of this one*, she wrote back, *you'd better just get the arm amputated.*

Various people had told me I really must go to India, so I returned to Bangkok by train and flew to Calcutta. For the next half-year I traced a jagged arc across the country's north. Other Western travellers – the kind who had careers and lives back home – would have needed no more than a month to tick off all the places I saw, but my approach to travel by now amounted to staying as still as possible, against exotic backdrops that gave this stasis a veneer of achievement. Whenever I moved on, I did so from a kind of politeness, a sense that it would be embarrassing if I just kept hanging around indefinitely. By drifting from city to city, I could maintain the appearance of motion when in truth I was going nowhere. On Christmas Eve, I got drunk on a Calcutta rooftop with a Norwegian girl whose head was shaved. The hangover breached my defences, and my body spent the next two weeks turning itself inside out. I was often too feeble to stagger to the corner kiosk for the daily bowl of boiled rice I was urged to get down me.

When I was better, I moved on to the sacred city of Varanasi, as otherworldly a place as could exist and still be on planet earth. Hindus from across India go there to die, then have their bodies cremated on the 'burning ghats' along the filthy Ganges. The motive of these death-pilgrims is instant *moksha*, release from the cycle of rebirth: grand prize in a faith that views worldly existence as an aeonic drag. I took Hindi lessons in the riverside home of a corpulent professor whose wife kept him fed with trays of snacks. He taught me to read the script aloud, even when I had no idea what it meant – the language is wholly phonetic, like Italian. I memorised a phrase with which to commence every faltering dialogue. It went something like *Tutti phutti Hindi bolsakta hoo*: 'I speak broken-shattered Hindi.'

After further meditation retreats in Sarnath and the New Age bastion of Rishikesh, in search of respite from India's clogged cities I travelled to Dharamsala, the airy town in the Himalayan foothills that is the home of the Tibetan community in exile. I hung around for a few weeks, eating dumplings and reading in cafes. There was talk of sightings of Richard Gere, though the Dalai Lama was said to be out of town. Prayer flags flapped in the wind. Monks carrying alms bowls walked the streets trailing burgundy robes. I attended a weekend retreat focused on death and dying, led by a white-haired American who felt there was nothing sadder than to expire in an indifferent hospital ward, the TV spewing out daytime banality. On the last day he guided us through the meditation practice in which one visualises one's corpse in advancing stages of putrefaction. I became a skeleton, strips of rotting flesh clinging to my bones. When I came down from the retreat, Isolde had emailed me pictures of her naked body. I covertly masturbated in the back of a dingy web cafe while gazing at them, my heart thumping. At temples I peered into mandalas, speculating about their affinities with the visions I'd experienced on hallucinogens. Like its aesthetic traditions, Buddhist cosmology and metaphysics had found ample space to grow strange and complex at the roof of the world, centuries before China's annexation of Tibet. The result was the psychedelic splendour of Vajrayana Buddhism.

In Dharamsala I read *The Tibetan Book of Living and Dying*, Sogyal Rinpoche's modern commentary on *The Tibetan Book of the Dead*. That book really is a trip. Famously, it describes the experiences we are said to undergo after death, adrift in a series of bardos – intermediate states – before being reincarnated. I read about these visions with keen but sceptical interest. Rooted in a materialist ontology – and, it seems to me now, intellectually blinkered – I equated truth with harshness: despair was proof that I was not bullshitting myself. I countered the woolly thinking of the dharma bums I met across India with a Nietzschean take on truth: each man is entitled to as much of it as he can bear. From the outset I had sought to practise a Buddhism without supernatural beliefs: it was not a faith but a contemplative practice grounded in empirical experience. I considered my resistance to soothing metaphysical fantasies a mark of good intellectual hygiene. The Vajrayana account of the afterlife, however, was hardly reassuring. Next to it, Western annihilationism seemed an easy way out, rendering not only death but life, too, weightless and without risk. The Tibetans believe that in the bardo following death, when one peers into 'the mirror of past actions' and the moment arrives to decide the nature of the next rebirth – hellish or exquisite, brilliant or debased – it is no external agency that issues the judgement, but one's deepest self. The idea struck me as terrible, profound and, in some sense, true.

From Dharamsala I headed north to Kashmir, where I based myself for a few weeks to pursue my studies. Specifically, I rented a houseboat on the Dal Lake in Srinagar, and the object of my studies was ketamine. This drug had never breached the Dublin circles I moved in; I knew little about it, except that it was a dissociative and, at least according to popular myth, a horse tranquilliser. An Israeli told me that with a little bribe you could buy ketamine in many Indian pharmacies. It came in bottles and you dried it out on a tin plate under the sun. In the evenings, with the sun sinking on the rim of snowy mountains encircling the lake, I insufflated lines of ketamine in the seclusion of my houseboat. It was incredibly weird, inducing a state of abstract derangement that was unlike any of the other drugs I had tried. It was like putting on a VR headset to enter the reality of a psychotic who was also strapped into VR while on shattering drugs. The day after a session, I would write up my experience at absurd length in my battered journal. I imagined I was conducting important research at the limits of consciousness, but I see now I was just getting fucked up on a boat. Later, I was dumbfounded to learn that ketamine had caught on back home as a party drug – people were taking this stuff at *nightclubs*.

After filling scores of pages with trip reports, I left the lakes and mountains of Kashmir and headed south. My intended year away had elapsed, but rather than return to *real life* I decided to fly to South America. When my money ran out I would find a job in a bar or cafe, build on the Spanish I'd learned at school. I had grown weary of asceticism; I missed being ruled by my appetites. The same factors that had drawn me to Buddhism now repelled me from it. In Buddhist psychology, the three so-called defilements of consciousness are greed, hatred and delusion. One thing I was not deluded about was being prey to all of them, but I was not ready to let go. Greed was wont to tear through my life like a tornado, yet it was the force that animated me, gobbling up books and pleasure and experience. As for hatred, the very word excited me: *hate, hate, hate.* I don't quite know where it came from, this vast capacity for hate, this hate-habit, which has never really diminished, fuelling daily reveries of carnage. It was present, certainly, in adolescence, when I would fantasise about smashing my father's skull in as we sat watching football, whenever he did something I loathed like bite his nails. The hatred I felt for my mother, who had done nothing to deserve it except create me, was extreme and pathological. Yet hate gave me fire. At bottom I did not want the peace that Buddhism offered – not yet. I knew that whatever discipline I had as a student of the dharma would dissolve when I left Asia. The thought did not trouble me.

I booked a flight out of Mumbai. Before leaving India, I spent a few nights in New Delhi, in a windowless hotel room high above the city's bustle. Throughout my travels in Asia, I had been keeping a blog, read by friends and family back home. It was conceived as an experiment in honesty, a bonfire of the inhibitions that would otherwise hamper the books I was determined one day to write. No matter how sordid or embarrassing my experiences, I typed them up and posted them on the blog. What happened next, though, in Delhi, was the one episode I declined to make public.

The day before I was due to leave for Mumbai, I poured my last bottle of ketamine on to the tin plate and left it to dry on the hotel roof. I spent the day sightseeing, and when I came back in the evening there didn't seem to be as much crystallised matter as there ought to have been. I persuaded myself that someone had knocked into the tray, spilled most of my ket. As the sun retreated on Delhi, I sat in my boxers in my hotel room and trained the fan on my body to cool the sweat. This was the time of the Iraq War. On the television screen, marines stalked the peripheries of Baghdad or Fallujah in the glow of night-vision green. I had my earphones in, the music on shuffle. Using a bank card, I crushed up the crystallised ketamine and divided it into two fat lines. Then I rolled up a banknote, leaned over and inhaled them both. I imagined it was about an average hit. Later, it would become clear that the entire bottle had been concentrated into those two lines. The word for this is overdose.

It came on fast and severe. I was in the war, clomping over scrubland amid tracer fire. The war was an emanation of the synaesthesic music that ricocheted through my skull, music I was creating with my thoughts. And then there was no war, no music, no coherent mind to grasp such concepts. There was pure existence, and this immanence was me, I was the cosmos moving through an event of sublime magnitude. The everything folded into the nothing till there was no longer any distinction: the world was the same as the Void, the Void was the same as the world. I had a sense of vast privilege at witnessing this transcendental climax. Then the Void grew tight and hot and ragged, as if Being were birthing and dying at once. It occurred to me that this was the end of it all, the eschaton. And then nothing. Aeons later, a scene slowly begins to cohere. There is blurred white light. It may be daylight, or fluorescence. There is a cube. A room. Someone is lying on the floor – a man, naked but for his underwear. He is face down in a pool of vomit. An indefinite moment passes before I realise it is me. I observe the tableau calmly, as if viewing a cadaver on a mortuary slab. Slowly the detached, hovering awareness forms an identification with the body, is drawn back into it. He twitches his fingers and toes. A hand clenches, unclenches. Finally he rises to his feet, groans, stands under the shower for half an hour. He is too out of it to feel shock – only the dull foreboding of it – at the realisation that he almost missed out on his own death.

I don't really have beliefs, but I do have an imagination, and now I imagine that I *did* die there, in that New Delhi hotel room, choked on vomit far from anyone who knew my name – and that I am there still, in that infinite instant, and all of this, the life that has happened since, is nothing but the judgement I have passed on myself, a torrent of visions ramified from who I was into what I have dreamed myself to be. Bleary and parched, beginning to apprehend the chasm I had peered into – all the shame and grief of those who loved me – I checked out of the hotel. In a daze that was like a dream of a dream of life, I cut my way through the throng, past the rickshaws and honking cars and limbless beggars, to the station, to board another train.

———

I agree with you about writerly self-pity. Nothing has given me more satisfaction and meaning than writing, though it can be so difficult. I won't kill myself (at least 'not tonight'), but I imagine that if for some reason I couldn't write, I would feel suicidal. Before I figured out how to write with the requisite competency to attract readers, life was a torment in part because I didn't know what to do with my experience: it wasn't enough, somehow, just to be. I was maddened by the idea that life may as well have never happened, that existence leaves no trace. Now I write about my existence, and in a sense I exist so as to write about it, so that the writing refracts the manner in which I live.

There was a storm on Saturday night. Now the trees in the courtyard are stripped bare and I can see the square and the Rue du Faubourg Saint-Martin from my window. I've been thinking about certain authors who haunt Paris or haunt me. I don't think I need to explain to you that I admit no separation between literature and life. When I write about other writers, other artists, I'm writing about myself, and when I write about myself, I'm writing about the universe.

My friend Sam came to visit for a few days. On the first night, we drank a lot of wine in a bar on Oberkampf with an old friend of Sam's, an English artist named Eddie, who has lived here for many years. Sam hadn't seen his friend since he too lived here, fifteen years ago. Back then, Eddie was thirty-five and seemed to the young Sam like a kind of god – the embodiment of freedom and individuation, living with his beautiful artist wife in a dazzling house they owned in Montparnasse. Upon seeing him again, Sam had to suppress his shock at how Eddie has aged. His hair is silver now, he has a bad cough from years of smoking, and he's lost the lustre he once had. He has long since separated from his wife, and lives alone in the thirteenth arrondissement.

It was unsettling to find Sam so taken aback: it confronted me with the inevitability of my own diminishment, the withering of all strength and grace. I've had the sense, over the past year or so, of enjoying a peak of life characterised by power and confidence. Hearing Sam talk about his old friend, I wondered if someone who knows me now, a young friend perhaps, would react in a similar way if they were to encounter me fifteen years into the future. The decline, the fading of the light, the falling short ... Is it deterioration from here on in?

Which reminds me, you never told me what you imagine death will be like. Do you think about it much?

Knife

For three years in my early twenties I underwent weekly psychoanalysis, lying on a couch in a book-lined study to talk about my most humiliating secrets, anguished intuitions and perverse desires. On the shelves of that study I noticed a number of books by Georges Bataille. Like many of his readers, I knew Bataille only through his early pornographic novel *Story of the Eye*. My girlfriend and I used to read passages of the novel to each other, and we were vaguely, perhaps dutifully, aroused by the imagery, but for the most part we were just amused. It read like a screwball Sade: a pair of young libertines enact weird erotic scenarios involving eggs, eyeballs, priests and even bull's testicles. At moments when I feared I was saying too much to my analyst, being too open about my aberrant thoughts, the sight of Bataille's books on his shelves reassured me: if he was reading this stuff, he could take anything I might serve up.

Bataille came to fascinate me, more for his theoretical works and for his life and personality than for his fiction. Two key words across his writings were 'ecstasy' and 'excess'. The words resonated with me, engaged as I then was in my own pursuit of ecstasy by means of excess, which, as it happened, often meant swallowing excessive quantities of MDMA at raves, festivals and concerts. I felt myself to be at war with the world. The values I lived by stemmed in part from the conviction, attained at the age of sixteen and never really discarded, that work, as it was generally experienced by people of my own working-class background – i.e. dreary toil that you didn't really believe in – was to be avoided as far as possible. Further, the exact contrary of such toil was the overpowering, life-justifying rapture that my friends and I found in music, clubs, art, books and drugs. Bataille, it seemed to me, had done the anthropological research to back up these ecstatic intuitions of mine. In his book *Erotism*, he argued that human beings had lost themselves in the work-world, rendering themselves means rather than ends. The systems of rationality and order we had erected to protect us from the dangers of nature had grown too rigid and powerful: they now enslaved rather than served us. Bataille was clear on what the solution was to this mass human self-abnegation: 'exuberant eroticism' and rapturous excess, which brought the sacred back into earthly existence, reinstating human 'sovereignty' against a dreary capitalist world that sought to deny it. Cosmic serfdom was cast off through useless acts of pleasure, self-destruction and sexuality.

Although I discovered him via my studies in philosophy, a large part of Bataille's appeal was the alternative he offered to philosophy's stock-in-trade, namely sober reflection and careful reasoning. While I found I could do very well in philosophy, intuiting what was needed to impress my lecturers and get good marks, I really wasn't into sober reflection and careful reasoning. When it got right down to it, I wasn't even really into philosophy. What had drawn me to the subject was its promise of astonishing flights of thought; shocking and dangerous ideas; a sense of vertigo; vistas of the sublime tinged with madness and horror. As the vast majority of academic philosophy turned out to be pretty antithetical to all that, I spent much of my time studying the subject in a state of catatonic boredom. During ethics lectures, unable to bear sitting through a meticulous unpacking of the complexities underlying the abortion or euthanasia debates, I would routinely skive off to play pool and smoke joints. For a while I considered dropping out, but I had come to philosophy after dropping out of an even duller subject, and to do so again would be to invite the dangerous conclusion that there was no subject that could hold my interest. Philosophy was all about the exaltation of reason, yet what got me through my studies was the often stridently *un*reasonable work of thinkers like Bataille and Nietzsche. While Bataille was treated warily by academic staff, he had far more draw for me than even such a colossal figure as Kant, who I could never really bring myself to read (which is a little like studying physics and ignoring Einstein). Like Borges, I viewed metaphysics as a branch of fantastical literature, embracing ideas not so much for their truth value as for their force of astonishment. When I finished my studies and moved into the great open world, these wild and unreasonable thinkers were the ones who stayed with me, who I continued reading, who I am still reading now.

In the spring of 2015, not long after I had stayed with my friend Zoé while researching Emil Cioran, I fulfilled a long-held desire and moved to Paris. I lived in the nineteenth arrondissement, first near the Canal Saint-Martin with my girlfriend, then by the Parc des Buttes-Chaumont, on my own. One afternoon in early summer, wandering through the Pompidou Centre, I came across a display detailing Georges Bataille's relationship with the surrealist movement and his influence on the avant-garde in general. Bataille was acknowledged as a central figure in the avant-garde's struggle to surmount the 'absence of myth' in the modern world. In black-and-white photographs taken on Paris streets, Bataille was as well groomed as ever, peering out from the past with those serene, kindly eyes that belied the rage and revulsion of his thought. Being at a loose end, I decided to visit some of the sites and addresses relating to the life of this weird author, whose work had marked my own weird youth.

On a drizzly late Sunday morning in August, I left my flat and took the Métro to Pigalle. As is not uncommon in Paris, there was a condom machine by the bottom of the stairway leading out of Pigalle station. Paris is widely known as the City of Lights, but to me it was the City of Condoms. Everywhere I looked I saw them. When I'd moved into my place by the park, a superlatively bohemian dwelling (it was falling apart, basically), the young woman I was renting from while she was away in Mexico had evidently been in too much of a rush to clean up the bedroom. I knew this because of the large, open box of condoms and the overfull ashtray on the bedside table – not to mention the clutter and dishevelment everywhere else. I didn't mind. In fact, I was pleased by it, this unwillingness to dispel the stereotype of the Parisian artist (the woman was a film-maker) – languid sex, dubious hygiene standards, chain-smoking. To me the condoms and ashtray were like the sweet that hoteliers leave on the pillow for when you check in to a room: a welcoming touch.

I emerged from Pigalle station on to the Boulevard de Clichy, one of Paris's seedier zones, with its sex shops, strip joints and the Moulin Rouge. The first time I'd come to Paris, a decade earlier, I'd had a nasty experience around here. After spending the day at the Musée d'Orsay, my girlfriend and I had decided to see a strip show. We entered, took our seats at a table in the darkness, and awkwardly watched women with ravaged faces and surgically remade bodies gyrate indifferently around a pole, one after the other. I remember being appalled and fascinated by one of the strippers in particular, a blonde with narrow, shaded eyes. Her face was harsh and run through with lines of age, but her breasts were immense, upright and gleaming. She seemed to me a kind of Minotaur. An enormous black man in a tuxedo appeared at our table and grinningly asked us what we would have to drink, pointing to a laminated menu he briefly held before us. We ordered 7Up and vodkas. A while later, just as we were deciding it was time to leave, the waiter returned and placed our bill on the table in a little black plastic dish. What it said was this: four hundred and forty euro. We rose to our feet in protest; the waiter's arm thrust out to block our exit. Two other men materialised and circled us, shouting in our faces. I said I wanted to call the police and their roars got louder. One of them poked his finger in my chest. Eventually we managed to convince them that all we had on us was twenty-five euro. I handed over the bills and we walked out of there with what dignity we still had, which was none. In hindsight, it seems unlikely that they would have assaulted us – I later learned that this is a common scam at strip clubs – but at the time I found it prudent to hide behind my girlfriend and suggest she sort this out because she 'knew French' (she could say 'please', 'thank you' and 'where can we find the Métro?').

Now the streets around Clichy were Sunday-quiet. Men sat outside cafes, nursing glasses of beer or coffees. Some drank pastis. One or two of them even wore berets. It is commonly said that the old Paris is dead and gone – the literary Paris of splenetic *flâneurs*, warring avant-garde factions and promiscuous philosophers. The real

Paris, this narrative insists, is now to be found outside the Périphérique, in the sprawl of the *banlieues*, which are addled with poverty and hate. In this reading, Paris's twenty arrondissements bounded by the Périphérique comprise a bourgeois enclave, obsolete and fated to be overrun by the scorned, the excluded, the enraged – all the post-colonial hens come home to roost. Sure enough, a week after I left Paris, an Islamist suicide commando would wreak carnage on some of the city's trendiest quarters, intensifying an era of fear and vulnerability. Glancing around Pigalle on this grey morning, though, it was clear that one could still live out the Parisian dream, or the cliché, with ample cultural props to flesh out the illusion.

For instance, this young, stylish, Doisneau-ish couple kissing and smoking over their thimblefuls of coffee on the Place ... André Breton. So I was on the right track, and sure enough, a minute later I was standing outside 42 Rue Pierre Fontaine, the address that Breton had commandeered as the headquarters of the surrealist movement for forty-odd years. The word 'headquarters', with its martial overtones, is apt. Like many of the avant-garde movements of the period, surrealism was run on near-military lines, with Breton as its ruthless general, calling the shots on who was to be purged and excommunicated, and allying his forces with the global struggles against capitalism and fascism. Reading about the spats and fissures, I wondered if they weren't all just playing around a little bit. It did look like fun, the art-militancy and bitchy factionalism. More likely, though, they were in deadly earnest, sandwiched as they were between two near-apocalyptic wars, and it was me and my video-game culture that lacked seriousness. As if in oblique sympathy with my thinking, the one-time headquarters of surrealism had since been transformed into the Comédie de Paris, a stand-up venue. On either side of the road there were sex shops and Vietnamese pho restaurants; a few doors down was the dilapidated shell of a Monoprix supermarket. A plaque on the wall commemorating Breton and the surrealists included a quote: *Je cherche l'or du temps*. As I stood there, a woman who I fancifully imagined was a prostitute walked past, smoking a cigarette and holding open a hefty paperback, reading as she strode. A thin, dark man began to roar into his phone in Arabic, gesticulating furiously. He turned the corner and the street fell quiet again. I watched a cute girl in tight blue jeans cross the road at the traffic lights. Idly, I thought about getting a prostitute. It would have been nice, just then. I found myself regretting that I didn't come from a culture in which paying for sex was easy and natural, a norm, like in South American novels.

My next stop was Rue de Rennes, south of the Seine, near Montparnasse. It did not take long to find the building where Bataille had lived, with his mother and brother, from the age of nineteen to thirty-one. This was the address where Bataille stripped naked in the darkness and, for reasons best known to himself, jerked off over his mother's freshly deceased corpse. There was no plaque on this house, even though masturbating over the corpse appears to have been a crucial, not to say seminal, event in Bataille's life, one that he wrote about recurrently. Christophe Honoré's loose film adaptation of Bataille's novel *My Mother* ends with a startlingly abrupt version of this incident: the adolescent protagonist bursts into the room where his mother is lying in wake, starts jerking off, and roars that he does not want to die. *Fin*. When I saw the film at the IFI in Dublin, the audience burst into laughter at this necrophilic money shot.

The years that Bataille spent living in Rue de Rennes were not ones of great literary productivity. The only real book he had written by his early thirties was *Story of the Eye*. Bataille's psychoanalyst, Adrien Borel, served as his editor, reading the novel chapter by chapter, helping his client refine it down from the unreadable pile of obsessive crap it would otherwise undoubtedly have been. Bataille claimed that it was his psychoanalysis that allowed him to write. Moreover, it allowed him to live: 'It changed me from being as absolutely obsessive as I was into someone relatively viable.' It was also Borel who gave Bataille the photographs he would fixate on for forty years, of a young Chinese man suffering the 'Torture of a Hundred Pieces'. (In Chris Kraus's annoyingly trendy novel *I Love Dick*, Kraus complains about the 'Bataille Boys' who imitatively gaze at these photographs, 'young white men drawn to the more "transgressive" elements of modernism, heroic sciences of human sacrifice and torture as legitimised by Georges Bataille'.)

My intention had been to walk from Rue de Rennes to the house on Rue Blomet in the fourteenth arrondissement, where the surrealist movement's second garrison had been based. Instead, with the afternoon sun breaking through, I found myself walking in the opposite direction, towards the Latin Quarter and the Shakespeare and Company bookshop.

Shakespeare and Company is perhaps unique in the world in being a bookshop that is at the same time a tourist attraction. People come to see it: they stand around outside and take photographs. Then they go inside and take photographs. Some of them stand inside and take photographs of their friends who are outside, or vice versa. Still others stand in the doorway, either to take photographs of friends who are inside or outside, or to be photographed themselves, standing in the doorway like dicks, blocking my way. Almost all of these snappers buy a book or two during their visit, many of which bear the names of such usual suspects as Kerouac, Bukowski, Hemingway and Salinger. Hanging out at Shakespeare and Company seemed to be a long-established tradition among young anglophone literary types in Paris – to the point of cliché, in the way that everything about young anglophone literary types in Paris was cliché. (It has to be said, however, that the selection of books in the shop was impeccable, and by this I mean that they kept my work in stock, which fact

I knew because I checked every time I was in there.) A few weeks earlier, at the peak of the heatwave that had ignited Paris for an infernal, beer-swilling fortnight, I had come along one evening to hear the English writer Geoff Dyer read from his work on the courtyard out front. 'I moved to Paris when I was thirty to live the life of the writer – which is all but indistinguishable from the life of a total loser,' he quipped, drawing somewhat deranged laughter from me and the other total losers who had gathered in the tormenting heat.

Poky and dim, Shakespeare and Company was always crowded, but I had never seen it more crowded than it was today. Seeking refuge upstairs, where members of a writing group were reading their work while young musicians took turns on the piano in an adjacent room, I became trapped on the stairs. A line of people was coming down, and another was coming up, but there was only space for a single file. Neither side seemed willing to give way, and I was caught in the squeeze. I began to suffer an attack of claustrophobia, which I wouldn't have thought likely in a bookstore; I considered kicking the man below me in the solar plexus. When I eventually made it back down the stairs, I ascertained that they did not have in stock the books by Bataille's theory-buddies Maurice Blanchot and Pierre Klossowski I'd hoped to pick up. Still, I was pleased to discover that the well-dressed German staffer who confirmed this for me had himself written a PhD on Bataille. He shared tips and suggestions, and for a few minutes we bonded over talk of sacrificial mutilation, the eroticism of violence and the ecstasy of war. I bade adieu to my fellow Bataille Boy, then spent a few minutes repositioning copies of my own novel around the shop so that they hid the books of rival authors. The door hinges groaned with another incoming surge of tourists: I decided I'd better split before a tragedy unfolded.

A week later, I woke up early – too early – on a Tuesday morning to catch a train to Burgundy. I'd drunk just a few bottles of beer the night before, but because only four hours had passed since I'd finished the last one, it felt like more. I shouldn't have gone to bed so late (or drunk beer), but then, had I gone any earlier, I wouldn't have been able to sleep. For a month I had been trying and failing to realign my quotidian rhythms so that I wasn't so unprofitably out of sync with French culture. All across Paris, bistros and restaurants offered excellent-value lunch menus – *formules du midi* – which began at noon and ended around two o'clock. After that, not only could you not order a lunch menu (starter and main or main and dessert), you couldn't order anything at all until dinnertime. They had their hours of convention, the French, and they weren't about to change for the likes of me, whose day only got slouching to a start as the waiters cleared up after the lunchtime crowds.

A few coffees got me back in the game. I boarded a train from Paris-Bercy towards the commune of Sermizelles in the department of Yonne in the region of Burgundy (all these administrative subdivisions meant nothing to me, but I enjoyed writing them in my notebook, the lexical trail connoting an odd mixture of bureaucratic staidness and the romance of foreign journeys). From Sermizelles it was a two-hour walk to the hill town of Vézelay, my destination. As we pulled out of Paris through the *banlieues* in the grey, misty morning, I alternated between reading Georges Bataille while feeling I should be looking out the window, and looking out the window while feeling I ought to get back to Bataille. I love being on trains and tend to get a lot of reading done on them, even if this reading is inevitably spoiled by a nagging sense of missing out on the landscape. Often visiting places is merely a pretext for a nice long train journey, the longer the better, with books, newspapers and my phone to keep me amused. I had been one of the last people I knew to buy a smartphone, but now that I had one, I was wholly reliant on it. I didn't really have any friends in Paris (Zoé had moved to Avignon at the start of the summer for her theatre career) but that was okay because I had my phone. There was little, perhaps nothing, it couldn't do, and I anticipated a long, rich, tender relationship with it, one lacking the myriad kinds of messiness that made human affairs, which on the whole had not gone so well for me, notoriously tricky. The key to getting the most out of your train journey was to resist tweeting or posting anything to social media en route, because if you did you would become distracted by checking what sort of response it was getting, and thus unable to read *The Accursed Share* or anything else.

When Georges Bataille founded the secret society of Acéphale in the tweetless years leading up to the Second World War, one of the rites its members undertook was to journey alone on a train from Paris to the tiny, remote station at Saint-Nom-la-Bretèche, where they would walk into the woods and congregate by the stump of a tree that had been struck by lightning. The members of Acéphale were sworn to secrecy and so we do not know exactly what they got up to out there, if there were orgiastic rituals (their highest aspiration was to carry out a human sacrifice), or whether they all just hung around in companionable silence, reflecting on what a spectacular nutjob Bataille had shown himself to be.

There were a couple of changeovers and I had an hour to kill at a station called Auxerre Saint-Gervais. It was pleasant enough, with its church perched on a hilltop and its houseboats and barges docked along the river. I didn't really know what part of France we were in, which department or region or commune or whatever: the feeling of being in a dreamy, interzonal nowhere-place was quite agreeable. There wasn't a single person on earth who knew where I was. I imagined staying on there indefinitely, checking in to a hotel or renting a small room by the river, blending in with local life, living out my days and never contacting anyone back home. Perhaps I would meet a local girl, marry, and remake myself as a provincial Frenchman, with his own Instagram page and Twitter handle.

An hour later, none of those things having happened, a coach carried me the rest of the way to Sermizelles. I disembarked by the small pale-yellow building of the train station, which was closed. There was no one around and, along with a few houses across the road, it appeared that the train station *was* Sermizelles. Forested hills rose up on either side of a river that meandered behind the houses. There were no signposts. Seeing a man packing things into the boot of a car, I asked him in French for directions to Vézelay. He replied in lilting, hesitant English:

'You turn right. Then go that way forever.'

He considered for a moment, then revised his estimation downwards: 'For ten kilometres.'

It had turned into a magnificent late morning. The Burgundy countryside I marched across was resplendently green, with the gurgle of the river – la Cure – the soft breeze, and the birdsong marred only by the noise of cars that zoomed past now and then along the road I was following. My tiredness had dispersed and I felt supremely cheerful in the sunshine and the country air. As I walked, my thoughts began to drift towards a realisation that had been dawning slowly on me these past few days: namely that Georges Bataille, whose grave and former home I was on my way to visit, was of dwindling interest to me. I had read him at a certain period of my life with great fascination, but now, in the Burgundy sun, I started to feel I wanted nothing more to do with him. His capacity for getting me high – blazed out in a trance of wilful irrationalism – had diminished. Everything about Bataille was starting to seem cadaverous, putrefactive, pitch-black, violent and obscene – I just wasn't on that trip any more. My thirty-third birthday was bearing down on me, an age that I had long associated, apprehensively, with Thomas Kinsella's poem 'Mirror in February':

I read that I have looked my last on youth.

Not to mention:

… they are not made whole
That reach the age of Christ.

I had imagined that it would be alarming to hit the milestone of thirty-three, yet as the date approached I had never felt more whole, less gloomy, further from death. I was getting older, but the truth of it was that in my youth I had been infinitely older, infinitely gloomier, more haunted by the death in everything. Bataille had helped to validate and clarify the lust for chaos, destruction and ecstasy that had governed my younger years, but now I sensed he was a writer I would have no further dealings with. If philosophers were musical subgenres, then Georges Bataille was death metal – and death metal was insufferable, its devotees a gang of dreary bastards. You liked to know it was out there, so extreme and absolute, but you were damned if you were going to spend your summer days listening to it.

It was lunchtime when I reached Vézelay. I had eaten nothing all day except a croissant that weirdly smelled of garlic back at Auxerre Saint-Gervais, so I decided to restore myself with a long, lavish meal. Vézelay was known for its wines, and I drank quite a bit over the course of the lunch, which, with the customary languor of French waiters very much in evidence, went on for so long that, by the time my dessert arrived (pear in red-wine sauce, which I washed down with red wine), I felt as if it was time for dinner, or at least for an aperitif, which I ordered, though it overlapped with the post-lunch grappa that had just arrived. I was a bit drunk. Some people claimed that alcohol was bad, but the truth of the matter was that it was actually very good, I reflected drunkenly. Yes, it was really, really good. As I noted this I also noted that, its other benefits notwithstanding, alcohol did not exactly lead to profundity or subtlety of insight. But who cared, when drinking it made you feel this good – so at home in the universe, so tolerant and benign. I would have recommended it to anyone. I took out my notebook and wrote: 'Alcohol is good. It makes you feel … like an emperor.' As I drank an espresso to try to clear my head, knowing I had work to do, it struck me how baffling it was that the French had produced such a formidable literature despite this custom they had of drinking wine with every meal. I loved wine, drank it copiously, but I did not see it as being compatible with writing. One glass of wine and my writing day was shot. Drowsy and lethargic, I would have to wait till the next day to even think about stringing some words together. The only thing I felt up to doing after drinking a glass of wine was drinking another – like the one I was now ordering to wash down my digestif, or aperitif, or whatever it was. Yet France had produced one of the world's richest literatures, whose practitioners were skulling wine the whole time. And you never even really heard of properly *alcoholic* French authors, the way you did with the Americans and the English, not to mention the Irish. The French got on with their drinking and their writing without making a fuss about either.

I checked in to my hotel, then strolled up the town's sloped, cobblestoned main thoroughfare, the Rue Saint-Etienne. Halfway up, facing on to the Place du Grand Puits, was the house where Bataille had lived, first in 1943 during the Occupation, then again for several years from 1945. Across the little square from the house was a bar. The French, like the Italians, use the word 'bar' liberally: in Sicily, a bar is where you go to eat ice cream or drink an espresso; in France it might be where you have dinner. But this really was a bar, because groups of tourists sat outside it drinking wine and beer. Some of them glanced up at me as I observed Bataille's house and read the blue plaque on the wall. Already I knew I was the only person in town who had come here for Bataille. These were pilgrims – not literary pilgrims or even pervert pilgrims, but the real kind (there were golden shells in the ground every few metres, indicating that this was part of the Camino de Santiago walk, with simple accommodation nearby). Or else they were just tourists, holidaymakers, content to have a few glasses of wine in a beautiful old hill town, watching the sun set over the lush Yonne valley. They didn't want to know about this wanker Georges Bataille, and who could blame them?

The town's stonework and wooden shutters were bright now in the evening sun, as the peal of the basilica's bells mingled with the relaxed patter of tourists. It was the idyllic French *joli village* – so *joli*, in fact, that UNESCO had declared the town and its basilica a World Heritage Site. There was even a Mary Magdalene angle, involving relics of hers that may or may not have been housed here (a rival village claimed it was they and not the Vézelayans who possessed the true relics). Attractive, smiling young nuns in pale-blue robes strode among the town's narrow lanes and arches, as did fresh-faced priests with hooded robes. Clearly, Vézelay was a devout place, and thus an incongruous one for Georges Bataille to have lived, yet he liked it enough to have wanted his remains to be brought back and buried here. Asking after him in the former house of the pacifist and spiritual writer Romain Rolland (which is now home to an impressive art collection – Picasso, Miró, Kandinsky et al.), I felt a twinge of embarrassment: I imagined I was lowering the tone of the place – touristic yet devotional – by bringing up this notorious deviant and blasphemer. Then again, Bataille's was an intensely spiritual, even religious, sort of atheism. The anguish that compelled him to plumb the depths of horror, decay and filth was indivisible from the intellectual upheavals Western civilisation had been going through since the collapse of the foundations of the Christian faith, weighed down under post-Enlightenment scientific knowledge – what Nietzsche had famously shorthanded as the death of God.

Bataille's filthy blasphemies emerged from a hinterland of loss and belief. In his adolescence, after a terrible childhood that had culminated in the traumatic abandoning of his incontinent, syphilitic father to a certain death at the hands of the invading Germans during the First World War, Bataille converted to Catholicism. Until his mid-twenties he was intensely pious, embracing his faith with the same zeal he would bring to bear on everything in his life. He even wrote a short and reverent book on Notre-Dame de Chartres Cathedral. For all the terror and evil of his writings, Bataille is, from one perspective, and like Nietzsche before him (himself the son of a pastor), one of Christianity's great anti-devotees. His eventual assault on the faith bore all the virulence of the former zealot who redirects his religious fervour into the most furious irreligiosity. The common, conventional forms of belief – like that of the pilgrims flocking to Vézelay and its basilica – were too lukewarm for Bataille's spirit; but so were the conventional forms of atheism. He had to take both where few others were willing to follow. An atheism of his kind – committed to preserving a sense of the sacred by the most appalling means – could not arise in one who had never been a believer. Even after he had renounced all faith he did not want us to mistake his intentions, the nature of his passion. 'WE ARE FEROCIOUSLY RELIGIOUS,' he declaimed in *The Sacred Conspiracy* (Bataille was given to shouty capitalisations when he got especially worked up). Even his fanatical hatred of bourgeois civilisation, with its denial of the ecstatic qualities of being, was an expression of his radical religiosity:

> A world that cannot be loved to the point of death –
> in the same way that a man loves a woman –
> represents only self-interest and the obligation
> to work. If it is compared to worlds gone by, it is
> hideous, and appears as the most failed of all. In
> past worlds, it was possible to lose oneself in ecstasy,
> which is impossible in our world of educated
> vulgarity.

Soon it would be twilight, and I wanted to find the cemetery where Bataille was buried before darkness fell. I tend to learn languages primarily from books, so that I often suspect my diction comes across as archaic and pompous. For instance, what I said to the little old lady I encountered on my way to the graveyard probably sounded to her something like: 'Matron, I seek the tomb of a venerable scrivener. Kindly point me towards the necropolis.' Point me she did, and I continued on up the paving-stoned slope, past the basilica. The cemetery was behind it, perched slightly beyond the town on the verge of the steep hill, so that it overlooked the valley splendidly. All in all, a nice place to be buried but, try as I might, I could not locate Bataille's grave. I checked every headstone, then I tried the older, more overgrown cemetery on a lower level of the hillside. Then I went back and checked the first one again. Nothing. Had it been any other philosopher, I might have conceded defeat. But here was the final resting place of the man who, more than anyone in history, had been transfixed, awed, entirely obsessed by death. To fail to find the place where death and Georges Bataille finally got it together – where he attained the object of his desire – was not acceptable.

I returned to my hotel and did a Google image search on my phone. A Czech photographer had come on a similar expedition a couple of years earlier, and she had taken a haunting shot of the grave. Once again the internet had proved that anything you might think about doing, someone else had not only done already but also documented online, with groovy filters. In the last of the day's light I hurried back to the cemetery and, with the help of the photo, quickly located the grave: it was one of the first I could see after stepping through the gate. In this little country cemetery on a hill, surrounded by the graves of the pious deceased, Bataille's headstone bore one of the more remarkable epitaphs I had seen:

One day this living world will pullulate in my
dead mouth.

On this serene summer's evening the phrase seemed beautiful – defiant in a manner that, for all Bataille's nihilism, was not deathly but affirmative, joyful, rapturous. Bataille had always denied that he was a philosopher, but a label he *had* accepted, knowing full well its provocative weight in certain circles (Sartre's, for instance), was that of mystic. In one of his most beautiful formulations, he evokes the mystic's yearning:

Without knowing it, he suffers from the mental
darkness that keeps him from screaming that he
himself is the girl who forgets his presence while
shuddering in his arms.

Nonetheless, as I closed the cemetery gates and left Bataille there with the living world pullulating in his dead mouth, the feeling persisted that I would not read much of him again. I continued to see beauty in waste; still believed, if not quite as often or as intensely, in useless acts, wreckage, lost causes, anything that went down in flames. But to hold Bataille's body of work close any longer would bring not inspiration but disease. I was, in other words, sick to death of his sickly deathliness. Time to move on.

That Friday evening, back in Paris, I walked to a bar in the eleventh arrondissement and watched the rain hammering down on the street outside. I ordered a bottle of red wine and stayed there until I had finished Michel Surya's definitive *Georges Bataille: An Intellectual Biography*, which I had been reading all week. It was after one o'clock as I walked home along the Rue de Belleville, deserted now with the rain still falling hard. I was drenched but I didn't care. Two black guys approached me. I tried to walk between them and found that one of them had clasped my wrist, firmly. I looked at him; our eyes met. I pulled my arm away but he held me tight. Then his friend was holding up a large, serrated knife that shone in the streetlight. He too looked me in the eye. I had sent the proofs of my new book off to my publishers that afternoon and now, with all the wine inside me, I reflected that I'd achieved and enjoyed a few things in life, and worse could happen than to die here, picturesquely, on a Paris street in the rainy night, to a gleaming knife. And then this passivity became active desire: a sudden, bright wish to die. Unexpectedly the guy let go of my arm. I walked off. They turned and cursed at me. I cursed back. I considered going after them and roaring in their faces, kicking and punching wildly. I lost my way in the rain, enthralled by visions of beating a man to his death – any man or any woman – not to cause pain but for the release of it, pummelling a face with my fists till it caved in, stomping a skull against the rained-on concrete. I was still raging when I got home – a euphoric, self-fuelling rage that craved eruption. That night I dreamed my own death. I knew that I was dying – the process was quick – but as I died I became suffused with joy because I knew that this death – of my self, my individuality, this bungled figment that called itself Rob and staggered through its world – was of no consequence, a mere transformation, the end of an illusion of separateness. A veil had been lifted and there was no boundary between me and all else: to have lived once was to live forever, merged with all that is in an infinite churning, where individuality is no more substantial than the patterns thrown up on the foam of the sea. I slept a good nine or ten hours and when I awoke it was a sunny late morning. I lay there feeling light, cheerful. A conversation in Spanish drifted up from the courtyard outside my open window. I remembered the dream, the brilliance of it. The ping of an incoming email sounded from my phone. Soon it was back – the anxiety, the plans, the craving to distinguish, preserve and disseminate myself. But the cheerfulness remained, the levity, and with it a lingering thought, or hope, or faith, which faded into the background ambience as the day progressed, that the dream had been the reality and that this lonely, curious existence was the dream.

Your photos made me laugh. It's hard to tell where they were taken, whether it's night or day, what planet we're on. The camera seems to be on ketamine. I've been walking and cycling all week, exploring unfamiliar quarters of the city. I sit by the river and watch people or read. The days are bright and crisp. In the evenings I call over to Eddie and he shows me his paintings, and we get drunk on red wine. I'm enchanted by his daughter Callisto, but also by his ex-wife. I tell him this: he laughs and refills our glasses. On Saturday night I ended up alone in a bar in the eleventh as students teemed around me. It was cheery there. Drunk, I worked and reworked a single paragraph in my notebook, till the page was a mess of crossed-out words and arrows and asterisks. It was a passage that had been coalescing in my thoughts for months: it felt time to get it down.

This morning I cycled to the quays in the nineteenth, where I lived when I first moved to Paris. The area beneath Jaurès Métro station has become a refugee camp. There are dozens of tents, children running about, men standing in clusters talking. It was one reality superimposed on another, as if the chaos had spilled out of the screen and now it's right there in front of you, invading the dream of Paris.

And here I am in a cafe by the canal, hunched behind my laptop. The couple across from me are arguing acidly, unaware that I speak English. She is blonde and slender, he is fat and dominant. Perhaps they have scorching sex, who knows. Nor do I know (since you ask) what purpose you will serve in my life — or would serve if we were to continue this correspondence till death do us part, rather than only for the time it takes to get these books written. In the meantime, you too are 'a diary that writes back'. Isn't that enough? It would be good if I could be you for a day – in your body, your mind – and you could be me, and then we might get somewhere. Meanwhile, a wave from across the gulf. Send more photos.

Tent

Nesrin was a Kurdish artist who claimed to have slept with two of the 9/11 hijackers, simultaneously, during a trip to America when she was seventeen, weeks before the men perished in a ball of fire above Manhattan. It was almost certainly a lie, but Nesrin used it as the basis for a video work, *Love Collision*, which was shown at underground galleries and club nights in Berlin. The work comprised a hardcore porn film in which Nesrin has sex with two men, intercut with footage of cities at night and hedonistic dance parties. The three performers have verses from the Koran inscribed on their bodies – a clear nod to Theo van Gogh's film *Submission*.

I knew all this because my friend Fran told me about Nesrin when he heard I was visiting Kassel to cover the documenta festival for an art magazine. Nesrin was living in the city, and Fran thought it worth putting us in touch even though she was, he wrote in an email, 'definitely evil, but in an original way'. Under no circumstances should I go to bed with her if the possibility arose, he insisted. It would not – 'repeat, *not*' – end well. I replied that there was more than enough scorched earth in my past already. 'Ah yes,' he wrote back. 'Scorched Earth Rob, lives his life like a retreating Nazi.'

Nesrin was an obscure artist in more senses than one. I read a few descriptions online of works she'd exhibited, but no search result divulged what I really wanted to know: what she looked like. I could find no photographs bar a couple of shadowy, indistinct portraits that suggested a slight, dark-haired woman dressed in black. I emailed her and explained that I was a friend of Fran's. I mentioned the dates of my stay in Kassel and said it'd be cool to meet up if she had time. Two days later, Nesrin wrote back that she would rather not meet, but asked if I would be willing to participate in an ongoing artistic production relating to 'art tourists' in Kassel. I wouldn't have to do much, she explained, just follow occasional instructions that she would send by email or text; for the rest of the time I could go about my visit as normal. Curiosity outweighed wariness; I agreed to take part.

Surrounded by forests and hills in the centre of Germany, Kassel was bombed to rubble during the Second World War. Documenta, the festival that was inaugurated there in 1955 by Arnold Bode, was meant to put Germany back in dialogue with the continent it had done so much to decimate, and showcase the kind of art that the National Socialists had suppressed as 'degenerate'. I arrived on the train via Frankfurt on a Friday afternoon that was sinking under rain. The city didn't look like much as I made my way from the station. I was renting a bedsit near the university, on the side of town inhabited by students and immigrants, its grey residential blocks serviced by hookah bars and kebab joints.

After picking up the key from a cheery young Muslim woman, I bought an umbrella and took a tram towards the city centre. The crowds milling and queuing around Friedrichsplatz, the main square repurposed as a multifunctional documenta headquarters, suggested that Europe's art festivals, or this art festival at least – which turned Kassel into an exhibition space for a hundred days every five years – were in fine fettle as commercial prospects. Despite being here to write about documenta, I was hardly an expert. I subscribed to a couple of art magazines, attended shows in whatever city I was in, but I had absolved myself of ever really keeping up with the scene. In lieu of extensive knowledge, I hoped that my combination of curiosity and scepticism would amount to a serviceable investigative method.

I took shelter in the press centre, equipping myself with maps and flyers from the information desk, where young women in black T-shirts issued directions and press passes. The first-floor cafe served as a convening point for grouped visitors, dripping puddles as they hunched over soggy maps like generals planning an invasion. I ordered a flat white and sat by the floor-to-ceiling windows, looking over the blurred geometry of Friedrichsplatz. The museums surrounding the square trailed long queues under canopies of brolly and parka, which I hoped my press pass would allow me to skip. My socks were wet. I sneezed with considerable violence. Now that I was here, the prospect of gleaning an aesthetically meaningful experience from documenta seemed dispiritingly effortful, especially under such waterlogged conditions.

Unless I was going to make up my article on the festival, I had to get out there, and so, resigning myself to squelching around in wet socks for the evening, I left the press centre and commenced my explorations right there on Friedrichsplatz. Planted on the grass-covered square in front of the Fridericianum museum stood the newly erected *Parthenon of Books*. This was the current documenta's spectacular centrepiece, the one you saw on websites and news articles, which rendered only partly redundant the experience of standing in the downpour to gape at it. The *Parthenon* was a full-scale replica of the real thing on the Acropolis in Athens, built not of Grecian stone but of books – specifically, books that had at some time and place been banned. These outlaw texts were wrapped in plastic, lining the columns and pediment, supported by a scaffolding of steel girders. I hovered near a walking tour (more accurately, a huddled and shivering tour) and freeloaded the key info, learning that this *Parthenon of Books* was in fact a reprise of the original work that the artist, Marta Minujín, had installed in Buenos Aires in the 1980s. Ascending the steps and passing between broad pillars, I clocked an assortment of Rushdies, Burroughses, Lawrences, Nins and Joyces, along with some less-expected outliers.

'Why is *Winnie-the-Pooh* here?' a bald man called over the noise of the rain to the tour guide, an Asian lady.

The guide smiled. That book had recently been banned in China, she explained, after it became a common joke among the populace that their leader, Xi Jinping, bore a resemblance to Pooh Bear. The bald man nodded, satisfied.

'And why's *Harry Potter* in there?' asked a white-haired old lady.

'Because it's shit!' offered an English lad in an Arsenal jersey who happened to be walking past, gripping his spray-tanned girlfriend in a near headlock. I let out a laugh – what were *they* doing here? – prompting the guide to glance at me reproachfully.

She turned back to her audience and explained that the *Parthenon* was installed at precisely this spot because it was here that the Nazis had publicly burned a mound of books they considered decadent, while in the adjacent Fridericianum hundreds of thousands of books had been incinerated when the edifice was annihilated under Allied bombs. She made it sound as if the Second World War had essentially been a war on books. The erection of the *Parthenon of Books*, she went on, was a tribute to the power of literature, which would always rise from the blazes lit by anti-democratic bad guys who sought to suppress it.

Spare me, I thought, intensely aware of my wet socks. We were encroaching on my professional territory here. I had a stake in the game, yet the earnest patter that followed about human rights, democracy and the struggle for justice had me siding with the tyrants and conflagrationists. Besides, censoring authors gave them the prestige of rock gods. When a book was deemed heretical enough to immolate – did the tyrants not see this? – it gained the impregnable glamour of revolt and edginess (though perhaps this did not apply to *Winnie-the-Pooh*). You couldn't buy the kind of publicity afforded by the blazing pyre – and what was torched in one country became a bestseller in another. I pulled out my notebook and sketched a maxim: *If a book is worth reading it's worth burning.* Or maybe: *If a book isn't worth burning it isn't worth reading.* I would hone it later. For Minujín's monumental work to redeem itself from ideological triteness, she would need to stalk up in the dead of night and set it ablaze – a layering of conflagrations in dialogue across the decades, infernally ambiguous. Perhaps it was just jealousy talking: I knew I was born too late to be in with much hope of a career-boosting ban. You could write anything you liked now and it didn't matter; everything was permitted because nothing was of consequence. The taboos had all been smashed and writers could run wild, on the understanding that their words had no importance whatsoever. The tyrants didn't bother to burn literature any more: they knew a senile cripple when they saw one.

A ban now and then indulged writers in the pretence of a swagger and virility their profession had long since lost. A cynic after my own heart, Jean Baudrillard had expressed a similar, quasi-ironic nostalgia in a passage I chanced upon while browsing the festival bookshop in the shadow of the *Parthenon*:

> Censorship makes it possible to conceal the worthlessness of a book or an artwork ... Now that this curse has been lifted, art appears in all its insignificance.

The *Parthenon of Books*, I soon found, was indicative of the overall tenor of the current documenta, which was avowedly politicised, abundant with art not for art's sake but for the sake of social change, the alleviation of world suffering, the bolstering of democratic-egalitarian ideals. The present curator, Adam Szymczyk – a man so hip he didn't even need vowels in his surname – had declared that the festival would address the multiple crises the world was currently enduring: mass migration, the renaissance of the far right, looming ecological catastrophe and so on. Leaving aside the crisis of his unpronounceable name, you could see Szymczyk's point – it really did feel like emergency time on planet earth – but this institutional yoking of art to political engagement seemed symptomatic of a broader cultural synergy: everywhere you looked, art was becoming indistinguishable from social work, progressivist politics, liberal guilt. To join the tribe called contemporary art, it was required that you loudly declaim a humanitarian worldview and place your work at its service. Often, when I looked at contemporary art, I sensed I was meant to fall on my knees and flagellate myself. In the programme there was even a listed event entitled *Shame on Us*, relating to the refugee crisis. That was it: Szymczyk would not feel satisfied unless everyone who visited Kassel crawled away in shame. The European Christianity of which art for centuries had been the efflorescence was finished – no hip artist would be seen dead with it – but its morality hung over the continent like ancient incense, and the scolding curators and shame-artists were its priests.

The rain was hopping off my umbrella, streaming through the streets. The heavy-metal mass of the sky suggested it would still be chucking it down when the next documenta kicked off five years later. I left the *Parthenon* and wandered – in the sense of splashed – amid the buildings surrounding the square. In addition to the work exhibited in galleries across Kassel, sculptures and installations were dotted about the city, in the wild, to be chanced upon or sought out using the documenta map, which, it was fast becoming clear, bore only a glancing relationship to the territory it purported to depict. Was this some postmodernist allusion to the breakdown of representation, the loss of meta-narratives and stable moorings? Perhaps, but as a guide to figuring out which direction to walk in, the map was all but useless – increasingly so as text and graphic crumbled in the rain.

I chucked it in a bin and stepped inside documenta Halle, where a wall of warmth enveloped me as I waved my press pass. Some of the art in this multi-floor gallery was memorable enough – huge musical instruments fashioned from migrant shipwrecks recovered from the Mediterranean; a very long painting that narrativised, in Stone Age cartoon fashion, the snowy lives and bloody rituals of Arctic tribespeople. It was the audience, though, who absorbed my interest, the art-punters themselves. What struck me was the overwhelmingly middle-aged demographic. The bustling gallery was not devoid of young people – that attractive Asian couple taking thoughtful selfies by a huge red vulva sculpture, for instance – but they were the minority, the guests of honour. Generally speaking, the young and the beautiful were elsewhere – dancing at nightclubs in Berlin, say. That was understandable. The pleasures afforded by contemporary art were, in the end, relatively slight. These stylish, financially comfortable couples and grey-haired friends – the earnest Dutch, the kindly Scandinavians, the eager Germans – suggested that looking at art was what you did when the intenser modes of cultural pleasure no longer worked, when the doors of ecstasy began to shut. Youth was the season of rapture: its fruits were sex and bliss, pursued at raves on beaches or in festival meadows, at orgiastic house parties or nightclub saturnalias that lasted till dawn and then dawn again. Youth was ecstasy's stomping ground, its home stadium – it accepted no substitute. Then you got old and you started collecting wine, or taking an interest in politics, or looking at contemporary art. Culture itself was a consolation prize, handed with a pat on the shoulder to Time's losers, those who'd fallen behind in the sprint of species renewal. The mild and refined pleasures of contemporary art were weak surrogates for real happiness but, wandering through the gallery's white rooms, adrift in a thirty-something liminality between youth and middle age, I found such thoughts quite soothing. Yes, I was getting older and would soon find myself excluded from the earth's true paradise, but there would always be a place for me, a safer realm of gentle pleasures and aesthetic titillation, without euphoria or terror.

I left the documenta Halle just before eight o'clock, as the festival was shutting up shop for the night. Walking along the hillside that rose from Friedrichsplatz towards the high point of the town, above the motorway and forests, I scanned the rain-soaked walkways and elevated gardens – all quite deserted – for stray artworks. Now and then I mistook real-life objects for artistic representations of themselves – like this tent, surely pitched by a refugee or a vagrant, perched on a hillside beauty spot, looking out over balustrades. But wait, it *was* a real artwork – as opposed to a real tent. I approached cautiously, just in case, but yes, it was made not of canvas but of sculpted marble, a creamy-gold hue, its folds and billows smooth and lovely under my palms. The tent seemed to radiate an inner luminescence, the brightest point on the wintry August landscape. I stepped around the front and found that the tent was open. Muddy footprints were splattered across the floor. I stuck my head inside to see if it reeked of piss: it did not. If I'd had a sleeping bag I'd have been tempted to buy a few cans and curl up in there for the night, looking out at the rain and getting plastered. I liked this sculpture. I felt a pull towards it, as if it were my home in another reality. True, I again had the sense of an artist wagging her finger at me – the ease of my life compared to the biblical sufferings of the refugees who flooded Europe – yet there was an optimism to this luminous tent, squat like a Buddha with its back to the middle-aged crowds of Kassel.

The next morning I hurriedly fixed a mug of instant coffee, skipping breakfast to make up for a late start, the students in adjacent blocks having kept me awake blasting hip-hop with bass that rattled the headboard. I read an email that had arrived while I was in the shower, from Nesrin. She instructed me to visit an address that Google Maps indicated to be nearby. Fifteen minutes later I arrived at a ground-floor address in a run-down block on a street that was deserted but for a dog that snarled weakly before descending into a pedestrian tunnel.

As Nesrin had indicated, the door was unlocked. I stepped inside, leaving it ajar behind me. In the centre of the small studio room was a bed, low and unkempt, whose soiled linen no doubt accounted for the reek of stale sweat that hung in the air. On the floor next to the bed were two red buckets, empty. Six words were written in black marker on the wall: *Eternity has never been so precarious*. Pasted around the text were a number of black-and-white photographs that, I realised with a start, had evidently been taken the previous evening: I was looking at myself, from a stalker's distance, wandering in the rain through the deserted gardens at the top of the city. I'd had no sense of being followed; the awareness that I'd been the object of covert attention brought a nervous thrill. Spotting a black marker on the floor by the bed, I picked it up and wrote the words *Fuck Arses* next to the first message. Two could play this game.

A short walk brought me to the so-called Neue Neue Galerie, not to be confused with the Neue Galerie up at the far end of the city. A nondescript building in the grimier part of town, the Neue Neue was already host to a chattering weekend crowd. I like a good video installation, and the work that detained me longest here was one such titled *Samsara Europa*. In a dark corner of the gallery, a film was projected from the back of a red van that had plants growing inside and which, I read in the accompanying text, had been driven across Europe by the Norwegian artists, a lesbian couple. The film was an oneiric road movie in which the van, emerging from the Mediterranean, made its way to Athens, passed through Kassel, and finally plunged into the North Sea. Along the way, naked beauties thumbed for rides at parched roadsides; a man in flames left an out-of-town bar and collapsed; a biker fired a shotgun into a murder of crows. I sat on the floor nestled against the van's back wheel as the film played on a loop, lulled by this dream of Europe, its scrapheap hinterlands and dusty southern planes.

As I watched, I thought of another film that my friend Kelly had evoked so passionately I felt as if I'd seen it for myself. Kelly had viewed the film on her twenty-third birthday, while high on LSD, at an exhibition of mystical art in Dublin. For hours she had sat in the dark, entranced by the lurid streets and verdant landscapes of Vietnam, where transvestites and grieving widows enacted rituals that marked the transience and cyclicality of human existence. Kelly seemed not quite able to unravel herself from the films she watched, the books she read, even from other people's minds – it was as if she never knew where she ended and everything else began. On the internet she called herself Tangle and I could see why. It seemed to confound her that she happened to be herself and not, for instance, me, or a village girl in Laos, or a sunflower. She spoke of this world as if it were one of any number where she might have found herself alive, and appraised its qualities as if against some metaversal template. 'It's such a *clever* world,' she enthused once, as we listened to a song whose synth line delighted her. Whenever I was in her orbit, reality acquired an implausible, bizarre dimension where the boundaries of the possible seemed to come unstuck.

Resting my head against the wheel as the screen darkened and then lit up again, I drifted in and out of wakefulness. I dreamed I followed Nesrin into a dim room beneath the streets. We had sex as two masked men with assault rifles roared at us. I began punching Nesrin's face as she howled in assent. I awoke with a start, disoriented and embarrassed. A little boy holding his father's hand regarded me serenely as they walked away. I got to my feet and shuffled towards the exit, feeling certain of two things: first, that I would find Nesrin if I could; and second, that if I did it would spell catastrophe – a blackness would spread from this German town to colonise my life, pitching us into a horrible entwinement. In the toilets I splashed water on my face and waited till the squall of lust and revulsion subsided.

By a coffee stand in the nearby park, I texted Fran about the dream. He was travelling in Japan with his girlfriend, but he replied promptly:

Sounds nuts … Did u meet her yet?
No. She's been following me taking pictures.
I warned u!
Yeah. How's Japan? Did u get to Kyoto yet?
Yeah Jpn is amaze. Florence and I haven't spoken in
3 days tho. It's a drag when yr travelling together.
Ha.

A photograph appeared: a shimmering city viewed through a train window.

Got to split. Arriving in Osaka now … in miserable silence. Chat later. Beware the Kurd!!!

I spent the rest of the morning seeking out permanent installations from documentas past, the imaginative sediment that had accrued over decades on Kassel's parks and squares. The rain held off and silvery light leached through the clouds that hung above the city, awaiting orders. A text came in as I walked towards the Hauptbahnhof – my curator friend Stavro in Berlin, telling me his friend Estefanio was in Kassel for the week; I ought to meet him, he'd know the best parties. On the plaza in front of the train station I descended a metal staircase into a disused underground station that had been repurposed as art space. Weeds sprouted from between the tracks. Long white sculptures resembling strands of DNA snaked through the cavernous structure. Whispering voices filled the air, emanating from unseen sources embedded in the walls. In the glow cast by erratic chandeliers, I noticed a woman on the other side of the tracks, further down the platform. She was dressed in black, with dark hair, and she was taking photographs. I stood watching her until finally she looked up. We gazed at each other for longer than seemed appropriate. Then she turned and walked through a doorway. After hesitating a moment

I leaped down, crossed the tracks and followed her. I entered a room where iridescent, digitised mosaics rotated and breathed on the walls and floor. I was alone: she had left through one of three doors, or via the staircase.

Back in daylight, I stopped for lunch at a Lebanese restaurant that bustled with map-clutchers. I ordered a falafel and chips. While awaiting my meal I checked my inbox: there was a new email from Nesrin, sent only minutes earlier. An inline image manifested over several data-sucking seconds. The photograph was in black and white, grainy like a CCTV still. Once more I was looking at myself, from above and behind this time, standing in the grimy studio I had entered hours earlier, with the buckets on the floor. The scene was as I remembered it but for one jarring difference: the bed in the middle of the room was not empty. In it lay the body of an unnaturally tall woman – or the black, scratchy outline of one. It did not look as if the image had been superimposed so much as burned away, an acid-corroded silhouette revealing an underlying dimension. The face was indistinct, but it was easy to imagine it was screaming. I scrolled down. A line below the image read: *Choose the caption you prefer.*

There was a list:

Endlessly disintegrating / My death waits like a witch in the night / Who I fucked and what it meant / Poetry from the past, projected into the future as violence /

*Love in an air raid / Love in a bomb shelter / Our
hate will never die / Only I know how much I loved
you / An infinite and magnificent sorrow / Blood
butterflies / Once and never again / Family of ghosts /
An investigation into my own disappearance / The
wanderer and her shadow / A knife without a blade,
that has lost its handle / I stay alive only to haunt you /
Whispering into a seashell on a beach in the north*

I copied *Love in an air raid* and pasted it into my reply,
adding no words to the message. Then I gazed again
at the photograph. I hadn't noticed any camera in
the room: it must have been well concealed above the
doorway. Again I felt that dark frisson of intimacy, a not
entirely unwelcome sense of violation. I sent another
one-line email: *Was that you in the underground?*

After my falafel I texted Estefanio. He replied while
I was drinking an espresso, suggesting we meet that
evening at an opening some young artists he knew were
having at the train station. And then maybe we could
head to a club.

Twenty minutes later I was standing over an apparently unremarkable square of sandstone on Friedrichsplatz,
in front of the *Parthenon*. If you didn't know it was there
you could walk right over it, which is what plenty of
people were doing as I stood aside and considered this
most suggestive of artworks. An inconspicuous plaque
confirmed that the stone square marked the top, and
only visible part, of Walter De Maria's *Vertical Earth*

Kilometer. In the centre of the slab was a metallic disc, several centimetres in diameter. Allegedly, this was the top end of a brass rod that plunged into the earth to a depth of, yes, one kilometre. It was a good gag – a work of massive proportions almost the entirety of which could not be seen. Constructed and buried in the seventies, the *Vertical Earth Kilometer* was, from one perspective, decades ahead of its time. Our digital epoch was busy making actual the dreams of presence and permanence – in a sense, of eternal life – that had haunted mankind immemorially. Everything that happened now would stay happened, and there was nothing that could not be searched for and found. At the twilight of impermanence, transience acquired a new mystique, and absence became charismatic. I thought of the mandalas created over many years by Buddhist monks in the mountains of Ladakh, meticulously drawn using pigmented sand, only to be wiped away the moment the final grain was in place. The *Vertical Earth Kilometer* stopped short of such extremism; to go the full way, it would have been necessary to cover over the sandstone marker, so that people walking above had no idea of the subterranean artwork below. Ideally, the work would never have been built at all. Then it would cross from the realm of the suggestive into that of the sublime – though there would be no one around who knew it. Since the only way such a perfectly self-erasing work could exist was in the imagination (as I had just imagined one), it left open the possibility that the world already contained many such secret artworks, invisible marvels at the dawn of omnivoyance.

After taking a photo of De Maria's tip-of-the-iceberg work, I spent hours wandering the galleries, numbly determined to encounter as much art as I could before leaving the following day. Towards nightfall, the rain that had been holding off finally burst. As thunder rolled I took refuge in a hushed, candlelit Austrian restaurant, where I had my first beer of the day, along with a schnitzel and some potatoes. Then I had my second and third beers while writing up my notes. As I scribbled and drank, I scanned the restaurant for a solitary woman, and although I saw none I felt as if Nesrin was watching me, as if I was in her lens. Every minute or two I checked my phone. My impatience for her to contact me hardened into annoyance, then anger, and the emotion swelled to envelop all of Kassel, all of the art world. I was conflicted: I had enjoyed the festival considerably, had found plentiful stimulation in the galleries and art-laden streets, yet I couldn't let go of my resentment at contemporary art for allowing itself to become a festival of piety and earnest political sighs. I had hoped art would provide an escape from the internet, but like everything else, it turned out to be the internet's reflection. Where were the outliers, the danger-artists who inverted the values of the group, threw matches at the powder keg just for the hell of it? Where were the neo-punks whose response to signs reading

Danger Ahead was to hit the accelerator? Documenta's anodyne, painfully woke fare had left me craving art whose intentions were purely corrosive, art that went against democracy and virtue, glorified evil, wallowed in destruction and chaos, art whose only dictate was hostility to the notion that art should ameliorate, edify, mould better citizens. And then it seemed to me that the kind of artist I longed to encounter was there all along: it was Nesrin, documenta's hidden shadow, stalking the fringes, excluded yet present and effective. I emailed her again:

> *I really want to meet you. I'm at the Austrian restaurant on the corner of Bremer Strasse. I'm heading to an opening later, inside the train station. I hope you'll come. If not, maybe see you afterwards. I'll be out all night probably. I'll let you know where we are.*

After sending the message, I texted Estefanio. Then I put away my notebook and called for another beer.

The following morning, I awoke with a hangover that felt out of all proportion to the amount I had drunk – even though I had drunk a great deal – until I blearily recalled Estefanio thrusting a pill into my fist in some packed, smoky club. The alarm on my phone was going off. I reached out to hit the snooze function, feeling as if a steel rod had been driven through my temples, a miniature *Vertical Earth Kilometer*. My laptop was open at the foot of the bed, an Erika Lust porn film paused on the screen – I must have tried to jerk off. In half an hour I needed to vacate the bedsit. Memories tumbled through my pounding brain. I remembered sharing a joint with a group of black guys, then them hugging me, then Estefanio throwing a punch and falling over. The causal link between these events was obscure. I wondered for a moment if I'd been beaten up, but my body appeared to be intact – the hurt was all inside. My alarm rang again. The day ahead seemed unendurable – trains and stations, pain and nausea. I turned my belongings inside out in a vain search for ibuprofen. Lying back in my boxers, I snatched up my laptop, minimised the Erika Lust video and checked my emails. It seemed I had sent no fewer than seven messages to Nesrin over the course of the night, the latest at 6:23 a.m. I read them through in rising shame: with each message my self-abasement intensified, until the last vestige of dignity was exterminated. Since I had no dignity left, there was no reason not to send her another message now:

My train leaves in a few hours. I'll be up on the hill again. Come and fucking meet me.

I had just clicked play on the Erika Lust clip when Nesrin replied – the first I'd heard from her since lunchtime the day before. There was no text in the email, just a link to what turned out to be a video. It took me a few seconds to realise what I was looking at: a large mound of severed cocks, a thousand of them, piled up in a concrete yard. The cocks were twitching, squirting blood, the nerve endings flailing. It could only have been a computer-generated vision but it looked all too real. I made it to the toilet just as my guts revolted. I clutched the white rim of the bowl as I spewed, spat, groaned. What came out of me was black, evil – I felt I was shitting from my face.

Out in the sunlight, with my wheeled suitcase at my side, I still felt like death, like shit, but it wasn't the extravagant pain I'd woken to. My train left in five hours. Slowly I wheeled my suitcase through the centre of Kassel, past whispering installations and cheery tourists who roamed in the Sunday-morning calm. In a Turkish shop off Friedrichsplatz I bought two bottles of wine and, although I hadn't smoked in years, a pack of cigarettes. Out in the street I sent Nesrin one last message, telling her again where I was going. I said I hoped she bled to death. I told her I would love her forever. I pulled my suitcase along the pathway that led up from the square, through bright gardens to the roof of the city. The hillside was deserted, as calm as a monastery garden. The marble tent looked no less lovely in the daylight. This time it did smell of piss. I chucked my suitcase inside. Then I clambered in too. I sat with my legs folded beneath me, in the doorway, looking out over the forest, and the autobahn that streaked to the horizon. Some dark-brown vomit had dried on my sleeve. The thought of catching the train no longer seemed compelling. In the high morning sun I opened the first bottle of wine and took a gulp. I felt the liquid pour down my gullet, sloshing through my insides to the pit of my stomach. With that first mouthful of wine I was drunk again, as drunk as I had ever been. I lit a cigarette, and thought maybe I would stay drunk forever.

Remember I told you about Eddie's daughter Callisto? She invited me for a week in Marseilles with some friends. We're staying in a large cool flat near the harbour, with a patio of white marble. I follow the narrow, scented streets of the Arab Quarter in a trance of sensualism and afternoon vermouth. If I squint my eyes I could be in Morocco, Tunisia, Algiers. Callisto's boyfriend came for a few days. I liked him. He seemed more manly than me, by which I suppose I mean he has more money. Their flirtatious friend Lucia teases me about the scenes of sexual failure in the novel of mine she borrowed from Callisto: Are they autobiographical? she asks. Lucia wears tight bright dresses, or denim shorts and T-shirts with the middle tied in a knot. I might fall on my knees in the daytime street and kiss her belly-button piercing, accepting all consequences. Yesterday we went swimming in the harbour and she wore a bikini that was like metaphysics. She knows I'm tormented, and we both enjoy it. She's seeing an engineer from Madrid. After a few drinks last night, she told me that once or twice a day she masturbates with him over video chat, and then she watched me imagine that.

We drink vermouth, rosé, glasses of beer, coffee, usually in bars by the harbour. For a while I had stopped drinking: I attained a long-lost clarity, suffered fewer debilitating depressions. I acquired the conviction that the drinking years were over – the possibility of happiness opened before me. And then, in classic alcoholic fashion, it occurred to me one morning that there was no abiding reason not to drink, to choose peace over euphoric destruction. I know by now

I can't pull off moderation (a sign of degenerate cultures and persons, according to Nietzsche). You told me once you don't consider yourself an alcoholic, but you do consider yourself a drunk. What was the difference again? Was it Duras who wrote something on the matter? She who drank wine in bed, all day long. I imagine having a brief and violent affair with her: it ends terribly, her slashing at my face. Once in Calcutta, I watched a goat being sacrificed on an altar to Kali. The head flew off with one blow of the sword, then the body twitched on the dusty ground, ejaculating blood from the stump.

Does it annoy you when I talk about these girls with their thongs that are almost there, almost not there? Sorry. Tell me about young lovers, what they've got that men your own age lack, so that I can learn what I'm in the process of losing. I've ordered another green glass of vermouth, and I've just swallowed ten milligrams of Valium. Nothing on earth can harm me, at least for the next five hours. Maybe I'll jump off the pier with the brown-skinned boys who seem to have clambered from the pages of Camus. That reminds me: I met an old guy on the beach who told me he killed a man in a fight over a woman. He served two decades in prison, was fucked and fucked others. He described the stench of shit, the hard cold eyes of killers. He had no regrets. He told me he believed we unconsciously seek out trauma, the extreme ordeal, when we have grown complacent ('Lost respect for the gods of shit and pain,' he said). Agony slams us back into life with terrified reverence. After we spoke, I swam in the sea and had the ecstatic drunken insight that everything is transient, everything is eternal, both statements are true. Also: that living your truth means loving even your suffering, and not masochistically. I imagine I can see Algiers from here, shimmering on the horizon, but it's just a high-noon mirage, my feverish brain.

Mediterranean

On the cusp of autumn, convinced, for reasons I will get into, that it was absolutely necessary for me to get out of Paris for a few days, I conceived the idea of making a journey to Blanes, on the Costa Brava in north-east Spain. The Chilean writer Roberto Bolaño had lived in Blanes for many years, and I had read about a seventeen-stage Bolaño walking tour that had been inaugurated there in 2013, on the tenth anniversary of his death. The *ruta literaria 'Bolaño en Blanes'* – and the article I would write about it to cover costs and pay the rent – seemed a strong enough pretext for me to leave Paris.

On a Tuesday morning I rode a crowded Métro train to the Gare de Lyon, and there boarded a train to Barcelona. It was a double-decker and my seat on the upper floor faced backwards, so that as we travelled the landscape receded in front of me. On the journey I read Mónica Maristain's *Bolaño: A Biography in Conversations*. The book is essentially a series of transcribed interviews with people who knew Bolaño, presented without much attempt at ordering or interpreting the material. Maristain is gushingly, irritatingly admiring of Bolaño;

it is hard to avoid the accusation of hagiography when a writer insists on comparing her subject to a saint. As I read on, every little thing Maristain wrote grated on me. I should have been enjoying the journey, but instead I was all tensed up with irritation towards this lazy biographer.

I closed the book, or rather turned it off, for I was reading on an e-reader, which I'd bought the day before moving to France to curb my habitual accumulation of physical books while on the move. I watched the landscape vanish before me as we sped towards the south. To put it bluntly, I was in a wretched nervous condition. It felt like weeks since I'd last had a decent night's sleep. Lying awake at two, three, four o'clock in the morning, I had been unable lately to slow the apocalyptic whirring of my thoughts. For years I had been living a largely solitary existence and it had never bothered me much. In Paris, though, it was getting to me badly. If you spend too much time alone, I reflected, then what would otherwise be a disturbing but transient thought will grow to immense, grotesque, obsessional proportions, so that finally you fear everything, emanating weirdness and menace on the streets and in the Métro. Your sleeping will go to hell and life will lose its flavour. Food, music, books, people, the days themselves – all of it will taste the same, taste of nothing. The very strategies you previously adopted to ward off paranoia and dejection – a good diet, exercise – will fall by the wayside. You will not eat well and you will certainly not jog. It will soon go from bad to worse, I reflected, so that when a friend comes to visit you in Paris, you will be terrified at the prospect of their arrival, for you'll have forgotten how to do the simplest things, such as shake someone's hand, make conversation, have dinner in company. In this abject condition you will walk the streets of Paris and you will look to the beauty that surrounds you, and this beauty will leave you unmoved. The women will not stir your lust, and it will seem that you will never lust again.

It was early afternoon when I reached Barcelona. I had managed to sleep a while, and the nap had untangled the coarser knots in my brain. I was glad to be on the move, and moving with purpose. Having a purpose, however questionable the purpose might be, was a relatively new phenomenon in my life. For years I had travelled to far-flung places, lingering for short or long spells before drifting on, with no purpose whatsoever – had gone to these places, even, *because* purpose would not bother me there, would leave me alone, let me be.

I dragged my suitcase away from Sants station into the hot afternoon, and stopped for lunch at the first decent-looking restaurant. Ordering my meal from the young, sullen waiter, I was pleased to find that my Spanish, dormant these last few years, was basically intact. On first moving to Paris, I had made considerable efforts to improve my French, which hitherto had been basic. I studied daily and soon reached a passable conversational level. Had I kept at it, I would have made significant advances in the months that had elapsed since that initial, assiduous period. By now I would have been confidently reading French novels, buying *Libération* and *Le Monde*, listening to current-affairs programmes and literary discussions on the radio. A couple of months into my stay, however, I broke up with my French girlfriend – a novelist I had met through my friend Zoé – and went to live on my own in a sprawling, shabby apartment in the nineteenth arrondissement that looked on to a vine-strewn courtyard. The end of the relationship removed any urgency to improve my French – it also foreclosed an entire future life, one that my girlfriend and I had dreamed up together and for a while believed in. In this foreclosed future we would live together in Paris, hang out with her artist friends, write side by side through the days and read to one another in the evenings, counting our blessings all the while for the children we didn't have. Of course, I had only ever felt partly committed to this potential future: as good as it seemed, it cancelled out all the other potential futures, and so I resented it a little, and finally it dissolved before me. Gradually it was coming to seem that the only future I *would* have was a stark, lonely one that was not chosen so much as drifted into – the kind of future you get if you persistently decline to make the decisive gesture.

In the solitude of my post-break-up life in Paris, as the summer ended and my days stretched on in silence, I became fixated on the idea that the difficulties of my life were intractable. At moments of extreme nervous tension, the anxiety aroused by such obsessional thinking provoked fantasies of suicide. In the quiet of my vine-covered apartment, I would look up from whatever I was doing and imagine myself hanging from the rafters in the spooky spare bedroom whose door hung open as if in dismal invitation. In the grip of these fantasies I would draft suicide notes in my head, carefully worded to inflict the minimum damage on those who survived me; I would consider how to hang myself in the least painful way, and wonder if it were possible to avoid traumatising whoever would find me there, swinging over the grimy floorboards.

Despite the recurrence of these fantasies, I was confident that I would not kill myself, for now at least. Having the *option* of killing myself sufficed. I basically relished life and wanted to keep living. From a more cosmic perspective, the existence of the universe had come to seem to me utterly implausible: all explanations of it were equally unsatisfactory, hence equally feasible. As a result, I wasn't fully confident that my life was not, say, an elaborate, hallucinated challenge – a sort of existential video game – in which the goal was to climb on to some higher plane of being by proving oneself in this one. Perhaps the unseen arbiters would look upon self-slaughter as the worst sort of failure, and I would thus be relegated to some more terrible sphere. Best to slog it out and leave the world by natural causes, just in case. Also, I lacked the physical courage to go through with suicide. Unless I could get some reliably fatal pills (but which kind?), the various methods of killing myself at my disposal – hanging, throwing myself from a tall building, slashing my arteries, plunging into a deserted stretch of the Seine late at night, and so on – were too painful and risky. There was only one way I would have the balls to kill myself and that was by shooting myself in the skull. That seemed by far the best way of doing it: quick, loud, bloody and – hopefully – painless. All of this was fanciful, though. I could not shoot my skull because I didn't live in a country where I could acquire a gun. The only country I knew where I'd be able to buy a gun was America, and I could never live there again: I would rather kill myself.

Besides, the last couple of weeks had seen an emissary of light enter my Paris life: a cat. My landlord and his wife were going on holiday and, for a modest deduction in rent, I had agreed to mind their cat while they were away. I had grown up with a mother who was afraid of cats (technically, ailurophobic), and so this was to be the first time I had ever lived with a cat. His name was Bobu. I spent hours with him each day, frolicking, observing his ways, courting his affection. The cat was mysterious to me. His habit was to leap up and plunge his fangs into my wrist, clawing me violently. After a few days with him, my arms were latticed with cuts. I wondered if this was the cat's way of 'playing', but it seemed likelier that he just hated me. I gazed into his eyes and comprehended nothing. I thought of how the ancient Egyptians worshipped cats as inscrutable gods sojourning on the earth. Despite his inexplicable rage, I relished frolicking with my Bobu, stroking him, holding his paws, taunting him when he ignored me so he would bite and scratch me again (being mauled was preferable to his indifference). I felt I was getting more out of all this than he was. He probably just wanted me to fuck off. But I had nowhere to go and nothing to do, so I would curl up next to him, making plaintive meowing sounds which he imperiously ignored. Like a wretched lover, I was scorned and humiliated by the object of my affections, pitiably colluding in my own abasement.

I wheeled my suitcase to the Plaça de Catalunya, from where my next train headed north out of Barcelona and along the Mediterranean towards France. I was enthusiastic about seeing this part of Europe, and the adopted home of one of the writers who inspired me most. At the same time, I was a touch apprehensive. By all accounts, Blanes was black with Bolaño pilgrims. I was conscious of the indignity of being one of many who travelled to Blanes for no other reason than that a writer they admired – a man possessed of prodigious literary gifts, but otherwise a man like any other – had once lived and worked there. It was true that peak Bolaño had passed. There had been a point, about five years earlier, when Bolaño was omnivisible in the literary culture. But even now, post-peak, devotees still reputedly flocked to the streets where their idol had once rambled, the bars where he'd hung out, the bookshops he'd browsed in. Often these devotees then went and wrote about their trips to Blanes. If all the accounts of awed Bolañoites who had journeyed to Blanes were compiled in a book, it would be thicker than even Bolaño's own brick-like masterworks *The Savage Detectives* and *2666*. A Belgian writer, Hedwige Jeanmart, had even written a novel called *Blanes*, about a woman who travels to the town and discovers that it has been overrun by enthusiasts, the most hardcore obsessives competing for nightwatchman jobs at the campsites where Bolaño once worked. During my brief, excruciating stint as editor of an online literary magazine, I myself had commissioned my then flatmate to write about the trip to Blanes she had undertaken. The same woman had a Bolaño tattoo on her forearm, comprehension of which required a knowledge of his oeuvre.

Here I was, then, another sucker rolling into Blanes, afflicted by a geeky strain of the deluded backpacker's complaint when he rocks up to whatever beach, cathedral or sacred valley and says: *Too many tourists*.

The train reached Blanes in early evening. Most of the passengers had disembarked at earlier points along the coast, a string of hotel-fronted towns looking on to the Mediterranean. Conveniently, the first stage of the Ruta Bolaño was right outside the railway station. There was an awkward moment: I had to ask two lady proselytisers to step aside so I could read the plaque, but they thought I wanted some of their Jesus flyers, one of which promised to reveal 'God's view on smoking' (I assumed He wasn't into it). The plaque was a red-and-black affair with an illustration of the author, and text in Catalan, Spanish, English and French. It also had a black-and-white photograph of the location, in this case with the same dark, dramatic clouds billowing around the station building as were currently gathering in real life. Along with a brief description of the location's significance to Bolaño's life in Blanes, there was a quotation from the author, with a shaky English translation:

> I do not know when I got here. All I know was, that it was by train and many years ago.

An unlikely claim, and typical of Bolaño in its self-mythologising. In point of fact, Bolaño moved to Blanes in 1985, when he was thirty-two years old and had already met his wife, Carolina López. He would remain with López for the rest of his life, and they would have two children in Blanes, though in his final years he spent a lot of time with his mistress, Carmen Pérez de Vega. Previously Bolaño had lived for a spell in Barcelona, and before that in Gerona, his first home after he had exiled himself from Latin America. He lived in Blanes until his death in 2003 of liver disease. (His sickness fuelled the groundless rumour that in his youth Bolaño had been a heroin addict – part of the lucrative myth of Bolaño as the reckless Latino literary renegade.)

My hotel, where I'd got a bargain deal, was located a couple of kilometres outside the town centre, looking on to a motorway intersection. Stepping out of my taxi and into the reception area, I was startled by the beauty of the young olive-skinned woman who checked me in and photocopied my passport. She had one of those marvellous smiles that have nothing guarded or cynical in them. I showered, then put back on the same clothes and checked my emails. Half an hour later I waved to the girl on reception as I headed out for dinner. She beamed at me.

The seafront of Blanes is lined with hotels, bars and restaurants, but by the time I got there everything was closed. It was late September, the beginning of the off season, and the proprietors evidently saw no point in staying open past sunset. The beach was attractively floodlit but there was nobody on the promenade. I walked in the low roar of the surf, preoccupied by hunger. Towards the edge of town I was met with a remarkable sight: out in the liminal dark, where the wet sand sloped into the surf, a magnificent and glamorous woman was fishing, entirely alone. She was immensely tall, about six foot five unless this was some trick of perspective, with thigh-high leather boots and a sumptuous, moonlike ass. She drew back her rod and cast with great assurance far out into the dark sea. All the time I was watching her she did not glance to either side, nor behind her, but remained focused on the black horizon, immersed in her actions like a Zen archer.

The following morning, I was surprised at the liveliness of Blanes: it didn't seem like the off-season after all. It was a gorgeous day with the temperature already in the mid-twenties, and the outdoor cafes were thronged with locals and tourists. The occasional bulging, crew-cut, fifty-something British male swaggered by, trailing an immense wife – reliable fixtures in any Spanish resort town. You could gaze at such a man and peer through the centuries: at whip-wielders in the colonies and plantations, overseers of vicious regimes, imperialist bullies and cruel enforcers. Ruddy-faced, swilled up, stranded in peacetime with no skulls to crack or natives to humiliate, they washed up on the Costa Brava and other sun-warmed coastlines, draped in Union Jacks, guzzling lager, vexed at having been born too late, in the hangover of Empire.

After breakfast I found the tourist office by a roundabout on the seafront. There, I picked up a Ruta Bolaño leaflet with a map indicating the locations of the seventeen stages. The blonde-haired lady at the desk mentioned that another Irish writer had been in just the other day, also enquiring about the Bolaño walk, and seeking a translator to accompany him to the botanical gardens further up the coast. I was intrigued by this writer who was one step ahead of me: for a moment I entertained a Philip K. Dickian – or indeed

Bolañoesque – fancy that the writer was really myself, a double, flickering in some eerie glitch in the space–time continuum; or maybe it was an emissary from the future, seeking to warn me of danger; or myself in an alternate reality where I had an interest in botanical gardens. More prosaically, perhaps the elusive author stalking up the Costa Brava was just John Banville, Anne Enright or Roddy Doyle, fleeing whatever demons tormented them. The lady checked her computer: the writer who preceded me was not my doppelgänger, nor Banville nor Enright, but a person with the fantastical name of Turtle Bunbury.

Before setting off for the remaining sixteen stages, I walked out on to the rocky promontory. From there I viewed the town, the coast and the hilltop Castell de Sant Joan, which stood sentry in the distance. There were some people out swimming, mostly elderly, and I regretted that I had forgotten my trunks, as I do every time I travel to the sea. The Mediterranean shimmered brilliantly under a high sun. The very word 'Mediterranean' had always been potent for me: I knew that when I wrote up this trip for my article, I would exploit every possible opportunity to use it. ('In Blanes I have the Mediterranean, the sea I prefer to all others,' Bolaño once said in an interview.) Back on the shore, I followed the beach away from the holidaymakers and covered restaurants. The second plaque was on the wall of what was now a fruit and veg shop, but which had once housed the jeweller's that Bolaño and Carolina López opened upon arriving in Blanes. In the photo, a goofy Bolaño grinned and made a peace sign outside his new business. López stood beside him, tall and attractive. She bore some resemblance to Patti Smith, herself a Bolaño aficionado. (Smith attended the 2011 inauguration ceremony of the Carrer de Roberto Bolaño, a street in Gerona. A video on the internet shows her stepping on to a windblown stage, daring a few words in touchingly awful Spanish, then singing a song in Bolaño's honour.)

The next point marked the site of a former beachfront bar reputedly frequented by junkies, fishermen and lowlifes, where Bolaño, a non-drinker, liked to pass the time and strike up conversations. The fourth plaque adorned the wall outside the Videoclub Serra, where he would talk movies with the owner, Narcís Serra. Film and dream are twin media of entrancement in Bolaño's fiction. 'Tell a dream, lose a reader,' said Henry James, but Bolaño had a singular ability to get away with it. A poet who turned to fiction (he liked to claim it was only for money that he resorted to 'the vulgarity of telling stories', but this is more myth-making), his novels and stories teem with recounted dreams. It is as if Bolaño the storyteller frequently wearied of the demands of narrative and compelled one of his characters to sleep, thereby permitting himself to exercise the inexhaustible resources of his imagination, generating pure imagery undiluted by the requirements of plot or realism. Flick through any of his books and you will encounter beautifully described dreams: burning chairs fall from the sky; a crazy man in the woods translates the Marquis de Sade with axe blows; rival gangs fight for a distant supermarket. There are dreamers who dream they are dreaming, while even a waking character might suddenly glimpse his author, 'as if he were in a kaleidoscope and caught sight of the eye watching him'. Or take this grandly superfluous dream from *Tres*, the posthumously published minor work I happened to be rereading:

> Giorgio Fox, a comic-book character, seventeen-
> year-old art critic, dines at a 30th-floor restaurant in
> Rome. That's it.

In Bolaño, characters dream, or they watch films, and the descriptions, which add little by way of plot or character development, are often indistinguishable: films are dream-like and dreams are cinematic. (Bolaño admired the Chilean film-maker Alejandro Jodorowksy, a surrealist who ignored the conventions of narrative cinema in favour of dream logic and the primacy of image.) In the Maristain biography, one friend remembers Bolaño doing nothing at all except read, write and watch TV, taking in late-night films as ravenously as the books he read.

Surprisingly, even in this era of streams and torrents, the plaque-bearing premises still housed the Videoclub Serra; a shabby, unlit neon sign outside read *Videos*. The outlet was now entirely automated. An old man was returning some DVDs through a hole in the wall with a furtive, suspicious air; I wondered if he'd been watching dirty movies.

Off a main road, on Carrer Aurora, was the site of one of the apartments where Bolaño had lived with his family. I dutifully read the plaque and took a photo. As I was walking away, a short man in his sixties gestured to me. It was Bolaño's one-time landlord, still the *proprietario* and happy to talk to me about the writer.

Was Bolaño *simpático*? I asked, unable on the spot to come up with a less inane question.

The landlord shook his head. 'No, no.' He insisted that Bolaño was locked in his head, unwilling to take other people's ideas on board.

'Obstinado?' I offered.

'Sí, sí. Muy obstinado.' A vigorous nodding.

I thanked the man, took a picture of him by the home of his bullheaded tenant, then walked across the road to the library, thinking that nobody ever got on with their landlord. The library too had a plaque outside and, inside, a conference room, the Sala Roberto Bolaño. In here, rows of silver plastic chairs faced a stage. A video showed residents of Blanes line dancing on a plaza, while John Denver's 'Take Me Home, Country Roads' played on a tinny loop. There was a stand displaying Bolaño's books (in Spanish), all published by Anagrama in artful covers. There were copies of a novel I had heard about but never seen before: *Advice from a Disciple of Morrison to a Fanatic of Joyce*, co-written with one A. G. Porta. It was Bolaño's first novel, not yet translated into English.

The conference room was empty. Glancing about me, I fleetingly considered stealing the volume in criminal tribute to the author who had been a prolific book-thief in his penniless, poetry-drunk youth. On the wall was yet another plaque, with a quotation in Spanish:

> I just hope to be considered a more or less decent South American writer who lived in Blanes, and loved this town.

I sat and rested for a spell, watching the line dancers. I was enjoying the walking tour, pleased by the town with its sea and sunshine. But what I was really looking forward to was getting back to my hotel and watching telly. I loved watching telly, could spend hours immersed in it. I did not own a television, hadn't done so in years, and whenever I had a chance to watch one – whenever I was staying in a hotel, essentially – I seized it. It was so much fun, sitting up in bed, hopping from channel to channel, drinking in everything from political discussions to music videos, to classic films, to women rubbing their groins while leering at the camera, to sports chat, to Islamic State gossip, to celebrity intrigue. You learned so much about the world: a night of TV was worth ten novels. When I was younger, I had automatically rejected television because it was what my parents did. Now that I had matured, a lifetime spent watching TV seemed about the most exotic and experimental kind I could imagine. As the rest of humankind migrated on to the internet, my return to TV took on the quality of a revolt against the spirit of the age: I would be the last couch potato, a brother in arms to that Japanese soldier who held out for decades in the jungle of some Pacific island, refusing to concede that the war was lost.

I needed to earn my TV binge, though, so I headed out to find the rest of the stages. Within an hour and a half I had ticked them all off. There were the promenades where Bolaño liked to sit, read, smoke and stroll; the cake shop owned by a bookish acquaintance with whom he enjoyed shooting the breeze; the bookshop where the staff always managed to get hold of the titles he requested; the gaming shop where Bolaño, a war-games geek, could meet fellow aficionados and buy accessories. It was all fairly interesting to anyone who had immersed themselves in the universe of Bolaño's fractal, allusive and often autobiographical fiction; but some of the texts on the plaques really were of a formidable banality: 'In this newsagent's situated near his home, he would go and buy the newspaper. He would often start up conversations with the shop assistants for the pleasure of debating current topics.'

Several of the tour stages were clustered in the old part of town, which was easier on the eye than the sprawl of high-rise blocks beyond the centre. Here, for instance, was the home where Bolaño lived after leaving Carrer Aurora and, on the same street, the studio where he wrote from the mid-nineties on. The studio had no telephone, which probably abetted Bolaño's astounding productivity. Even now, with the author twelve years dead, new titles kept on appearing, plucked from the seemingly bottomless well of manuscripts and computer files he'd left behind. Some of these posthumous publications, such as *Woes of the True Policeman*, are worthy additions to his oeuvre, while even the more mediocre works have been received gratefully by Bolaño addicts. Being one such myself, I had even read *The Third Reich*, a weird and interminable novel I finished in the same spirit in which it had clearly been written: sheer perversity.

Bolaño's prolific output troubled me because it was at odds with my personal ethic of writing. Over the past few years, I had come to believe that there were simply too many books in the world. The situation, I sometimes imagined, had become so critical that it ought now to be regarded as a criminal act to publish a book that did not absolutely need – in a sense I could not precisely define but which had something to do with urgency and perhaps suffering – to exist. Obviously, this was a demented, reactionary position, and most of the time I was able to recognise it as such while getting on with my own reading and writing. Still, the underlying point felt valid: one would do better to publish strictly when animated by urgency and conviction. ('One should speak only where one cannot remain silent,' wrote harsh old Nietzsche; '… the rest is all chatter, "literature", bad breeding.') Experimenting with the practical implications of all this, I had made it a point of pride to write only when I felt like it. The problem was, I almost never felt like it. What I did feel like doing was watching telly or pornography; sitting in bars in the eleventh arrondissement; going to the canal with a beer and a book; loitering in the Parc des Buttes-Chaumont; listening to music while lying on the couch; playing with my cat; texting friends; or doing nothing at all.

In perambulatory homage to the Julio Cortázar novel beloved by Bolaño, I hopscotched around the later stages of the tour rather than visit them in linear order. I made sure, though, to reach the final, melancholy stage last. The seventeenth plaque marked the author's last studio. 'In his later years,' the text read, 'aware of the countdown the serious diagnosis had started, he committed himself entirely to his writing.' In the year he died, with his private life becoming painfully complicated, Bolaño actually moved into this studio, on the lively Rambla de Joaquim Ruyra. It was the site of his final, exhausting effort to salvage as many of the words, dreams and visions as he could before it all went dark. The result of this last great push was *2666*, the unfinished, enigmatic masterwork that is certainly one of the great books of the century so far.

By mid-afternoon I had completed the tour. I climbed the hill to the Castell de Sant Joan, from where there were views over Blanes, the Costa Brava beyond, and the Mediterranean. When I reached the summit, thirsty and tired, my first thought was that this was a view worth photographing. A pang of sadness followed. For years, I had travelled around the world, passing through many places of beauty, and for all that time I had made a point of not owning a camera. Naturally I'd had an urge to capture moments, seize hold of images so that what I experienced would not be obliterated in time. The wager was that, by not having such an option, I would be forced to appreciate every moment *in* the moment, to embrace and honour the flux of my existence in all its singularity and transience. Everything I saw, heard and tasted would, I hoped, be intensified, bearing as it did such a weight. And now here I was, another schmuck with an iPhone, snapping happy, angling for his pano-rama shots, already wondering to whom he would send the pictures when he got back to a Wi-Fi zone. This was what all our devices were leading to: a world of perfect communication wherein nobody was interesting enough to be worth communicating with. I used to be interesting once, I thought glumly, framing the sea.

I returned to the hotel with the feeling that I'd earned my night in with the telly, only to find that there was no telly. This had escaped my notice the previous evening, when I'd crashed straight out after getting back from the seafront. Bereft of the box, I went downstairs and drank a couple of beers at the hotel bar. I was served by the beaming receptionist, who tonight wore a lovely, cream-coloured shawl. I pretended to read my book while she flitted between the bar and the reception desk. As she was putting on some music I glanced up at her. She smiled at me, then laughed and looked away. We started chatting: she was Romanian, and her family owned the hotel. Just then her sisters came in; all three of them were magnificent too. We chatted away, they were charming and vivacious, and I was feeling very good about the situation indeed. The mother and father presently appeared, which I was less happy about. The eldest sister, a blonde, told me she was studying fashion; she wanted to show me the dress she had designed, her first, to wear to a wedding that weekend. She took the dress from its protective sheath and held it up before me: it was long, pink, diamond-encrusted and tantalisingly translucent. I asked her whether she would wear anything underneath it and she said yes, flesh-coloured underwear. I told her I was certain she was going to be famous one day and she agreed. Just as I had turned my attention back to the receptionist and worked up the nerve to ask her out, the father, who did not say much, closed up shop, turned out the lights and ushered them all into the car, home for the night.

I paid for another couple of bottles and took them to my room, where I squandered the rest of the evening on the internet, posting tweets of an aggressive banality. I had spotted no other guests since checking in and assumed I was alone in the hotel. Around 2 a.m., however, the quiet was pierced by a woman's unbridled erotic screams – a full-throated, prolonged howl of ecstasy. Such a noise goaded its hearer: someone else was having this rapturous sex tonight, not you. For a jealous moment I imagined it was the goddess from the reception desk, wearied by my indecisiveness and now gifting herself to some other man who doubtless couldn't believe his luck, his entire life justified by this one night. Lying there in my TV-less room, with the shrieks so loud it was as if the fuckers were in the bed with me, I felt momentarily sorry for myself. Then I began to laugh. The thought was inevitable: it might have been a Bolaño story, one of those faintly hallucinatory narratives about a drifter who turns up in some town, has an inconclusive encounter or two and moves on, having learned nothing and finished up more lost than when he started out. I remembered some lines from Bolaño's last interview, with his biographer Mónica Maristain for *Playboy Mexico*, when the shadows were drawing in:

What are the kind of things that make you laugh?
My own and other people's misfortunes.

What sort of things make you weep?
The same: my own and other people's
misfortunes.

I slept badly, my dreams toxic with alcohol. The next afternoon, hot and tired, I returned to Barcelona and boarded the late train to Paris. Return journeys are always longer than the outward trip, and glummer. The promise of the journey has been spent: instead of an open horizon of possibility, the only destination now is familiar. You sign up for the melancholy of returning the moment you determine to undertake a journey. I brought my book to the cafe carriage. The hours dragged past. The train broke down deep inside a tunnel: I struggled to ward off a claustrophobia compounded by mental images of jihadists stalking through the carriages with AK-47s, executing anyone who couldn't recite a page or two from the Koran. (A month earlier, passengers on a French train had avoided such a fate due to the fortuitous combination of a jammed assault rifle and the presence of two off-duty US marines and a British civilian.)

I was looking out the window when a dark-haired woman I had noticed earlier took the stool next to mine. She ate a salad and when she was finished she did not get up to leave. We got talking: she told me she was Algerian, had been living in Spain for a decade, was on her way to visit her sister in the north of France. She showed me pictures of her two children, who were beautiful. Her ex-husband was a communist, she said. She had left Algeria 'because of the mentality'. Too many people she knew had died violently. We spoke in French that was peppered with Spanish phrases, and a few English ones. I found I was enjoying myself. Twilight was blazing out across the French countryside, the fields all darkening. I bought us a beer each: she laughed and said it would be a scandal in Algeria for a woman to drink alcohol, especially on a train with a strange man. The carriage was empty now, the vendors having retreated behind the counter. Our conversation had reached a comfortable pause. The woman glanced up at me and smiled, turned away, looked at me again. I touched her forearm and after a moment she ran her fingers over my own. We kissed. She drew me in close and I trailed a hand along her thigh, up inside her denim skirt. Her knickers were a thin, silken slip: I parted them and slid a finger inside her. Behind us the automatic door hummed open and we drew apart, giggling like teenagers, hiding in our hair. She said I shouldn't think she was the kind of person who did this often, and I replied that neither was I.

It was past midnight when we arrived in Paris. The rain was coming down hard. She was staying the night in a hotel in Montmartre, would catch another train in the morning. Outside the Gare de Lyon there was a long queue for taxis. The cars arrived slowly, in ones and twos. We stood in line, holding each other in the rain. The night was cold. We moved slowly in the queue, pulling our luggage along beside us, like we were a married couple, a man and a woman who knew each other.

———

After I got back to Paris I didn't see anyone for days. I haven't been right at all, with hot coals in my skull. I've been drunk for a week, pouring Brouilly in my room when I wake up, wandering the grey city as in a dream. This constant oscillation between the desire to live forever and the desire to end it all right now. The suspicion that everyone gets everything he wants. I have an uncle who's an alcoholic. He left his family, lost his job, now he sleeps in a hostel for destitutes where they give him three meals a day, money enough to stay drunk all the time. I imagine him happier than he's ever been, free-falling through destiny.

I have all the chapters fanned out on the floor, in front of my desk. I hover over the pages, getting a sense of the whole and what it requires. At such times, when the work is going well and you feel its substance begin to cohere, there is respite – more than respite.

And what about your book? Is it vicious, or funny, or what? Are the men all awful? You make having children sound like hell, by the way, which is how so many novels I've read make it sound. In a parallel world, I never encountered certain books, ideas, works of corrupting art, and now I'm raising two kids, the age my father was when I was six or seven, sweating to pay off the mortgage, envying my bachelor friends their casual lovers, drinking up the courage for a first adultery.

Last night I joined Eddie for a party at the house on Villa Seurat where he and his ex-wife raised their children. She and Eddie are still friends, and their current partners attend the family gatherings. Eddie and I stayed late, dancing with Callisto and her friends till all the wine was gone. The family is half Greek, so their soirées have none of the stifling reserve of bourgeois Paris parties. Or to put it another way, Eddie and I got magnificently hammered. He told me that if he didn't have children, he'd have no reason not to kill himself. I thought of John Berger's insistence that suicide should not necessarily be seen as the tragic derailment of a life – what went wrong? – *but may be part of that life's destiny.*

I still believe in amor fati – *I wouldn't exchange my existence for any other. Nietzsche wrote that anyone who has a* why *in life can put up with almost any* how. *For as long as you are working, you have a* why: *when you reach the end of a project, the* why *dissolves. You are left alone with yourself, in all the pain from which the work had offered relief. But there is another perspective, more comforting and no less valid: with the completion of every book, it gets easier to disappear.*

Nightclub

When I was younger than I'll ever be again I fixated on the idea of moving to Berlin. I spent a couple of years drifting around the world, and every place I went, the most interesting people I met would say: *Berlin.* By the time I returned to Ireland, I wanted so badly to move to Berlin that I began learning German, read up on the city's history, packed my belongings, and finally moved to Sicily.

The reason I moved to Sicily back then and not Berlin involves my Berliner friend Linda, and the notorious week I spent at her apartment in Friedrichshain, prior to my planned move. But I'll get back to that, or maybe I won't. For now, suffice it to say it was a real shitshow, and consequently I only got round to living in Berlin a decade later, when I spent a winter there with the aim of researching a novel.

I arrived in the city in late November, just when everybody else wanted to leave. The winter was tightening its grip – the days were over before they began. I worked in my room in Schöneberg each afternoon, and in the evenings I rode the S-Bahn around the city. Because it was dark whenever I took the train, it was impossible to get a sense of Berlin's visual character, what distinguished one neighbourhood from another. The streets seemed deserted as I soared above them, peering in the windows of cuboid offices – it was the emptiest capital in Europe. The Berliners wore black-hole clothes that sucked in whatever light there was – the city hid itself in its citizens, and vice versa. After a week or two the colourlessness of Berlin began to unsettle me. It wasn't long before I came to believe that it was all a reflection: I saw no colour because I was colourless myself, saw no light because a light had gone out in me.

It was on one of my aimless night journeys, as a shoal of grey citizens poured off the train at Hauptbahnhof, that the thought hit me: I was jaded. The suicidal mania I'd endured in Paris and Spain had relented, but it had left in its stead a condition of surfeit and indifference. As the train trundled out of the station over the dark city, it seemed to me more shameful to be jaded than it did to be heartbroken or suicidal. Those were distressing experiences, obviously, but they were violent conditions, the consequences of passion gone awry. Jadedness was a more contemptible kind of defeat, a death in life without dignity or valour. *You were so jaded when I met you*, a woman had said to me once. She was right that I had been jaded, and right to imply that it was through her I became unjaded. There are worse descriptions of what it is to fall in love than that: an unjadening. The event of encountering an unanticipated, amazing other destabilises your categories, overturns your certainties, so that it is no longer viable to go on as you have been. But that – love – was in the past, and possibly in the future: in the present there was solitude, and a habit of promiscuity that iterated with diminishing zeal so that lovers had come to seem disposable, interchangeable, like the faces that scroll past on a dating app. I sensed I had strayed too long and lost the thread of return. The prospect of ever again being so enchanted by any one person that I would commit to making a life with them – or, if I did meet such a person, that I would be un-fucked-up enough to make them stay – seemed remoter as the years fell off. Already looming on my horizon were the stark years in which virility would dissipate, when my body would become as repulsive to the young as those of the middle-aged had been to me. I would continue to desire what I had always desired – the love and physical intimacy of women – but these longings and my efforts to satisfy them would increasingly find me branded a predator, vilified in a society that now endorsed the hatred of men, and reviled especially those past a certain age who have neither married nor renounced their sexual hunger. As I exited the S-Bahn at Alexanderplatz, I caught a glimpse of my reflection in a window. I thought, that is the face of a man who is jaded. Then I thought, that is the face of a man who used to be handsome. I wished I didn't care so much about the fading of my looks, but looks were a sign of youth and I had never taken an interest in very much beyond youth culture, nor made any plan for getting older. Before moving to Berlin, I had asked my barber to put some dye in my hair for the first time, and got a spiky, youthful new haircut, but what I saw reflected in the station window was merely the haircut of a man trying to look younger than he was. At a certain age, when you shamble into the bathroom in the morning, instead of thrilling narcissistically at your reflection you start to avoid your own gaze, like that of a lecherous creep on the subway. I was almost certainly in the grip of Seasonal Affective Disorder – being a SAD bastard – but I was convinced the truth was written in wintry lines all over my face: somewhere along the way I had become the kind of man of whom it could be said: *The years have taken their toll on him.*

On a Friday evening I met Linda and her friends at an Italian restaurant in Friedrichshain – the sixth-best Italian restaurant in Berlin, according to Linda – for a pre-club meal. Linda and I had reunited at a bar in Mitte the previous week, for the first time since my notorious stay years earlier. Linda had gamely offered to facilitate my explorations of the Berlin techno scene, in which she and her friends were immersed. Over vodka and Club-Mate I'd told Linda of my ambition to write *the great Berlin techno novel.* I had no sense of what this novel might look like, except that it would include an ageing expat druggie who dances a lot. In the meantime, its notional existence gave a sense of purpose to my intention of hanging out in grotty clubs every weekend, buying drugs in the toilets while friends in Ireland started having kids and buying homes.

Friedrichshain was thronged and we had to wait for a while even though we'd made a reservation. Smoking cigarettes outside the restaurant, Linda's forty-ish friends looked like well-paid office workers at the end of the week, which is precisely what some of them were. But when they took off their elegant coats they revealed black, stylish clubbing gear – hoodies and techno T-shirts and runners. The waitress placed menus on the table and we ordered bottles of sparkling water, most of the group being straight-edge. Linda's edge was anything but straight: she ordered a beer, then began rolling a joint under the table. The friends chatted about their week, mostly in English for my benefit, although I urged them not to.

'So what are you currently writing about?' asked Marc politely. He had a narrow beard and a shaved head and he was a DJ.

I extemporised about the sedimented psychic histories of Berlin, layers of memory and hallucination. What I didn't mention was that, ever since we'd sat down at the table, I'd become fired up on the idea of writing about *them* – Linda and her stylish, not-so-young techno friends. Clubbers who were pushing into their forties seemed to me a milieu worth exploring, one that might illumine a host of confluent themes that engaged me: what it meant, for instance, to age in twenty-first-century Europe, and the new kinds of family that emerged when the nuclear family blew itself up. Naturally, nightclubs teemed with sexy young things who could wear any ill-fitting, outlandish clothes and still look edgy and mesmeric. The techno kids danced with animal assurance because they knew the world was about them: they were the future and we – anyone over thirty – were already the past, sinking inexorably into it. Better to leave the gorgeous twenty-year-olds to their photogenic bliss: I would write about Linda and Marc and Thorsten, Julia and Katarina, and in writing about them I would be writing about myself, my own reckoning with the ancient headfuck of ageing, which was the dinosaur in the room of any club I danced at from here on in.

I gestured to the waitress and ordered a glass of wine, while the others studied the menus.

'Prego.'

Hours later I sat in a grotty toilet cubicle at Griessmühle, a marvellously dilapidated club on the banks of a canal, hidden amid factories and business premises. The MDMA I had taken after we got inside was coming to life, and among its effects was an urgent quickening of the bowels. Outside the cubicle, girls and boys laughed and smoked and chattered, sitting on sinks overlooking a shadowy yard. Ostensibly these were the girls' toilets but that did not matter: the toilets were a hangout, a chill-out room away from the actual chill-out room downstairs. Realising there was no toilet paper, I took the notebook from the pocket of my jeans, ripped out two blank pages and used those instead.

I found Linda dancing on the lower floor, a joint in one hand and a beer bottle in the other, a head shorter than the guys around her. The beat rumbled in my viscera as lasers lanced through the darkness. I sank into a tattered leather chair at the back of the room to watch: when Linda dances, there is no one cooler on the planet. She had not changed much in the years since we'd last met – but why should she change? These days she lived alone, on the tenth floor of a GDR-era high-rise in Lichtenberg. A fierce intransigence of character – along with a prodigious sexual appetite – had meant that traditional monogamous relationships were never going to work out for her, and now she dwelled in a wise, relaxed zone somewhere between polyamory, self-sufficiency and openness to the possibility that things might yet play out differently. She still took photographs, was active in radical politics, smoked weed every night after work, and cared nothing for what anyone thought of her. Seeing me sprawled on the armchair, she smiled from amid the dancers. Then she turned back towards the sound system, silhouetted in white strobing light.

Early on Sunday morning we were still out in the city with my friends Conor and Stavro. I took no more MDMA, but the high left a glow that lasted not only through the weekend but long after the chemicals wore off, so that in a sense I never really came down. There was more to it than drugs, and yet there was something in all this I had forgotten: taken at the right time, MDMA can effect a shift that is not ephemeral nor merely chemical. A gloom is dispelled. The world becomes altered, brightened, clearer – an unjadening occurs.

As life got its colour back, my attention flowed outwards again. I recorded my days methodically, as if the life I was living were the first draft of *the great Berlin techno novel*, and all I had to do was get it down. There would be no plot, but the book would carry itself on pure tone, buoyed by my happiness at living in the city that, as Nietzsche had once said of Paris, was the only home for an artist in Europe. Most evenings I attended art openings or parties with Stavro, or drank with him and Conor in Tannenbaum, their favourite bar. At weekends I took to the club scene with the zeal of a twenty-five-year-old, like the one I had been on my last visit to the city. When I was out dancing, high on drugs I consumed in reasonable, mid-thirties dosages – unlike the over-dosages I'd caned with Linda a decade earlier – sentences would appear fully formed in my mind, or would lengthen throughout the night, becoming increasingly complex and beautiful, clauses linking elegantly amid the laser lighting and subwoofer quake. I quivered in the tension between wanting to be present in the moment and standing perpetually outside of it, projecting myself into a future in which I would sit at my desk and distil what was going on here. Now and then I would leave the dance floor to shut myself into a toilet cubicle, anxious to jot down a phrase before it vanished in my brain's neuronal hum. When I left the toilets – concealing my notebook in shame at my compulsion to record – young clubbers would enter in pairs or threes, pulling baggies from their pockets before the door shut behind them. These ecstatic nights out nourished me with insights that felt desperately poignant, and this poignancy would ramify through the recognition that I had become so alienated, so cut off from the natural outflow of empathy I recalled from childhood, that I needed drugs to feel that way again.

In December the famous Christmas markets started sprouting up around the city. Or so I heard: I hadn't the slightest interest in visiting them, and their existence to me was a matter of hearsay. Meanwhile, I moved apartment. Stavro helped me find a sublet in the Kottbusser Tor area of Kreuzberg. 'The most excellent neighbourhood in the best part of town,' he insisted. Stavro was biased: like everyone in Kreuzberg, he venerated the area while nurturing a disdain for Friedrichshain, Kreuzberg's rival neighbourhood across the Spree and formerly across the Wall.

After I moved to Kreuzberg, Sylvia, a girl from Montreal who worked in a Paris wine bar, came to stay for a long weekend. We had met at a party in the autumn. That night she had worn gawky clothes, and later, when she took them off at her flat in the tenth arrondissement, the perfection of her body had stunned me. I'd told her this, that the perfection of her body was stunning to me. To which she had replied, abstractedly, that she had the same body as every other woman on the planet. The insight had confounded me: I suddenly felt I'd lived my life in thrall to a confidence trick, making myself ridiculous by panting and gasping in pursuit of an illusion. We both insisted we didn't want a relationship, but we had been meeting ever since, either at hers or mine, never in public, as if we were having an illicit affair. Sylvia liked to be treated forcefully, which is putting it mildly. One night I'd fractured her finger by beating her too hard with my belt. After that we used a safe word: 'creative non-fiction'. I suggested it as a joke, but she thought it was perfect. In Berlin we visited sex clubs, taking part in orgies with other couples. These nights delighted me in that they were free of jealousy and the dominance hierarchies that usually form among males when women are involved. The sex parties were characterised by generosity, playfulness, the pleasure of giving pleasure. At one, a man reached out to jerk me off as he penetrated his partner, while I parted Sylvia's labia and slid my fingers inside her, and she licked the nipples of the other woman, who lay back on a raised seat, coming loudly. I had never been pleasured by a man before; it happened so fluidly that it didn't feel like a first of anything. That night culminated with Sylvia squirting voluminously over the leather bed where she kneeled on all fours while I, and a man whose girlfriend

I had made love to earlier, joined hands in a fraternal clasp and thrust our fingers into her dripping cunt.

On her final night in Berlin, Sylvia told me she'd had sex with two men since we'd last been together, one younger and one older. The latter was significantly older than Sylvia and, she said, a serious pervert. As she described the things he did to her, rather than hatred or jealousy I felt a kinship with this man, a fellow-feeling that linked us across European capitals, he who was beyond all restraint in his will to suck the tit of life while it was still within reach. I imagined him wheezing and debauched, contemplating his end in some squalid hotel, a wrinkled condom slumped on his tired prick. In turn I admitted that I'd had sex with a prostitute – for twenty minutes at a cost of forty euro, in a brothel in Schöneberg. Sylvia insisted on hearing about the encounter in as much detail as I would provide.

'It sounds humiliating,' she said when I finished.

'It was.'

Sylvia flew home and then, a few days before Christmas, Stavro and Conor flew home too. On Christmas Eve, I visited Linda at her flat in the high-rise in Lichtenberg. She cooked pumpkin soup while I reclined in the hammock that bisected the living room at an angle, rolling one-skinner joints for Linda to smoke in the narrow kitchen while she told me stories about her travels and love affairs. To me Linda embodied all that was vital and underground in Berlin: when I thought of Berlin I thought of it as the city where Linda lived. But now she was thinking about moving away – at least, she'd had enough of the winters.

'I want to go where there are hammocks out of doors,' she said.

'Tenerife,' I said, before licking a cigarette paper.

'Maybe Ko Samui, for the trance parties. But actually I want to go to Mexico.'

'The place I want to go is Kyoto, though I like imagining it as much as I'd enjoy being there. They have temples, cherry blossoms, poems about the moon.'

'Even in Kyoto, hearing the cuckoo's cry, I long for Kyoto.'

Drawing on a fresh joint, she told me she'd finally got round to reading my books. She said she found my writing brave. I shifted in the hammock and replied that it made me uneasy whenever someone described my stuff as 'brave' – it made me think I'd humiliated myself in ways I hadn't quite intended. She asked me what I was working on, and when I told her, she wondered if I ever felt I was living a certain way only so that I could write about it. If Linda's phone hadn't rung just then, I might have told her that the time when I could have understood such a question had passed, that I had long since solved the problem of authenticity, of making existence adhere to itself. I might have told her that my life was the research for the book I was writing about my life, and that this book, which was many books, would justify that life. Linda might then have smiled sadly, and concluded that writing was a symptom of the sickness for which it was also the cure.

Instead, she told me a story in which she decided to have a child with a man in India, before realising, at a point when it might well have been too late, that this was imperfectly wise. The story surprised me, in that I had always viewed Linda's commitment to childlessness as an inviolable element of her nature. This had intrigued me when we first met in South America. Moreover, I could relate. The difference was that, whereas Linda was concerned with political issues and worried about the direction society was taking, these days I appraised myself to be not only child*less* but child*ish* – that is, I lived like a child, concerned exclusively with novelty and selfish delight, relating even to geopolitics and the prospect of planetary catastrophe as modes of entertainment. Sometimes I judged myself brutally for this, but even the self-reproach seemed a kind of decadence, an exquisite late-capitalist masochism. More often, I gave myself over to pleasure with ease of conscience, enjoying the spectral glow of what felt, on so many nights, like the twilight of a jaded civilisation. I seemed to myself nakedly symptomatic of a general decline – when an epoch started producing the likes of me, you knew the game was up. It was nice to live like a child, though – better than it was to live as a man. Being a man was a grim slog of duty and sacrifice and repressed desire. Men had built European civilisation,

217

driven its expansionist phase, and now it fell to us – history's children – to squander it.

Linda and I talked for a few hours, then I went home. We did not have sex. This was hardly remarkable, yet it was striking too, because a decade earlier that had been all we did: have sex. We had never been explicitly *in a relationship*, so it wasn't exactly that we had broken up and were now simply friends. Linda was getting older, and I was getting older too, at precisely the same rate. What had once been a raging blaze was now an affectionate glimmer. This was what ageing meant: you had less sex, even with those with whom you once had record-breaking amounts of sex. Lust waned and friendship blossomed. And this was okay. It was nice.

Alone in Berlin, I spent Christmas Day wandering out at Tempelhof, where the Nazis had built a characteristically grandiose airport, its environs since repurposed as an immense city park. Kitesurfers and kite-flyers busied the grey sky, and I thought about Sicily, where the sky was blue, and kites flocked the coastal horizon at San Vito Lo Capo. I had gone to Sicily to write a novel – *the great backpacker dropout novel*, or something like that – but I abandoned it at the point when writing about my prior life had come to feel like infidelity to the vital present. Some Indians, or perhaps Pakistanis, played cricket on the airstrip, jumping on the spot to stay warm. I watched them until the cold moved me along.

My friends gradually returned to the city, and on New Year's Eve, Stavro invited me for dinner at his new place in Friedrichshain – 'I've become a traitor!' – along with Conor, an American DJ named Midge and a Swedish poet named Dani. The noise of fireworks intensified as the day progressed: by ten o'clock it was a constant barrage.

'What *is* it with Germans and fireworks?' wondered Midge, looking out the window at the illuminated skyline over the Spree. 'It's like they wage war on their own city every year.'

Stavro had a theory. 'It's atavistic. The Germans love artillery, and this is as close as they can get in peacetime. They're compelled to re-enact the Battle of Berlin, over and over.'

After we'd been out to the bridge at Warschauer Straße to ring in the new year amid screaming rockets and machine-gun bangers, Dani told us it was a tradition in Sweden for each person to give a speech outlining their hopes for the year ahead. She stood on a chair and began: she hoped to finish one book – about loss – and start another – about krakens. When it was my turn, I surprised myself by admitting that in recent years an intense gloom had descended on my life. A confluence of appalling shocks had laid me low when I ought to have been at my happiest. But lately the gloom had dispersed, and I entered the new year with a cheerfulness – I realised this as I spoke it – that I had never quite known before. I said something vaguely Nietzschean about an open horizon, a clear sky, the necessity of living with courage. I was not used to speaking this way to people I did not know intimately and I trailed off, embarrassed. Next Stavro stood up – he is a mountainous man whose presence fills a room. He too spoke about courage – the chief virtue, he called it, the one on which all the others are predicated. He was talking about art, the life in art. We were all meant to be cynical and post-everything, he said, and we were discouraged from voicing thoughts such as these, but the truth of the matter was that art was a heroic endeavour, it was not for cowards. Every step of the way was beset by angst and uncertainty – about status and confidence, money and the future. You lived with the waves rolling above your head, fighting for air, and the struggle would never abate. When you committed to a life in art, he said, you had to accept that the only way it was likely to end was in failure and oblivion. The others spoke in turn, and afterwards Stavro poured us glasses of vodka and Mate for a toast.

More of Stavro's friends bundled in from a different party. The music got louder, people began dancing. Now Dani and Conor were kissing, and Midge and I were talking about techno, and Stavro was wondering if he should move back to Kreuzberg. And so it was that a new year began, right where the old one ended.

It was still a new year the following morning, when Conor and I pushed into the crowd that danced under a barrage of gut-shaking beats on the main floor at Berghain – the immense club in a former power plant by the river – for the last day of the epic New Year's party. My euphoria at getting in – after a tense moment's hesitation by the doorman – blossomed into wonderment at what this place really was. Throughout the New Year's party all areas were open – including the gay-sex dungeon below ground, with its warren of crannies and dark rooms. Everywhere connected to everywhere else, so that you could simply walk in any direction and eventually get to wherever you wanted to be. Berghain was too much to have anticipated and too much to take in. Every freak in Europe had apparently converged here – the mutants of a weird emerging era. I left Conor dancing near a huge speaker and roamed the building. Naked men sucked one another off on couches by the heaving dance floor, or fucked in elaborate group formations atop tables, while women with bare breasts and fetish gear danced frenetically, each dancer distinct from the others and yet *for* the others, a gathering in ecstasy whose constituents, by conforming to no set way of dancing, formed a collective in beauty. This was why I loved clubs in Berlin, why dancing had become as needful to me as reading or laughing: the ease of access to a state of unselfconsciousness. There was always someone older or younger, nakeder or weirder than you, and the fact that photography was forbidden (they put stickers over your camera at the entrance) and there were no mirrors anywhere reinforced the ethos of participation over gawking, immersion over separation. In the crowd you lost any distinction between dancing and being danced, broke clear of selfhood right at the point where the self became exalted and sovereign. This did not feel like decadence – this was political. These men and women would go back out to the world empowered and awake. The assembly was like some rogue faction from *Mad Max: Fury Road*, a futurist goth convoy enjoying one last techno orgy before roaring into battle. The gloomy industrial interior – dark corridors, steel platforms, abyssal shafts – recalled not a film but a video game: the iconic nineties first-person-shooter *Quake*. On the main floor the music was menacing and intense – up here at the Panorama Bar, where the shutters let sunlight stream in whenever the beat dropped, it was celebratory and joyous. Techno was like contemporary art: the terrain was so vast that even if I tried to keep up to speed, I would always be chasing a scene that shifted faster than I could track it. Techno in the twenty-first century was a self-replicating code in constant, restless mutation. The names changed as soon as you learned them, but it didn't matter because it was all one ur-track, an expanding aural singularity that throbbed in bedrooms and squats and clubs and flowed through fibre-optic cables, which individual DJs tapped into and redirected through pulsating Funktion-One systems like these.

'I'd forgotten, but I'd forgotten I'd forgotten,' said Conor when we rested against a balcony above hundreds of dancers, surveying the scene. 'It's like when you take psychedelics: you get back to that place and you think, Oh *yeah*, of course! How could I forget? But you're not able to *not* forget. The experience entails its own unrememberability. It's like entering another dimension.'

At some point in Berghain's atemporal carnival, I wandered into the subterranean labyrinth, seeking the disco that was down there amid the dark winding tunnels. I stepped into a dim, tight room lined with urinals. The walls and floor were grey brick. I seemed to have crossed into a murky and haunted underworld because, as I stood over a urinal, a disembodied head floated towards me with eerie slowness. That was how I saw it: a head floating in the darkness, stopping inches from my cock. A man – topless and tattooed, in leather trousers – had crawled on his hands and knees across the slosh of piss and filth, and now he was kneeling at my crotch. His expression was urgent and solemn, as if we were performing a ceremony. I figured he wanted to suck me off and I shook my head. He gazed at the flow of my piss, entranced. As I was finishing, I waved it and splashed some on his face, over his lips. He grimaced in pleasure. As I zipped up, he withdrew and slithered back into the shadows with the same otherworldly slowness.

'That was insane,' I said when I found Conor perched on a giant swing alongside a dozen others. 'There was a guy down in the toilets who wanted to drink my piss.'

'Oh yeah, the toilet guy.'

I saw him again as the day wore on, in other toilets throughout Berghain, always alone, stalking the urinals with a fixed, pathetic cringe. Who was he? What had happened to make this his destiny – crawling through filth to drink the piss of strangers? He was abjection incarnate, a being who had sunk further into abasement than anyone I had encountered. I felt a sympathy, a tenderness, for him. He seemed to me both admirable for fully inhabiting his perversion, and terribly sad – he *must* have been broken to seek out such humiliation. I envisioned a childhood of rape in dank basements, a howling obscene mother. When the night outside synced with Berghain's perpetual night, I sought out the dungeon urinals again, following narrow passages past rooms where men fisted, sucked and got as far inside one another as they could. I knew he would be there, and that he would come to me. In the dark toilets I unzipped. Immediately he emerged from the shadows, the same cringing face. This time I let him drink it all. It streamed over his mouth, his lips. He gulped, gurgled, his eyes rolled back in ecstasy. I pissed long and hot in his abject face. He swallowed all he could and the rest overflowed on his chin. As the stream relented, he glanced up and met my gaze.

'Danke!' he rasped. 'Danke!'

In the weeks that followed, the pages in my notebooks filled up more slowly, then stopped filling up at all. It was as if the experiential supernova of Berghain had nuked my will to affix a mesh of form on to the formless real. I kept going to clubs with Linda and Conor and other friends, but I no longer tried to remember anything, letting myself be swept up in the flux of dancing and techno. I registered the first inner shifts towards an acceptance that *the great Berlin techno novel* might be yet another write-off on the scrapheap of my ambitions, no more than the memory of a book I had once contemplated writing. During this blissful period it dawned on me that this was the book I had been writing all along: an anthology of the abandoned books that didn't get written while I was busy documenting the rapturous decline I underwent while I was failing to write them, otherwise known as my life.

The week before I left Berlin, Linda, Conor and I met on the platform at Alexanderplatz. We ate some of the magic mushrooms that Conor had grown the previous summer using a kit he'd bought online. We took a train out to the Grunewald forest on the edge of the city. It was a grey morning, the kind of sky that is always about to rain but never does. We marched through the forest, past the looming ruins of the old NSA listening post at Teufelsberg. A few kilometres from the tracks stood the 'Cemetery of the Nameless'. Nico was buried out here, and Conor wanted to take a picture of her grave for an article he was writing about *thanatos*, the longing for death in popular culture. As we followed a narrow trail through the woods, I told Linda I'd given up writing, which meant I'd given up asking more from experience than itself. She said she didn't believe me, and I replied that maybe it was more of a thought experiment.

We came to the cemetery gate. A sign indicated that it was open daily from ten till four, but as there was nobody around for miles, the cemetery's openness or closedness seemed to pertain solely in the minds of visitors. When Conor pointed this out I found it very funny indeed, which is how I knew the mushrooms were coming on. Nico's grave, like that of Serge Gainsbourg in Montparnasse Cemetery, which I'd happened upon while visiting E. M. Cioran's, was well stocked with offerings of wine, beer, joints and even what looked like a vial of speed or cocaine. Someone had left a red notebook in which visitors wrote messages: lyrics from Velvet Underground songs, expressions of gratitude, druggy soliloquies. Conor took a couple of mushrooms from his pouch and placed them by the headstone. Linda crouched down to write in the notebook.

Conor began dancing, as if odd-shaped waves were passing through his body. Perceiving myself inhabiting the action instants before I did so, I leaned to pick up the notebook and read what Linda had written.

Come, see real flowers of this painful world.

It was probably some time later when Conor remarked that ancient civilisations showed admirable pragmatism when they equipped the dead with useful, quotidian items for their journey to the afterlife.

'What should we put in your grave when you go?' I asked.

Conor considered this. 'My headphones.'

'I'll need my coffee maker and some tobacco,' said Linda. 'No question.'

They asked me what I would need. I settled on my steel-toecapped Doc Martens, which I'd been issued when I worked at the Dublin Mail Centre many years earlier. It would be important to have dry feet and look tough in the underworld, I said.

A bird squawked and flew from a bush. The noise reverberated, ripples in the stillness. Then silence enfolded the forest, and I stood with my friends among the graves, imagining how it would be if I weren't holding on to any of it.

I like these new photos, how they make my own city seem as foreign to me as it is to you. Phoenix Park flattened under grey skies; the north side like Berlin after the war. I wonder if this is how we are, only seeing afresh and feeling alive in countries where we weren't born. It's amusing that you felt compelled to go there to finish your book – I've always needed to get away from the place to write with any clarity.

I've resumed recording my dreams after a decade's hiatus. I did it in my twenties, writing them down each morning when I was travelling in Asia. Writing out dreams is a drag, so now I use the voice recorder on my phone. Because I've been ill, with a scorched and bleeding throat, the recordings sound like the tapes of Colonel Kurtz they play at the beginning of Apocalypse Now, *rasping his insane visions of slugs crawling across razor blades.*

Speaking of dreams, I had a momentous one on the night of the full moon. I was in the countryside in northern France, sleeping with my girlfriend. I dreamed that she and I were shapeshifters who had travelled back in time from the 81st millennium, to fight in a cosmic war on terror. It was the type of dream that occurs only every few years, so freighted with emotion, so numinous and vivid, that when you wake up you know something deep has taken place. The difference with this dream was that I believed it was real even after I woke up, or half woke up. I was convinced not only that my girlfriend had shared in the dream, but that she had long known about the epic conflict it depicted. I lay there in amazement, waiting for her to open her eyes and acknowledge what had happened. When she did wake up I gave her meaningful, expectant looks. Gradually I realised she had no idea what I'd dreamed about.

To answer your question, I used to write mainly to hurt people, to violate them. Their happiness was intolerable to me – I couldn't let them off the hook. And I did hurt them: that craving was slaked. Now I would say I prefer to contaminate people with my puzzlement. My friend Paul likes to say of his intentions as a painter: not to solve the mystery, but to deepen it. You make fun of, and probably despise, what you call my 'alarming tendencies towards mysticism'. I don't mind. 'Register the cultural moment,' you say, but increasingly I fixate on the essential, which is what's fascinating where everything else is interesting. I let questions of relevancy take care of themselves. It's not as if I'm shielded: the cultural moment is coming at me hard and fast.

Sometimes I still like to hurt, to abuse.

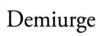

Demiurge

Every now and then I will attend a conference or a lecture on some topic or other, not so much out of an urgent interest in what the speakers have to say, but because it is imperative to get out of my silent room here in Paris, where if I stay too long I lose the sense of trusting myself. In such instances it is as if I am no longer me, but *he* and me, the two of us locked together like starved rats in a cage, one of us more cunning and satanic than the other.

At one conference I attended, my friend Michel gave a talk on literature in France after the 2015 terrorist attacks, concluding that it would be much the same as it had been before the attacks. Afterwards, milling about and drinking as much free red wine as I could, I listened as Michel and a colleague of his named Natasha discussed a show that was running at the Palais de Tokyo, by the artist Tino Sehgal. Natasha was not only an admirer of Sehgal's work, she was part of the show too. Sehgal's art is deeply interactive, she explained (I knew nothing about him); the only materials he employs are the bodies of the people who perform it. Intrigued, I decided I would check out the show later in the week.

I drank too much wine and, when I got home at 3 a.m., I couldn't find any headache tablets. Foolishly I rooted in my bag of toiletries for the Seroquel pills my girlfriend had left behind after visiting me in Paris, Seroquel being an antipsychotic that is prescribed by some desperate psychiatrists as an off-label treatment for insomnia. My girlfriend had been prescribed the drug for both purposes in turn, but she had come to loathe Seroquel for its bludgeoning crudeness and had sworn off it. I knew from experience that the pills were potent, in the sense that a train running you over is potent. My rationale was that I would take only a third of a pill, then sleep right through the hangover and wake up smiling late the next morning. After biting off a segment, though, I looked drunkenly at the remaining crescent and thought: fuck it.

When I awoke it was dark. I felt impossibly heavy, as if my limbs were weighed down by chains. The pressure in my bladder forced me to shamble into the bathroom to piss. Then I curled back into bed. There really was a lot of street noise for the pre-dawn hours, I noticed foggily, reaching for my phone beside the bed to peer at its illuminated face.

It was 9:30 p.m. I was too groggy to feel more than a dull remorse at having slept through an entire day, though I did glimpse an image of myself in advanced old age, ruing my fecklessness. I felt as though I hadn't slept at all, had taken the pill mere minutes ago and jolted forward a day, the earth having spun on its axis around me.

I made a pot of coffee and sat in bed with my laptop, brain circuitry slowly humming back to a semblance of normal function. I decided I would stay awake through the night and see the Tino Sehgal show the following day. Meanwhile I peered into my screen, reading all I could about Sehgal: interviews, commentary by art critics, the bitching or praise of his peers. Apparently Sehgal was something of a phenomenon, among the most lauded youngish artists on the contemporary scene. He lived and worked in Berlin, like so many current artists, and in interviews he sounded like a lecturer in critical theory, also like so many current artists. Towards dawn my phone pinged with a WhatsApp message from my girlfriend in Dublin. There was a perplexing series of emojis, including a banana and two of the aghast-cat faces she used relentlessly, and then the following:

Did we hallucinate a world?

I assumed it was another line from Philip K. Dick's novel *Flow My Tears, the Policeman Said*, with which, it would be no exaggeration to claim, my girlfriend had become obsessed. She was writing an essay about it, not to publish or show anyone, but for herself, to comprehend her fascination with this novel she had described to me as a 'mystical text', the key to some profound revelation about the nature of reality, language and God. She spoke of the book as if it were the Kabbalah, saturated in encrypted meaning that wizened initiates could pore over for centuries and still not exhaust. The book could drive the reader mad, she said; indeed it was *a machine to drive the reader mad*. I was fascinated by her fascination but unable, even after a close reading, to tell whether her sense of the novel's eerie ontological depths was legitimate or just the refraction of her own incandescent, volatile mind. By way of reply I sent her an alien-head emoji.

Dawn broke as I read more about Tino Sehgal. It seemed he did not seek to undermine the museum as an institution, unlike many of his peers who, following the belligerent tendency of the twentieth-century avant-garde, condemned it as an engine for the reinforcement of bourgeois subjectivity. In museums, Sehgal observed admiringly, you were able to look around and say in the future-perfect tense, 'This will have been the past.'

Around noon I cycled along Rue la Fayette towards the Palais de Tokyo, an art deco monster in the sixteenth arrondissement, across the river from the Eiffel Tower. As I was parking my bike, a great wave of exhaustion rolled over me. I needed to lie down, just for a moment – and why not right here, on one of the large stone blocks lining the museum's courtyard. No one else was around. I gazed up at the low grey sky, listened to the quiet sounds: traffic along the Seine, the breeze. I closed my eyes, thoughts drifting like curls of incense. Now a pale girl was taking me by the hand and explaining that Tokyo was above all a 'fatal city', the place where I would meet my desires. Several Japanese women led me into a radiant, jewel-bedecked room, where they each held a card before them with a number printed on its surface: 3, 34, 49, 88, 27. Every number indicated a different 'trouble zone', said the pale girl: I had all day to explore the 'phenomenal realm'. I said I would rather stay with her; she replied that this was impossible.

I got to my feet and brushed myself off, chilled from lying on the stone block. Traffic sped past, into a tunnel between the Palais and the river. I wrote some notes in my black notebook. Then I crossed the courtyard to the entrance. The queue was surprisingly long for a weekday afternoon. As I neared the ticket desk I turned on data roaming. Another WhatsApp message:

That intangible malignity which has been from the beginning …

As I read it a new message appeared below:

All that most maddens and torments, all truth with venom in it.

I wrote back *Indeed … Gotta go am at P Tokyo thing!* followed by an aghast-cat emoji, then killed my internet connection. The girl behind the ticket desk looked at me expectantly as I pocketed my phone and took out my wallet. Absently I placed my notebook on the desk in front of me, in plain view of the two stylish twenty-something women queuing behind me. As I took my ticket I noticed the mislaid notebook and snatched it up. It had been open on the page I'd last written in:

THIS WILL HAVE BEEN THE PAST

Tokyo as 'fatal city', place where I'd find all my desires.
Japanese women lead me into many-coloured room.
Holding cards showing me numbers: 3, 34, 49, 88, 27.
Desire for pale girl. Think back to therapist.

I glanced at the women. One of them was oblivious, handing over cash; the other met my eye and grinned knowingly – she thought I was part of the show. Pulling my hat down to my eyes, I gave her the most enigmatic, lingering smile I could muster: pretty hokey. I recalled what Michel had said, how the charm of Sehgal's work was that you were never quite sure where it began – or where it ended. Then I turned and scuttled off past the gift shop and towards the exhibition hall.

The Palais de Tokyo is huge, and the idea behind the 'carte blanche' series to which Sehgal's exhibition belonged is that the entire space – 22,000 square metres – is given over to a single artist. I pushed through a curtain of glass beads, like the entrance to a boudoir in an Arabian-themed porno, and joined a new queue, which I took to be leading into the show proper. Or perhaps this *was* the show, an endless series of queues – a commentary on consumerism and futility.

When I reached the top of the queue, a young guy in the room ahead broke from the group he was part of and singled me out, making continuous dance-like motions as he asked, 'Quelle est l'énigme?'

I froze. The enigma? Jesus …

Assuming I hadn't understood, he said, 'Maybe English? So … What is the enigma?'

I had no idea what the enigma was. He was waiting for an answer. I repeated the question to buy some time.

'Yes,' he said, sadistically. '*What is the enigma?*'

Frantically I tried to think of anything at all to get this freak away from me and move the wretched show to its next stage. I should have gone to see some Impressionist paintings or something. I was too inhibited, too awkward, at bottom too Irish for this kind of carry-on. And still he was there, dancing like a twat, waiting for my answer.

'The enigma,' I finally muttered, 'is … who are you?'

'Your answer leads you … *here!*'

He flamboyantly directed me through the next entrance. I moved along, rattled by the encounter, doubting the wisdom of attending a heavily interactive show while jolted on coffee and not having slept. A little brown-skinned girl emerged from the side of the room and trotted alongside me as I made for the opposite door.

'Qu'est-ce que le progrès?' she said.

This wasn't so bad. Little kids were all right: you could fool around, say silly stuff, it didn't have to be embarrassing.

'Le progrès,' I improvised, 'est l'évolution de l'esprit, la mentalité, et la moralité.'

She wrinkled her nose in derision. 'Progress is the evolution of mortality?' she replied *en anglais*, enunciating each syllable to emphasise how much of a silly fool I was.

Glancing about me, I felt like a paedophile, as I always do when left alone with kids, legacy of the anti-paedo hysteria that had seized the culture since the nineties – guilt is assumed and a child molester lurks behind every lollipop. But I was quite stirred by the answer I'd given and felt an avuncular duty to elaborate and edify.

'Yes, that is progress. But not mor*ta*lity – mo*ra*lity. It's a struggle, I'll admit.'

A massive black lad appeared – for a second I thought he was a nonce-basher. The girl informed him of my views on progress, then skipped off. So it was a relay effort – or else they had a protocol to keep little girls away from glazed-eyed loners on antipsychotics. My new companion led me through more rooms with blank white walls and bare cement floors. Interrogating me further, he established that I was Irish, and that, yes, I supposed I did feel that Ireland had evolved over recent years, in certain, very circumscribed ways. The interaction was a little stilted, and frankly I was finding it exhausting, craving, as I so often do, to be left alone, free of the enervating demands of human engagement. But the fucker wouldn't let up: questions, questions. Then a third party joined us – an older man with thin white hair – and the black guy was gone.

Holy shit, was it going to continue like this for the duration? I'd avoided reading reviews of this show in order to preserve the surprise, but if a relentless series of one-on-ones was in store, I'd have to bail. Perhaps there was an emergency exit … Meanwhile the old boy was yammering away, recounting an anecdote about a book he'd read by an Arab author. Around the time he was reading this book, his wife left him and his father died, leaving behind a house in the countryside. My interlocutor felt entitled to the house, but knew he'd face resistance from his brother and sister. A meeting was held by the three siblings and their lawyers. Imitating the Arab hero of the novel, the man said little during the meeting, remaining inscrutable, letting his familial rivals talk themselves into the thick of whatever judicial spiderweb he had spun.

Frankly, the old codger wasn't coming off all that well from the narrative – and he'd seemed so nice! – though perhaps I was getting it all wrong, had misunderstood something crucial (we were conversing in an Anglo-French melange). There was something about his sister being a 'murderous slapper', but again it's possible I misheard. His story trailed off with him living in a house facing the sea: the house had three walls, and its fourth wall was the sea view. He liked to stand and watch the blue horizon that was framed by the walls, meditating on infinity. 'That sounds very nice,' I offered. We arrived at a door; he held out his hand. 'Bonne journée,' I said, confused.

Thank Christ: no one stepped in to replace him as I entered a large, high-ceilinged hall, like a vacant hangar, where scores of people were ambling about. After the series of rapid engagements, this, I felt, was something like the calm a river feels when it finally meets the ocean. Scanning the diffuse crowd, I had no idea who was part of the performance and who was the audience. I entertained a *Truman Show* paranoia that *all* of them were in on it, and I was the lone innocent.

I sat against a pillar to observe. Some people were talking in pairs or small groups, others roamed alone. At first the crowd circulated randomly, but now I noticed that five people towards the far end of the hall had begun walking backwards, fanned out in a loose parallel. Others joined them as they slowly made their way across the length of the hall. Now there were twenty or more, all walking backwards in a curving line. The effect was otherworldly, like a film in which the hero can see the spirits of the dead abroad in the world. Forty-strong, the flock of backwards-walkers drifted to the other end of the hall, as if drawn by a magnetic current. Most people had fallen silent to watch. There was the sense that something was impending: a climactic event, some species of crisis or revelation.

I took out my phone to capture the eerie row of figures in case I wound up writing about all this (I no longer trust my memory, which plays by its own rules). After snapping it I enabled data roaming and read another message:

'... *the tower is everywhere* ...'

It took me a moment to realise that these words were not from Philip K. Dick but from Thomas Pynchon's *The Crying of Lot 49*, a novel that had for a period obsessed *me*. The quote referred to a painting by the surrealist Remedios Varo that the heroine, Oedipa Maas, views in Mexico City and is thereafter haunted by. In the painting a group of maidens sit trapped in a tower, forced into the production of a vast tapestry that flows out the windows and over the landscape, into the surrounding void. In the novel we are given to understand that the tapestry is the very fabric of reality, traced through with the inexplicable hieroglyphs of being. In reply I bounced back a line my girlfriend had already sent me:

I sought refuge in a nightmare of meaninglessness.

To the side of the hall there was a dark corridor: I saw a woman walk in and vanish. As I followed her into the deepening black I heard music, weird and primordial, full of chanting and strange syncopations, like a rave in another solar system. I came to the entrance of a room that was pitch-dark. Stepping inside, I raised my hands before me and couldn't see them. An archaic terror came over me and I resisted the urge to get out. The music seemed to come from many sources. I moved carefully into the darkness, feeling my way. Something brushed against my hand. Now I understood: the music was not coming from speakers or instruments; it was being chanted, shrieked and groaned by a mass of people all around me in the inviolable dark. There must have been a dozen of them – a shifting *a cappella* biomass. A voice near my head hissed freakish incantations. A glimmer of light appeared from a source on the ceiling: I could discern shapes moving around me, mole-people with night-vision eyes. The glimmer went out: purest black.

Back in the main hall, the group who had walked backwards were now running the length of the floor, weaving deftly between the scattered visitors like antelopes on a Eurasian plain. I followed another corridor and entered a large room. A few dozen people lined the walls, watching each other across the floor. A smaller group frolicked around before turning their backs to the rest of us. In unison they began to chant in English:

'The objective of this piece is to become the object of a discussion!'

At first they whispered it, repeating it more loudly each time. The chant suggested that what I was seeing here was something like a *pure* conceptual art piece, self-reflexive to the point where the object vanished into its own discourse – or, less generously, up its own hole. I had long suspected that, since the turn towards conceptual art however many decades ago, *talking about* the artwork – conceptualising it – had become more important than the encounter with the work itself. When I looked at art in galleries and museums, the first thing I always did was read the accompanying text on the plaque beside it, and in many cases I was happy to leave it at that, the work itself adding nothing besides a sense of the disparity between what the text on the plaque told me I was supposed to think and feel, and what the artwork actually provoked me to think and feel, which was often nothing. Some of them were really quite stimulating, the texts, the concepts. Under the reign of conceptualism, it wasn't enough to produce art, you needed to be able to articulate precisely *why* you had done it, and this 'why', this articulation, *was* the art. Artists today were philosophers, academics, theorists in drag, auto-critics. At some point, the way we were going, art would merge into the everyday, an invisible conceptual film that would hang over reality to render it itself yet not quite – which, come to think of it, was sort of what Tino Sehgal's work was like. After the performers had recited the line for the fourth time, a voice from the crowd along the opposite wall called out:

'I love Marine Le Pen.'

There were scattered laughs, a ripple of unease. Some of the audience were black or Arab and all of us bore the sartorial markings of urban sophisticates – not part of a demographic who looked kindly on Le Pen. Looking around to see who had spoken, I was astonished (and yet, punch-drunk with derealisation, not really surprised) to discover it was an acquaintance of mine from Ireland named Declan – Art Deco, as he was widely known. He stood a head taller than everyone else, wire-thin with dark curly hair, wearing a red scarf.

A new chant began:

'There has been a comment!'

Then the performers discussed Declan's edgy intervention while he gazed on, poker-faced behind black-rimmed glasses.

I can't remember what was said because I was still trying to process the fact that Art Deco was here, now, at the same Paris art show as me. Was he part of the performance? Or was he just a spectator, throwing a curveball into proceedings by declaring his love for the Front National leader? Provocation was by no means uncharacteristic of Art Deco. I'd had no idea he was in Paris – but then, it had been a while since we'd been in touch. Before I'd ever met him, Art Deco had been a near-mythical figure in certain Dublin circles: performing with bands, involved in art projects and literary journals, generally considered an eccentric, enigmatic dude who might one day do something either great or catastrophic. He had studied at the National College of Art and Design but, although he was the most promising student in his year, dropped out on the eve of his final exams – four years of study down the drain. The legend grew that this dropping out was intended as Art Deco's first major artwork: a punkish meta-commentary on the careerist art establishment and the university system; perhaps a celebration of nihilism, a potlatch gesture of waste and extravagance.

After I'd got to know him a few years later, however, Art Deco told me it was all bullshit: the truth was he'd dropped out of NCAD in the pits of a shattering 'nervous crisis': extreme paranoia, panic attacks, suicidal delirium. He bitterly wished he *had* finished art college: that way his life might have turned out differently. He might have succeeded in 'professionalising his psychodemons', as he put it (he had a way of saying such things without sounding pretentious or self-aggrandising), rather than channelling them haphazardly through the vague collaborations and low-key projects that had punctuated his twenties. Art Deco and I had been in sporadic contact over the past five years: the last I'd heard, he'd moved to Berlin and was living in a huge residential block on the outskirts of the city, inhabited by artists, punks, anarchists, dropouts and refugees. He'd gone out there to write a novel, provisionally titled *The Lord of the Universe*, which I gathered was a frenziedly paranoiac, metaphysical enigma. Art Deco had sketched out the plot in an email: living alone in a bedsit on Kienitzer Straße, the young narrator smokes a great deal of weed and starts to believe that the graffiti on the streets and the U-Bahn tunnels contain coded messages meant for him and him alone. He is ultimately led to an abandoned fairground outside the city, where he confronts a 'messianic' hunchback (presumably the titular 'Lord', though only our narrator believes him to be special). The encounter triggers some sort of dire cosmic unravelling.

The chanters suddenly started yelping. Then they hopped and skipped out of the room, signalling a break in the performance. I approached Art Deco, gesturing till he saw me.

'Rob, what's the craic,' he said, his voice betraying zero surprise.

I was glad to see him: we weren't particularly close but we'd had some lively conversations at Dublin house parties and in London cafes. We chatted about the overlapping lives of our friends, then I asked him if he was part of the show. He shook his head.

'Just passing through. I'm still out in Berlin.'

I asked him how the novel was going.

'Grand. I get very involved in it, maybe too involved. Like, I'm writing about my life, which is fair enough. But then I start to suspect I'm also *living about my writing*. Do you know what I mean?'

'Kind of.'

'Like, I wander around Berlin looking at street art, putting myself in the head of a guy who's doing the very same thing – Bertolt Schultz is his name – except he sees hidden meaning everywhere. And then I realise it's *my* head I'm putting myself in. I'm Bertolt Schultz inside the book, imagining my life into being – this life out here. Without me, Bertolt Schultz wouldn't exist, but without him I'd exist differently – in other words, I wouldn't exist. When you walk around and imagine seeing meaning everywhere, it *generates* meaning. I write it down, but the more I think about it, Bertolt Schultz is the one writing me, on a Möbius strip.'

I was really losing him …

'Like that Spacemen 3 album', he continued, '*Taking Drugs to Make Music to Take Drugs To*. Anyway, that's why I had to come to this show. Twelve hours on the train from Berlin. I thought it would do me good to decompress in a space where everyone is pretending to be *themselves*. Usually they're pretending to be someone else, and that makes me nervous. I can already feel the benefit of coming here today. I'll walk out renewed. Do you have any ganj?'

I told him I hadn't really smoked in years – it made me paranoid.

'Fair enough, man. We're all hanging on by a thread.'

We swapped phone numbers and agreed to meet up before he left Paris. After we parted, I roamed the space for hours, discovering new rooms, returning to the main sites to find them transformed into fresh variations. The show was a continuous flux, so that you could never determine the final parameters of the artwork: it mutated even as you observed it. There were no texts to read, no plaques on the walls to fix Sehgal's evanescent human art: the work would leave no trace other than memories, emotions, words between friends, critical response. For someone like me, whose very career was an avoidance strategy of touching from afar, as safe and distant as a drone operator from his victims, Sehgal's art administered shocks of presence: face-to-face encounters stripped of the numb rituals of politesse, the opiate of functional chatter. I was, in fact, finding it seriously destabilising.

Periodically I would turn on my phone, fancying that my girlfriend's insistent, emoji-adorned PKD quotes were part of the game, a subliminal commentary hurled out to alter my perceptions and scramble reality.

> *Borne along by a current of abandon*
> *she dreamed of disembodied voices in the stellar dust*
> *her essence a symptom of some deeper cosmic pathology*
> *Through open wounds the cold drifted, a wind across*
> *the plane which reality had become*
> *And now it came to her, as if in a whisper …*
> *There could never be a test for what she was*
> *pregnant with.*

This last one, about a pregnancy, was not what I needed to see. Why had she sent that? It was one of those frazzled and defenceless days, the nervous system coiled against some imminent shock of revelation. In the main hall I sat against a pillar and rested. Outside the skylights, darkness had long since fallen. I scribbled notes around the fanciful idea that Tino Sehgal was a gnostic demiurge who had choreographed all of creation: his show was the universe, enacted by everyone I had ever met and everyone I hadn't, every generation who had tended the earth and all who ever would. The tower, I wrote, was everywhere. While I was bent over my notebook, a man in a beret broke from the shoal of backwards-walkers and approached. He hunkered down beside me and said:

'I like to burn books.'

I asked him if he'd repeat that, please.

'I like burning books.'

I laughed; he smiled.

'Are you a Nazi?' I said.

'Well, that's the question,' he replied.

He told a story: his parents had died and left him a house in the Brittany countryside, which was full of books. In the months following their death, he would drive out to the house at weekends and sort through the books, some of which were valuable as literature, whereas many others were trash – potboilers, romances and such. He would burn the worthless books in the fireplace. Before chucking a book into the blaze he would read a few lines or paragraphs, honouring an impulse to bear final witness to these stories: after all, someone had once laboured over them, even if it wasn't quite Proust or Balzac.

One Saturday afternoon, standing before the crackling fire, he randomly opened a book on a scene in which one man was viciously humiliating another, employing the vilest epithets. The victim of the humiliation was a

Jew. There followed a scene of appalling violence. He flicked through the book: it was foul with the rhetoric of anti-Semitism. What the hell was this book? And why had his parents owned it? The cover had been ripped off so he had no idea who its author was. He flipped to another page and found a passage from the Talmud, which seemed to him profound. He read it many times, memorising it. Then he flung the book into the fireplace, watching it curl and crumble in tongues of flame.

So what was the quote from the Talmud, I wanted to know.

He smiled. 'I've forgotten. It was something to do with the Word, and the true name of God. Perhaps I was meant to forget – the message so bright it erases itself, a blank space in the psyche that beheld it.'

He asked me what I reckoned: was he right to have burned the book?

I shrugged. Why not?

Then he suggested, citing some metaphysical school or other, that he, I, everyone who lived, had consented to all this in advance; that the soul, in some pre-terrestrial limbo, had viewed its coming adventure: every hurt and embarrassment, every idle afternoon and schoolyard humiliation, all the laughter and each instance of tenderness – the whole and specific human confusion. The soul had foreseen all this, in the knowledge that it would be forgotten upon arrival in our world. And the soul had said yes, let it happen, let it be, and so here we were, out of our depth in life. 'What do you think?' he said. 'Does that seem astonishing? Would you indeed have said yes to this life, knowing what you do?'

'I dunno,' I replied.

'This piece has now concluded,' he said coldly.

I left the Palais de Tokyo and cycled through the lit-up streets near the Champs-Élysées, heading vaguely in the direction of home. Above the boulevards hung the fattest moon I'd ever seen, a shining yellow disc like a Seroquel pill. Stopped at a red light, I read another message on my phone:

She passed imperceptibly from one scene, one age, one life to another. There was nobody who could shield her from malignancy – think back to the rapist

On Rue Washington, I locked my bike up and stepped inside a little Vietnamese restaurant with bright fluorescent lights. A plump middle-aged woman took my order. I ate a bowl of pho, the hot soup warming my insides as I read over my notes, jotting down reflections before they dissolved in the frazzled wiring of my mind. Like Art Deco writing his novel, I tried to imagine how I'd have experienced Sehgal's show if I were psychotically paranoid, beset by an ego that perceived connections everywhere, the symbols of an absolute conspiracy. How would it feel to drift in a space where the borders had broken down, a metaphysically altered limbo, if one were caught in the centrifugal pull of an ecstatic delirium? I sketched out a story in which I was trapped inside a story that took place within the Tino Sehgal show, right up to the scene where I saw myself enter a Vietnamese restaurant and begin writing in my black notebook, and for a shocking instant I had a sense of being authored, of perceiving the vision behind it all, he who guided my pen and wrote me into being at once – a vertigo of tunnelling fictions falling away to infinity.

I turned on my data again, like a smoker reaching for his pack. Art Deco had emailed to tell me I was going in his novel. What *is* progress? he asked. Progress is the absence of reason, he suggested. Progress is falling down a staircase in the dead of night. Progress is retribution, upheaval and murder. Did I want to come to a party in Bastille on Saturday? A message arrived from my girlfriend.

Get out of my skull

I strained to remember where this line appeared in *Flow My Tears*, but it didn't seem familiar. I sent a reply: *hmm?* and a puzzled-face emoji. Another message appeared.

Get. Out. Of. My. Skull

Some motion caused me to glance up. The Asian woman behind the counter was staring at me; her lips were moving as if she were silently talking to herself, or praying. My phone emitted a volley of pings.

Get out of my skull
Get the fuck out of my skull
… Robert
Get OUT of my skull

My eyes darted between the screen and the woman as messages flooded in – it was as if she were mouthing the words as I read them.

Get OUT OF MY SKULL
GET OUT OF MY SKULL
GET OUT OF MY SKULL GET OUT OF MY
SKULL GET OUT

Now the woman appeared to be weeping silently, tears glistening on her cheeks. I turned off my phone, put it in my pocket, and finished my noodle soup.

Some days ago I met with Niko, a writer from Georgia who lives in Berlin. He was here visiting his girlfriend. We had coffee in Belleville, then he brought me to a flat on Rue Clavel, where he gave me fistfuls of pills I'd never tried before: prescription stuff called tramadol and Lyrica. Also more Valium, in case I need it, which I do. He talked me through which combinations and dosages work best, and issued a vague warning about addiction.

Niko has lived in Berlin for twelve years. He was forced to leave Georgia by the conservative and religious forces he'd pissed off there. The drugs he's on – medication and recreation seem to blur – constitute a delicate balancing act. It was uncertain as to whether he'd be able to meet me at all – an unnameable fear often prevents him from leaving the house. He says he hates Paris anyway.

Niko and I talked about my friend Linda, whom he knows in Berlin. I can't recall whether I've told you about her. We met more than a decade ago, when I was twenty-three and she was thirty. We travelled together in South America for a while. A year later, I stayed with her in Friedrichshain, for a week of monumental unwisdom. I lost all sense of limits. On one of the last nights, at a club, I decided I would finally confront the tormenting problem of sexual jealousy – there and then, by asking Linda to fuck some other guy. This being the kind of logic that pertains when you've been hammering drugs and going without sleep for a week straight. She screwed a guy in the toilets while I sat out at the bar. It was early in the morning. The drugs were dragging on me and I started to doubt what we were doing. So I walked in on them – and that was everything blackened between us for a long time afterwards.

These days I trust Linda, which is to say I feel I can tell her anything. For instance, I can tell her that I look back on my youth as a campaign of revenge against women – a war of attrition with unforgivables committed on both sides. Nowadays an eerie calm prevails; a belated peace seems to have dawned. The result, I think, of pure exhaustion. I come to women these days as a friend, waving a little white flag. Perhaps there were easier ways to acquire this modicum of what, with a little stretch, might be called wisdom. But they weren't my ways.

And yet, I wonder how true all that is. The longer you and I stay in contact, I think the greater the likelihood that we'll somehow maim each other. Did you ever have that dream of no control, the one where you're not walking, you're being *walked, towards a precipice?*

Psychopomp

When Kelly came to Paris to work on her photo essay, she smuggled four tabs of acid past customs at Dublin airport, wrapped in a sliver of tinfoil hidden in her knickers between a sanitary towel and the press of her flesh. She didn't tell me she was doing it because she knew I'd be obligated to try and dissuade her, but she knew I'd want to take the acid with her too.

Despite several admissions to St Patrick's psychiatric hospital since her teens, Kelly enjoyed psychedelic drugs with a casualness and frequency that were foreign to me. It was she who had introduced me to the concept of microdosing. 'All the kids are doing it, daddyo,' she'd said, joshing me about the difference in our ages – though not, she insisted, in our levels of maturity. Microdosing, she had explained, meant taking a small amount of a psychedelic such as LSD on a daily basis, just enough that its effects would shimmer at the edges of your experience without overrunning it. Subtly under the influence, you could conduct yourself quite normally: for instance, while working part-time in a Nepalese restaurant in Temple Bar, as Kelly did;

or studying; or painting. Before I met her, Kelly had been microdosing for several months and had become a committed advocate of the practice, whose benefits included enhanced lateral thinking and being a bit high all the time.

'My tolerance is greater than other people's,' she had explained once at her flat in East Wall, 'so I can take more than what's usually considered normal for microdosing.'

'In which case,' I'd pointed out, 'you're not microdosing at all, you're macrodosing.'

At this she had smirked, put her black Russian beret on my head, and snapped a photograph of me reflected in her lipstick-smudged mirror.

Kelly's photo essay was to be based on André Breton's novelish memoir *Nadja*, in which the leader of the surrealists recounts his enchantment with a fragile, preternaturally sensitive young woman, against the backdrop of Paris's streets, cafes, squares and gardens. Of particular interest to Kelly was the mystical, even supernatural, undertone in Breton's reflections on chance and 'synchronicity' (Kelly, not Breton, used this word with its Jungian baggage). Breton had failed to recognise the true import of his encounter with Nadja, she believed, because he was blinkered by 'the atheist superstitions of the twentieth century'. She had bought a map of Paris on which she'd marked out all the sites mentioned in the book. I was happy to tag along: it was an excuse to get away from my desk, where for weeks I'd made zero progress with the memoirish novel I was supposedly writing about, as I'd told my agent over the phone in an extempore flourish, 'sex, death and clubbing in post-Bataclan Paris'.

The night Kelly arrived, we went to a party that my friends Ellie and Seb were throwing at their apartment in Belleville. Red wine was poured and cans of Leffe were handed out in abundance. After a couple of drinks, Kelly was feeling euphoric. 'We're in *Paris*!' she said, flopping down beside me on the blue couch where I was guzzling Leffe. A moment later we found ourselves talking to a woman named Charlotte who had arrived a few days earlier from the US. She was a novelist, palmist and perfume maker – 'though not necessarily in that or any other order' – and was writing a book that had something to do with perfume and astrophysics. Kelly asked Charlotte to read her palm. When Charlotte did so, she frowned, then looked up at Kelly and seemed to hesitate before speaking. Still holding Kelly's palm between her fingers, she said it was as if Kelly couldn't possibly exist: she had two life lines running from opposite ends of her palm, zigzagging in contrary directions. Charlotte had never seen such a pattern before: it suggested Kelly was some sort of 'quantum aberration'.

'I told you!' I cried.

'Hmm,' said Kelly.

We puzzled over this a while, then Charlotte told us how she'd been having lucid dreams for years, and had finally decided to study the phenomenon. I said

I envied her: for a long time I'd wanted to have lucid dreams and had read everything I could on the subject, but had managed only on one occasion to realise I was dreaming without the excitement of it waking me up.

'What did you do?' Charlotte asked.

'I flew around for a while.'

'Aha. That's the first thing most people do. The second is –'

'I tried to have sex with everybody. And that's when I woke up.'

'But did you really wake up?'

I made the thinking pose, like Rodin's sculpture.

'I dunno,' I said.

'Maybe this is the dream, and that was the true world,' said Charlotte.

'It seems unlikely,' I said.

'Maybe I dreamed you,' said Kelly. 'Have you ever seen *Lost Highway*?' She put on a spooky voice like the bald freak in the film. '*I'm in your house right now.*'

'Yeah, well, you're just a quantum aberration.'

Charlotte had recently decided to use her lucid dreams to have sex with children. Not, she insisted, because she was a paedophile, but because she wanted to do the most extreme thing she could think of, in the consequence-free realm of the dreamscape. It was all set up: six wide-eyed children were in a line before her, pliable and nude; she knew they would give her intense pleasure. Just as she was about to commit the transgression, however, it occurred to her that she could not be certain that such an act truly would carry no consequences. Somewhere in 'the multiverse', who could say that this act would not cause suffering? Who could say our dreams aren't realities elsewhere, and our travails here the dreams of others?

She gazed at Kelly and me in turn, sipping her wine.

We woke to a bright, cold October morning. We were mildly hungover, which according to Kelly was the optimum state in which to conduct this kind of city-roaming mission.

'It makes you sensitive,' she said. 'You're less rational, more intuitive.'

After a breakfast of bacon, blueberries and coffee, we rented bikes on the Vélib' system and set out along the Canal Saint-Martin. The city felt oddly deserted as we curved up the Boulevard Richard Lenoir where the canal dips underground, with only homeless people on the streets.

'All these refugees,' Kelly called from behind. 'Did you see that family by the bridge?'

The light turned green and we traversed the broad Avenue de la République. We had a lot of sites to get through. Kelly's plan was to limit her photo essay to exactly forty photographs – the same number as the 'plates' in Breton's book that illustrate the locations, people and artworks mentioned in his story. Kelly would photograph the sites as they stood nine decades after the book's publication, and substitute people she encountered in Paris for Breton's surrealist friends (she had taken a portrait shot of Charlotte the night before, and one of me just after I'd woken up, sitting red-eyed on the edge of the bed). I'd read *Nadja* a year or two earlier and recalled a vague, digressive, insubstantial book whose core story – that of the meeting between Breton and Nadja – is over as soon as it begins, with Nadja left languishing in a mental institution and Breton pompously philosophising about why he doesn't feel like visiting her. I'd been flicking through Kelly's copy since she arrived, interested not so much in rereading *Nadja* as in reading *Kelly*. Her slim, battered Penguin Classics edition was busy with underlinings and marginal notes, in red ink and delicate, precise handwriting.

Though Kelly had a lively interest in the early-twentieth-century avant-garde, I sensed that the thrust of her intended photo essay was essentially autobiographical – Kelly fathoming herself through the words of André Breton, who peered through the prism of Nadja, who gazed out at the reader from the kaleidoscope of her encroaching madness, and finally me in turn reading it all – her, Kelly, *Nadja*: a loop of gazes like a serpent swallowing its tail. Some of Kelly's marginal notes were enigmatic – 'he dies here'; 'Nietzsche's tears as he embraces the horse'; 'like Stalingrad!' – others prosaic. On page thirteen she had written the phrase 'abominable sentence!' next to the following:

> Such reflections lead me to the conclusion that criticism, abjuring, it is true, its dearest prerogatives but aiming, on the whole, at a goal less futile than the automatic adjustment of ideas, should confine itself to scholarly incursions upon the very realm supposedly barred to it, and which, separate from the work, is a realm where the author's personality, victimised by the petty events of daily life, expresses itself quite freely and often in so distinctive a manner.

What a mess! Perhaps such tormented syntax was a surrealist strategy to derail the reader, sabotaging reason and loosing the forces of the unconscious. Or perhaps Breton just didn't write very well. I'd tried to read the sentence several times but its meaning dissolved in the time it took to traverse the pile-up of qualifications and subordinate clauses from capital 'S' to full stop. You wandered into such a sentence and lost your way back out, mislaid the thread of return, like a madman running through catacombs. I'd wondered if it was a bad translation, only to discover that it was executed by none other than Richard Howard, the poet who had achieved such superb translations of E. M. Cioran.

We parked our bikes at the Place de la République and walked up the Boulevard de Bonne Nouvelle to the arch of the Porte Saint-Denis.

'Breton used to walk up and down here every day, past this arch,' said Kelly, framing a shot. 'He had a premonition that something of profound significance was going to happen here.'

'And did it?'

'He doesn't say. Perhaps it did and he never recognised it.'

A motorbike rider pulled a wheelie as he tore up the boulevard, prompting a trail of Parisians to shake their heads at his noisy display of vulgarity. I sat on a bench with *Nadja*. I opened the book at random and found the following underlined: 'Anyone who laughs at this last sentence is a pig.'

Kelly was on the bench beside me. I hadn't noticed her sit down.

'Extremely handsome, extremely useless,' she said.

'Thank you.'

'That's Breton's description of the Porte Saint-Denis.' She flicked to the relevant page and pointed to the underlined phrase.

'Oh.'

'Shall we take acid?' she said. 'You'll see a city you never knew existed.'

We did it on the terrace of a cafe, washed down with Picon Bière, then rode the Métro from République to Porte de Clignancourt, at the end of line 4. When we emerged from the station the Boulevard Périphérique loomed before us, streaking past on a concrete flyover like a great medieval wall.

'The edge of the city,' Kelly said.

Whereas the heart of Paris had seemed deserted, out here it was teeming: Africans and Arabs hawked their wares – runners, tracksuits, watches, jewellery, phone accessories – at tightly packed stalls that ran beneath the flyover and out towards the *banlieues*. We could have been at a bazaar in Algiers or Mogadishu. The strip of stalls led to the gateway of the Saint-Ouen flea market, our next destination.

We walked beneath the Périphérique flyover, in its long broad shadow.

'It's like crossing into a different country,' I said.

'All of Paris is like that,' said Kelly. 'Different psychic atmospheres that you can feel changing within the space of a few metres.'

She took my hand and we ducked into the flea market off the bustling street.

'This part is called the Marché Vernaison,' she said. 'With antiques and stuff.'

We roamed through narrow, quiet aisles, some of them covered, others open-air.

'No wonder the surrealists loved coming here,' said Kelly, gazing at the jumble of incongruous items – paintings, old newspapers, statues, knives, crystals, musical instruments, clocks. 'There are so many *things* in the world,' she noted, before drifting into a shop full of

Japanese fans, with the words *Objets Interdits* emblazoned across its front. I stepped through an adjacent doorway and found myself in a room full of gods: Vishnu, Shiva, Ganesh, Buddha, Ra, Osiris, Celtic spirals, totems and demons. I peered through a glass case at a statuette of Anubis, lord of the underworld, with his head of a dog and erect human body. I recalled that Anubis was the judge of souls, the weigher of hearts; an obscure disquiet passed through me, the echo of some childhood terror.

Standing alone in a corner of the shop, flanked by two glass cases of African deities, was a large, metal statue of the Buddha in a dark tinge of green.

'From seventeenth-century Laos,' said the grey-haired proprietor, emerging from behind a wooden desk.

The Buddha sat in the lotus posture, one hand palm-up on his lap in a gesture of exquisite grace and poise, the other resting on his calf. The figure emanated serenity. I peered at it, drawing its peacefulness into myself as my body tingled with the onset of the acid. I wanted to meditate again, give up my dissolute habits, ascend from the sewers of suffering to the clear skies of the Buddha mind. It really was an enchanting statue, a point of stillness in the surge of the world. For two thousand years Buddhist artists had striven to perfect this and a handful of other figures in their sculptures and paintings, seeing no need to innovate. Originality to them was the whim of chattering, immature cultures, destined to be washed away in the ebb and flow of aeons, while the Timeless alone remained, the –

'We'll be closing soon,' the owner said with a trace of apology. I had been gawking at the statue for an age. 'Perhaps you would like to buy something?'

'How much for the Buddha?'

'Two thousand seven hundred euros.' He rubbed his nose with the tip of a forefinger, where the frame of his spectacles rested. 'But I can do it for two thousand five hundred.'

I pretended to mull this over. Then I said, 'What did the Buddhist say to the hot-dog seller?'

I waited a couple of beats.

'Make me one with everything.'

He didn't even smile. By now, I should point out, the gods all around me were very much alive, humming with energy, grinning or frowning, playful or enigmatic. Some were livelier than others, which I put down to the relative skill levels of the nameless artists, those legions of craftsmen in the eras of anonymous creation that preceded the civilisation of the selfie. I asked the proprietor whether he minded me taking a photo of the Laotian Buddha – he didn't, so I did. As I left the shop of the gods, Anubis's head turned to follow me with its gaze from beyond the world.

Out in the aisle, Kelly was floating like a long, slender flower.

'Alright, mate,' she said.

'Anubis was staring me out of it,' I said. 'I felt he wasn't impressed with the state of my soul.'

'He's the god of embalming. A theosophist once told me I was an embalmer back in ancient Egypt. I met her in St Pat's. Do you believe in reincarnation?'

'I believe in everything.'

'Me too. But look.'

She nodded towards a man who sat in an open-fronted shop, surrounded by a chaos of old framed paintings.

'He looks like a genetic splicing of Roberto Bolaño and Jean-Paul Sartre,' she said.

It was true, he did! Kelly began giggling as the man glanced up and grinned. He beckoned us inside. A little dog with huge floppy ears and a lustrous coat of fur scrambled out of the shadows and leaped on to the vacated chair. Another man, unshaven in a creased check shirt that wasn't tucked in, appeared from a back room.

'Vous êtes touristes?' asked the first guy.

'Oui, plus ou moins,' I replied. 'Mais j'habite ici à Paris.'

'Et de quel pays venez-vous?'

'Irlande,' Kelly and I said together.

'Ah, l'Irlande. Alors, je parle français. Lui' – he pointed to the other man – 'il parle anglais. Et puis lui' – he pointed to the floppy-eared dog, who barked at his finger – 'il parle tibétain.'

And what was the name of this Tibetan-speaking dog, I enquired.

The men said together:

'Microsoft.'

With that, Kelly crumbled into the kind of psychotropic hilarity I knew could last long enough for the men's amusement to turn to offence. To distract them I tried to explain that Schopenhauer ('le grand philosophe,' I clarified unnecessarily) thought that the best gauge of originality was what one called one's dog. However, I confused the word for 'dog' with the word for 'cat' – or thought I did until I realised I'd actually used the word for 'cunt', which is perilously similar. I reckoned it best to mumble a farewell to Microsoft and his human companions, leading Kelly by the elbow and deeper into the market.

'That's the thing with psychedelics,' I said when we were in the clear. 'Everything becomes so implausible. Stuff happens that would never happen were you not on psychedelics, and so reality becomes doubly questionable. If you see what I mean.'

'I don't know that I do,' she said, wiping tears from her eyes.

Drawn by a sparkling window display, we stepped inside a white room full of crystal. The face of the young man in a black polo neck who welcomed us throbbed and pulsated – I couldn't look at it for longer than a glance. We were in a crystalline zoo: crystal birds frozen in the air; glinting crystal lizards; lions, serpents and fish whose crystal bodies were pools of void and light.

'Swarovski,' said Kelly.

'Huh?'

'Swarovski,' said the man with the melting face. 'All of this crystal is Swarovski. High quality.'

Kelly was bending over a statue of a bird in flight, shimmering with tints of colour.

'You can pick it up if you like,' said the seller.

She held it before her. 'It's so heavy.'

I drew my face in close, peering into the depths of its translucent body. Kelly's single eye watched me from the other side, calm and soft, her blue iris multiplied in the crystal's innumerable sides, fractal symbols from myth or religion.

'My mother always said if you surround yourself with beautiful things, your mind will become beautiful,' she said.

'But the world is so ugly now,' replied the crystal seller, who stood politely by while we peered through the bird.

'Yes, but does it have to make us ugly too?' said Kelly, gazing at me from crystal ponds.

'It is not yet knowable,' said the man. 'We may have it in us to resist.'

'Beauty will save the world,' said Kelly, and her million eyes blinked softly.

'We can defy. We can overcome. Or we can simply turn away,' he said.

'But where can we go?'

'To the stars, perhaps.'

The man laughed and it rang out in that white room for a long time, a laugh that engulfed all else, breaking free of the one who was laughing to ring on and on, delighted and predatory, tumbling into the universe.

We left the crystal menagerie and wandered among piles of decades-old newspapers and magazines, yellowing photographs of long-dead wives, husbands, lovers, families.

'There's the theory that all of time exists simultaneously,' said Kelly. 'There's no difference between the primordial past, and this moment with you and I walking here, and the deepest future, when humans are long gone. The passage of time is an illusion residing only in the mind. That's what the mystics say too, but only today have I ever understood it.'

'It might be the drugs,' I said.

Soon the market would be closing. The sellers were slowly packing their wares in boxes, counting bills, recording profits in little notebooks.

Suddenly we were out of the labyrinth of aisles and in a large room so incongruous it might have been disturbing were it not so marvellously tacky and lurid. We had seemingly been teleported out of Paris and straight to Mexico (the most surreal country on earth, according to Breton), into a gaudy cantina whose every surface was cluttered with knick-knacks: fairy lights; bunting; religious baubles and icons; beer advertisements that flashed like Tokyo hoardings. On a low wooden stage a grizzled Latino with a toothpick protruding from his mouth played a synthesiser over a tinny beat. Perched high on a stool at his side, a pot-bellied man in a sombrero gestured flamboyantly, while singing a gushing love song to the scattered customers who sat over glasses of beer or pastis and plates of food.

'When did we come in here?' I said. 'I don't seem to remember stepping through the door.'

'Well, we must have done,' Kelly reasoned, 'because we are definitely in here as opposed to out there.'

At a long table in the centre of the room we sat down on red plastic chairs. A man with sallow skin shuffled over to present us with menus. The song fizzled out and the singer waved us a drunken greeting. He turned to his keyboardist and made a fisting gesture, said something about 'esta mujer!' and started cackling. The duo embarked on an even more melodramatic song as we ordered Picon Bière.

'The great thing about Picon Bière is that it has beer in it and liquor too,' I said. 'Not just beer, and not just liquor either. Picon Bière.'

Kelly gazed about in wonderment as the drinks arrived.

'This … can't be real,' she said quietly. The shadow of some suspicion darkened her face. It lasted an instant and then her expression became neutral again.

Looking back, it was then that I should have recognised I was out of my depth, that we urgently needed to wind this down, get clear of that place, turn the trip around. We did none of these things: I just said, 'It's not real. It's not even surreal. It's simply unreal. In fact, we're in an unreality TV show. Congratulations, honey.'

'*Stop*,' she hissed.

'It's like *Celebrity Big Brother*, but with no celebrities, no house, nothing.'

Her hands covered her face. The Mexican wailed lyrics about the endlessness of love, the ardour of his heart, the misery of his nights without his betrothed.

As the song climaxed, Kelly lowered her hands and rested them on the table.

'Okay now,' she said. 'It's okay now.'

'Will we have another?'

'Yes.'

When we got back home she seemed herself again, jocular and affectionate. We were tired, overstimulated from the day, the acid wearing off but still lapping over us in gentle washes.

Down in the street a group of friends laughed and shouted, heading out for the night. Then it was quiet. I poured two glasses of gin and splashed in some flat tonic water.

Kelly said, 'Let's not sleep at all, then take the rest of the acid at dawn. There's only a few places left we need to go. We mustn't stop till I take the last photo. Then I'll understand what it's all been for.'

We undressed each other slowly, kneeling in the lamplight and the green glow of the *HOTEL* sign on the rooftop opposite my window, whose first two letters were bust and unlit. I kissed her mouth and my skin tingled. She lowered her hand and pressed two fingers against herself, then held them up to examine. Her period had started.

As we coiled across the bed we left dabs of blood on the white sheets, lurid and pretty in the lysergic afterglow, like animals bleeding in the snow.

'There's so much of it,' Kelly said as we lay there afterwards, finding our breath. 'It can't all have come from me.'

I laughed. 'Then who?'

'It's like we've been murdered,' she said.

'Maybe we were. In the multiverse, by paedophile children.'

I must have blanked out because now it was dawn, murky light inching under the blinds. I felt for Kelly's shape in the bed beside me but she was not there. I looked up: she was sitting at the desk, writing in her black notebook.

'What are you writing?' I said quietly.

She snapped the notebook shut, turned to me, her face strange and feral. 'Automatic writing,' she said.

She glided over to the bed, lay across my chest. I stroked her back, her neck. With her fingertip she traced spirals on my chest, which was smeared with gore like warpaint. 'I'm not awake and I'm not asleep,' she said. 'Let's go out now.'

It was foolish to take the acid but we took it anyway. I poured drinks, more gin than tonic. We drank by the window, looking over the courtyard and the fallen leaves. My hands were shaking. 'Je t'aime,' I said. 'Oh, oui je t'aime.'

I topped up my glass with gin and turned on the little radio I'd bought at a one-euro shop. A voice said in English: *God may have forgiven you, but I have not.* There was a din of shrieks and hisses, some hellish avant-garde broadcast.

'Turn it off,' Kelly said.

We cycled towards Bastille, past the boarded-up skeleton of the Bataclan. The city was domed under a bleak sky as we reached the point where the canal flows into the impassive Seine. We clinked the bikes into automatic locks by the river, traversed the Île de la Cité on foot, and found our way to the Place Maubert. There was supposed to be a plinth bearing the statue of some historical figure. But there was no plinth, only a dismal city square, some pigeons bickering by a drain.

'Breton said this place filled him with unbearable dread,' said Kelly, raising her camera.

I knew where Breton was coming from: everything filled me with unbearable dread that morning. Life's surface was fraying, peeling off to reveal a prospect of nightmares. I needed to drink.

We sat on the terrace of a cafe that was sleepily opening up, and again ordered Picon Bière. A motorbike farted past, on to the Boulevard Saint-Germain. Some men gruffly heaved crates off a truck down a side street. On the table next to ours, someone had scratched the words *NO ONE HERE GETS OUT ALIVE*. I hurriedly covered it with a red napkin so Kelly wouldn't see. I drained my beer. As I signalled through the window for another round, Kelly began speaking about an article she'd read. Physicists were claiming that the universe may be a simulation. An unseen mega-intelligence, or our posthuman descendants in the depths of the future, had initiated the code that emanates all that seems to be in our hallucinated universe. What were their motives, I wondered. Kelly didn't know – entertainment, or sheer evil.

'But it doesn't matter,' she said, sounding far away. 'The world is ending now, whether it's real or not. It's all coming asunder. Don't you feel it? Look there.'

She pointed at a window in the second floor of the old building across the street. 'It's dark now, but soon it will be red.'

I watched the window, drunk. In no more than a minute the light in the room came on, illuminating the curtains in a reddish glow. I felt nauseous; I walked into the cafe and downstairs to the toilets, where I dry-retched over the bowl. I pulled down my jeans and shat freely, hot and liquid. I put my forehead on the sink and rested there. It was cool on my skin. I closed my eyes and saw fractal shards, silent gods, a bloodied eye, fires at the edge of a city, snakes giving birth to humans, funeral pyres by a filthy river, Anubis silhouetted on a hill.

When I came back out, Kelly was weeping. Feebly I put my hand to her shoulder but she shrugged it away.

'It's all wrong,' she groaned, shaking her head. 'It's all wrong.'

I stood there, tired and indifferent. A tramp shambled past. I sat down and gulped my beer.

'This was a terrible idea,' I said. 'Let's go home. We can knock ourselves out with your pills, and hopefully when we wake up things will seem right again.'

'There's one more place we have to go,' she said.

I left too much money for the beer and we walked wearily past Notre-Dame, over the bridge to the island in the river. We stepped through the narrow alley that led from the Pont Neuf into the secluded square of the Place Dauphine – the loneliest place in all of Paris, it seems to me now. The wide square was lined on two sides with restaurants and cafes, but there was no one, not a single person to be seen. Drops of cold rain wet our faces; a wind blew through the alleys, past the chairs and tables on deserted terraces. It was as if the world had fallen to plague, a planet drifting through space like the *Mary Celeste*. The Palais de Justice loomed at the far end of the square: it appeared to me as the temple where hearts are weighed as souls cross into the underworld. Its bleak facade sent a wave of fear through me, like a prisoner being dragged to the site of his final agony.

'They burned them here,' Kelly whispered.

I did not ask.

'Imagine the screams. Imagine the pain. Oh God.' She dug her fingers into my arm, so hard that I gasped.

'They're burning her,' she said. 'She's burning. She's screaming. She's signalling out through the flames.'

She was babbling now and I thought she would faint or have a seizure. I led her to a bench in the middle of the square. The rain was falling heavier. Kelly was sobbing, dejected. I was numb to the cold; shivers of euphoria coursed through my misery. Dark clouds raced across the sky, far too quickly in all directions. Some windows in the Palais de Justice began to blink on, one by one, a dim red glow like the building was on fire. I could hear chanting, as if from an immense crowd. I drew Kelly into me, tried to comfort her.

'Is it true?' she murmured. 'Did they die? Where is she now? Oh God. Do we get out?' She moaned and I squeezed her hard, as if crushing our ribcages together, fusing us.

'Please, Kelly,' I said.

'Oh God,' she whimpered. 'Oh God.'

I could feel her tears soaking through my jumper. She rocked softly, trembling. I flickered in and out of consciousness. Voices gabbled as shadows swarmed the sky. I don't know how long we were there. Gradually her trembling stopped. She was heavy and still in my arms. In the distance, beyond the Palais de Justice, thunder boomed. Rain pelted the cobblestones across the deserted square, as the doorway to the Palais slowly opened and the shadow of a lone figure emerged.

———

Sunday was the warmest day this year. All of Paris was out on the streets and in the parks, drinking on the terraces. Students played football in the courtyard. A Brazilian religious group sang songs and danced in the building across the street with the doors and windows open. I set out and walked for hours: down to the Seine and past Notre-Dame, through the teeming Marais, along the Canal Saint-Martin, into Bastille and the eleventh arrondissement, up the sloping streets of Ménilmontant and Belleville. I arrived finally in the Parc des Buttes-Chaumont, where I watched the sun sink from the hillside. It was one of those simple days when you delight in being alive, the warmth of the air, the colours and sounds of the city, free of anxiety and gloom.

The book is turning out differently than I anticipated. I've changed as I've written it – the process of writing it has changed me. I no longer believe what I used to believe when I started it, nor disbelieve what I didn't use to believe. I've told you, haven't I, that my intention from the outset was to write a book that, through whichever blend of memory, dream, learning and invention, was a celebration of elsewhere, of life played out anywhere except the place you happen to be from, which is the only kind of life I've ever really imagined. But it's also an account of the changes that have occurred, are occurring, and will occur – the timelines are tangled, as if time is folding in on itself – between the moment I first set pen to paper and the moment I type the final full stop, when everything will become possible again. I've held nothing back, but there is much that it's still impossible to write about, that it will take ten years to see clearly. That, I think, will be the why *that sees me through the* how, *whatever the* how *looks like (at the moment, it looks quite good).*

I know all this means that an ending is approaching, which means that you're soon to disappear from my life, and I from yours. Then we can get back to the lifelong, meticulous work of disappearing from our own lives. And now all that's needed is a final chapter.

Threshold

For years DMT – the most mysterious thing in the universe – was conspicuous in my life by its absence. Then, suddenly, it was everywhere.

I had first heard about DMT while drinking yagé in Peru and Colombia, and reading everything I could about the psychedelic plant brew. I learned that the psychoactive component in ayahuasca is DMT (N,N-dimethyltryptamine), a molecule produced naturally by the human brain. Smoked or injected in its pure form, DMT differs from ayahuasca in that it is extremely quick to take effect, short-lasting, and intensely powerful. Whereas an ayahuasca trip lasts for six or seven hours, with DMT it is all condensed into about ten minutes. After I left South America, my fascination with plant psychedelics gradually subsided under the myriad distractions and projects of life. I maintained a vague hope of smoking DMT but did not actively seek it out. In part, this was due to an apprehension that the reports I had read of DMT experiences instilled in me. Smokers of DMT, including the drug's great fanatic Terence McKenna, reported bewildering hurtles through 'hyperspace' – being blasted right out of a familiar reality (to the accompaniment of a tremendously loud tearing noise) into realms that are unimaginably bizarre, and populated by non-human entities with baffling intentions.

After leaving South America, I lived in London for a few years. There I attended the first UK screening of Gaspar Noé's film *Enter the Void*. It was on a Wednesday night at the Rio, a one-screen theatre in Dalston. I went with my friend Zoé, who was in London developing a play. Gaspar Noé was present at the screening – an intense, bald, walrus-moustached man. Before the film, he flitted between rows of seats as the mostly young audience nudged each other and nodded towards him. I had high expectations: from what I'd heard, *Enter the Void* contained so many elements that mirrored my own fixations – Tokyo, drugs, expatriate slackers, underworld sleaze, techno, mysticism, sexual obsession – it may as well have been written with me in mind.

The red curtains parted and the film began. In the electrifying opening-credits sequence, words forty feet tall in lurid neon colours flash past at incomprehensible speed, as an industrial-ambient soundtrack ignites into the brutal breakdown of LFO's 'Freak'. Pummelling and brash, the sequence makes clear that this will be no casual experience – this is cinema as ceremony, ordeal, total immersion.

Now we see the world through someone's eyes. More exactly, we see a grungy apartment, cluttered with drug paraphernalia, movie posters, psychedelic trinkets and a copy of *The Tibetan Book of the Dead*. From the blinking point of view of what we now realise is a young American man – his barely awake thoughts are mumbled in voiceover – we step out on to the balcony. Below us is the Tokyo night: rooftops, flashing signs, a warren of streets and alleys promising limitless sin and danger. A gorgeous young woman joins us on the balcony, wearing only her underwear. 'Oscar …' she says sleepily. It's the young guy's sister, glowing with a forbidden sexuality. An aeroplane appears on the horizon and trails across the night sky. We point towards it. 'Imagine being up there, like, looking down on all the lights and stuff. All the people would be like tiny insects.'

'I wouldn't want to be up there,' says the girl sullenly, turning to us, lurid in the city's reflection.

'Why not?'

'I'd be afraid of falling … into the void.'

The sister leaves for her night's work – she is a stripper in a club called Sex-Money-Power – and it is at this point that the DMT appears.

Back in his squalid flat, Oscar lights up a vaporiser pipe. He draws deeply on the fumes as the pipe's contents smoulder in an orange glow. This drug tastes like shit, he thinks. As it takes effect he lies back and gazes at the ceiling. A heaving vortex opens up above him – a breathing, pulsating mass of tendrils, plumes and weird snaking shapes. He draws again on the pipe, then once more. For the next seven or eight minutes, in one of the more original uses of CGI in mainstream-ish cinema, we drift out through the elaborate, eerie psychedelia of Oscar's DMT trip. It's an audacious piece of film-making – minutes tick by and what we are seeing adds nothing to the story, gives no insight into character or motivation, only visual entrancement and hallucinatory splendour for their own sake. Ambient noise and the gibbering, staccato DMT voices all garble together, carried on a plaintive synth wave. In its bold psychedelic grandeur, this remarkable scene, like all of *Enter the Void*, is Noé's bid to emulate his highest cinematic ideal, Kubrick's *2001: A Space Odyssey*.

After the screening, Noé spoke about the technical challenges the film had presented and what he had been trying to achieve.

When the discussion was opened up to the audience, Zoé raised her hand. A microphone was passed along the aisle, to facilitate the exchange I would later mythologise as 'Zoé versus Noé'.

'Did you smoke DMT when you were making the film?'

Noé nodded. 'Yes. Several times. I took ayahuasca too. Maybe I didn't take enough – I never had the out-of-body experience that people talk about, where you leave it behind absolutely and this world vanishes. I wanted to, but it didn't happen.'

'What was it like, the DMT?' she asked.

Noé drew his fingers along his moustache, like a bald Nietzsche. 'It is very strange, very intense,' he said.

'There are weird realities, other entities. Some people even feel like their minds are being raped.'

A global cult has grown up around DMT. The drug's appearance in *Enter the Void* is among the first signs of its acknowledgement by the broader culture. In the decades since its discovery by Western science, startling claims have been made about DMT's effects and implications – claims that, to anyone who has never tried it, must necessarily seem preposterous. The loquacious and impassioned spokesperson for psychedelics, Terence McKenna, questioned why the religions hadn't put DMT forward as their 'central exhibit for the presence of the other in the human world'. To him, the shocking nature of the DMT trip was an instant paradigm-shatterer: 'The entire construct of Western reason disappears into that dimension like hurling an ice cube into a blast furnace,' he insisted. Whenever he smoked DMT, McKenna would find himself transported to a dimension more real than reality and inhabited by 'self-transforming machine elves' who were '*frantic* to communicate with human beings *for some reason*'. After first encountering the drug as a young art historian and anthropologist, his path in life was set: 'We should stop fucking around and go off and grapple with the DMT mystery,' he told a friend. A DMT trip, he maintained, is the most dramatic experience one can go through 'this side of the yawning grave'.

As a consequence of drug laws created in response to anxieties around psychedelics in the 1960s, very little research has been done into DMT's potential psychiatric applications, let alone its significance in terms of understanding consciousness and the nature of reality. One exception is the unique research carried out by Rick Strassman, a medical doctor and professor of psychiatry at the University of New Mexico. Over five years in the 1990s, after a torturous struggle to obtain funding and permission, Strassman studied the effects of DMT on dozens of volunteers. In the wake of his investigations, documented in his book *DMT: The Spirit Molecule*, an unnerved Strassman admitted that DMT may possess properties as seemingly far-fetched as those ascribed to it by McKenna. The volunteers' testimonies forced him to consider the possibility that the dimensions accessible via DMT are 'freestanding' spiritual realms, rather than mere hallucinations. As Strassman counsels: 'There is intense friction between what we know intellectually, or even intuitively, and what we experience with the aid of DMT.'

While not as well known as its tryptamine cousin LSD, DMT is in many ways the apex of psychedelic drugs ('There is something peerless about the spirit molecule,' insists Strassman). The term 'psychedelic', which means 'mind-manifesting', was coined by Humphry Osmond in a letter to Aldous Huxley, whose book *The Doors of Perception* endorsed mescaline and other drugs for their mystical, aesthetic and spiritual benefits (though not for everyone: Huxley insisted that they should only be available to a cultured elite). The psychedelics are divided into two groups: phenethylamines, which include mescaline and MDMA (a mildly psychedelic stimulant), and tryptamines such as DMT, LSD and psilocybin. Psilocin, which is produced when magic mushrooms are ingested, differs from the DMT molecule by only a single oxygen atom.

The first psychedelic found to be endogenous to the human body (produced in the brain and spinal column), DMT is pretty much everywhere else in nature too: in most mammals and many plants, for instance. It was first successfully synthesised in the West in the 1930s by a Canadian chemist named Richard Manske, but he did not become aware of its psychoactive properties. That discovery would occur in the 1950s, when a Hungarian chemist, Stephen Szára, grew intrigued by ongoing research into the psychiatric implications of psychedelics. Living behind the Iron Curtain in Budapest, and thus unable to obtain the LSD being disseminated by the Swiss pharmaceuticals company Sandoz Laboratories, Szára synthesised DMT in his lab and administered an effective dosage to himself. All this happened in good time for DMT to join the array of drugs that young people would embrace as part of the countercultural upheaval of the sixties. It remained curiously underground, however, as if too weird and disturbing even for the open-minded hippy generation to feel comfortable with.

As Szára realised, DMT must either be smoked or injected in order to have any effect. When it is ingested, the human gut produces the enzyme monoamine oxidase (MAO), which immediately breaks it down, foreclosing its psychoactive effects. The *ayahuasceros* of South America, who have used DMT in a shamanic context for thousands of years, found an ingenious way around this: by adding a DMT-containing bark to the vine *Banisteriopsis caapi* (the 'vine of the dead') and drinking the foul-tasting brew, the inhibiting stomach enzyme is neutralised, enabling longer, less overwhelming visionary trips. Ayahuasca is thus a kind of folk technology that renders more coherent, manageable and spiritually beneficial the DMT experience, which, in its pure form, has been described by one writer, Daniel Pinchbeck, as 'the psychedelic equivalent of bungee jumping'.

The day before my friend Matt arrived on the train from Dublin with his newly bought vaporiser pipe, DIGI scales and a gram of DMT, he sent me a text:

I had a dream last night in which I encountered a 'stealer of worlds'. He said, 'Soon.'

Matt was coming to stay with me in Rosslare Harbour, where I was living again. He was among my oldest friends and one aspect of our friendship was a shared enthusiasm for drugs, although this had been on the wane in recent years. Matt's life was a perpetual low-level crisis of a sort that, by virtue of its longevity, was indistinguishable from stability. Recently he had started seeing a psychoanalyst. During his latest session, Matt had talked about his interest in DMT, how he had long wanted to try it and now the possibility of doing so had arisen. He suggested that psychedelic drugs might have therapeutic properties not to be found in mainstream psychiatry. The analyst listened for a while and then shut him down: he insisted that DMT was 'just a drug' and therefore of no relevance to Matt's analysis. When Matt pressed him, the analyst admitted he hadn't heard of DMT or ayahuasca. To Matt this smacked of intellectual parochialism and a crashing incuriosity, traits not conducive to the respect required for the analytic relationship, with its delicate interplay of transference and projection, to work. He soon decided to terminate the analysis.

On the first night, Matt and I set up on the kitchen table. He laid out the black battery-operated scales and the glass pipe.

'I wish we had some Buddhas or something,' I said. 'As talismans.'

Matt nodded. He too felt a foreboding about the drug.

To begin with, we measured out 20 mg hits, a moderate dosage. We took it in turns, one of us waiting quietly as the other took a hit then sat back and closed his eyes as the DMT came on. When I smoked it, the effects were immediate and vivid, but manageable, although I did experience an intense inner vibration that alarmed me. Matt was reassured by his experience on a moderate dose – nothing terrifying had happened, only a familiar, delightful psychedelia: brilliant, swirling, kaleidoscopic patterns; a sense of numinosity and wonder; bursts of colour and rapidly shifting landscapes.

The online database we had consulted designated a strong dose as between 40 and 60 mg. For his second hit Matt upped the dose to 50 mg. Sitting across the table as he vaped the powder, I made sure not to stare at him while he was under the effects of the drug. When I did glance at him, it was obvious he had gone deep. His eyes were closed and he was utterly still, as if he were in a state of meditation. Minutes later, as it wore off and he gradually returned to his senses, the first thing he said was, 'I recommend taking less than fifty milligrams.'

He had believed he had died. Information, noise and imagery had come hurtling at him with bewildering speed and density as he was propelled through a 'wormhole', accompanied by an extremely loud vibration. Then his consciousness had become completely separated from his body; he had found himself in an utterly alien realm, full of what appeared to be intricately patterned machinery. Moreover, it was inhabited: he had been met by an array of strange, insectile beings, some of whom had prodded him with friendly curiosity.

'One of them … probed me,' he said, visibly nonplussed at what he was saying. 'It came towards me and sort of … inserted something into me. I was scared but they sort of put me at my ease.'

We brought the pipe, scales and mound of DMT into the sitting room, with its lamps and candleholders. In that more amenable space we smoked late into the night, taking time between each hit to compare our experiences. Each time he smoked a high dose, Matt was consistently transported to the same machine-like realm where he encountered what he described variously as 'jesters', 'workers', and 'data-things'. They spoke in a rapid and incomprehensible language, also emitting 'code' and 'language' directly from their bodies. Meanwhile they were restlessly at work, constantly flitting about. Growing more at ease in this realm, Matt attempted to communicate with the entities; he realised that this could be done telepathically. They did not frighten him, and some of them were gentle, reassuring, even loving. Were they good? he asked them. No, they said. Then were they bad? No, they were not that either.

My own trips revealed a hurtling, shifting psychedelia that was marked by speed and a sense of urgency. That first night, I could not overcome my fear sufficiently to take what the online forums called a 'breakthrough' dose: enough for familiar reality to be replaced by an entirely different world. Every time I smoked enough DMT to get right to what felt like the threshold, I had the distinct sense that another consciousness was present. This shapeshifting being guided the experience, creating elaborate and startling geometric effects, leading me through swirling, mandala-like corridors, generating layers of beauty and artifice. The strong impression was that the presence was utilising the brief window of the DMT flash to urgently signal its existence to me, vying to impress like a peacock flaunting its feathers, beckoning me to travel further. It was only the following evening, after meditating and taking a walk on the beach, that I would finally screw up my courage to go over the edge.

Matt was more cavalier. Around 3 a.m. on the first night, he hit a 60 mg dose. By now we were both smoking while in the cross-legged half-lotus posture, which seemed to instil confidence. He held the lighter above the glass pipe till all the powder vaporised, drawing it into his lungs. I waited in silence, focused on my breathing. About ten minutes later, Matt began to shift. I looked up. His eyes were open and wet with tears.

'That was it,' he said. 'They showed me everything.'

In 1938, the Swiss chemist Albert Hoffman synthesised LSD-25 – lysergic acid diethylamide – under the aegis of his employer, Sandoz Laboratories. Thus was instigated an era of vigorous research into psychedelic drugs, which were studied for their applications in the treatment and understanding of mental illness, and for what they revealed about the nature of consciousness. As Rick Strassman writes, 'Psychedelics were *the* growth area in psychiatry for over twenty years.' Then it all started to go wrong.

In the 1960s, Timothy Leary and colleagues of his at Harvard University conducted studies into the effects of psilocybin and LSD that quickly gained notoriety, and were soon feared to be getting out of control. Leary went rogue: shunning Aldous Huxley's preference for a trickle-down, elitist approach to psychedelics, he became a vocal advocate for LSD's widespread usage as a consciousness expander: acid would lead the human race to a higher plane of being, freed from the greed, neurosis and narrow-minded aggression of the past. The authorities shut him down. Leary was jailed for cannabis possession, and soon legislation was put in place banning all psychedelic drugs, despite the protests of many in the psychiatric community. The nascent project was stalled.

The Controlled Substances Act passed by the US government in 1970 marked the beginning of the 'war on drugs' that rages still. Visionary plants that have been revered in tribal cultures for thousands of years – and other substances, both natural and synthetic – have been demonised, their users criminalised. Terence McKenna, who remarked that 'the notion of illegal plants and animals is obnoxious and ridiculous', insisted that government bans on psychedelics are motivated not by concern that citizens may harm themselves while under the influence, but by the realisation that 'there is something about them that casts doubt on the validity of reality'. Drugs like DMT and psilocybin are disturbing to the powers that be because of their gnostic quality, the mainline access they afford to experiences that threaten established paradigms. In short, 'they open you up to the possibility that everything you know is wrong'.

Years before Matt visited me in Rosslare, I had settled for a time in Bogotá, following a period spent wandering in South America. I taught English in the city and lived in a series of apartments around La Candelaria, the cobblestoned heart of the old town, where students hung out in cheap bars and played music on the plaza. While living there I befriended a middle-aged woman named Consuelo. Erudite and impressive, Consuelo was deeply involved in the experiential and philosophical study of yagé. After I had undergone several *pintas* – ayahuasca ceremonies – at the house of her artist friend Daniel in the hills outside of town, she invited me to spend a few days drinking yagé at her remote farmhouse in the countryside.

Consuelo had studied philosophy at the Sorbonne in Paris under people whose books I had read. Afterwards, she returned to Colombia to teach aesthetics at the Universidad Nacional, until she retired out of disillusionment with the 'supermarket' mentality of contemporary higher education in the country. On the long bus journey out of Bogotá to the farmhouse, she spoke about Nietzsche, Bataille and Blanchot, relating them to the immanent philosophy of yagé and Amazonian shamanism. She told me about the doctoral thesis she had written on 'the aesthetics of cruelty'. The type of cruelty that interested her was not the sadistic bloodlust of the Romans but that which Nietzsche advocated: the cruelty that stimulates life, growth and strength by sacrificing comfort and happiness – a cruelty often directed towards oneself. Antonin Artaud had found this kind of noble cruelty in Mexican peyote rituals; drawing on her own experience, Consuelo discerned it in the yagé-imbibing ceremonies of South America.

During the drive, she recounted various stories of yagé's Nietzschean cruelty. Though she had undergone harrowing ordeals, Consuelo continued to drink yagé with confidence, trusting in the harsh wisdom offered by what she called the 'teacher plant'. She tended to speak about yagé in personal terms, as a conscious and intelligent entity. For instance, she told me that although she had a great admiration for the Marquis de Sade, she rarely read him any more because 'the yagé doesn't like Sade'. This was due to Sade's excessive rationalism rather than the extreme violence of his writings, she said.

It was after midnight when we reached the farmhouse. The following morning we enjoyed a breakfast of cheese arepas, scrambled eggs, coffee and papaya out on the long veranda. Consuelo had grown up on this land. Both she and her daughter Maya had learned to swim in the lagoon where we would bathe during our stay. Consuelo came out here to think, write and pore over philosophy books as chickens clucked and iguanas lurked about her. The ninety acres constituted Consuelo's private ecological project. She cultivated nothing on it, so that the diverse flora and fauna of the region could thrive. Neither had she installed electricity on the farm. There were only candles and the sun and moon for light. No television, radio or internet marred the peacefulness, as the brook gurgled and the surrounding jungle teemed with noises. Consuelo hoped the farmland would instil a forgotten respect for darkness and anticipate a time when it could no longer be dispelled with the flick of a switch.

That evening we greeted the young shaman (or *taita*) Crispin, the artist Daniel, and the half-dozen friends who arrived with them. The group got busy preparing the site for the ceremony. Crispin constructed an altar beside the bonfire we had erected earlier. Candles were placed along the veranda and under trees. In time, we all sat down by the bonfire on mats or plastic chairs.

Now that we were settled, Crispin began. He thanked Consuelo for her hospitality in his usual polite way, and then spoke for a while about yagé, as he always did before a *pinta*. He said that what we were doing was building 'the great church of yagé'. *Yagécito*, he called the brew, as if he were talking about a lover or a child.

'Salud con todos,' I said when it was my turn to drink, as was the custom. 'Salud, y buena pinta,' replied the others in chorus. The taste of yagé is unbelievably foul – I struggled not to retch after gulping down the bitter orange gunk. Afterwards I lay on my back to gaze at the stars. Crispin, dressed in his ceremonial get-up, appeared to doze in his chair, exhausted by the day's travelling. A middle-aged man walked off a few yards to throw up. Far on the horizon, a lightning storm began. Daniel walked serenely among the trees, the white robes he had donned for the ritual draped over his pudgy belly. I watched it all in the silent illumination of distant lightning.

When the rain started to fall, everyone gathered under the shelter of the veranda. The stars had fled and now the lightning was close, the thunder rumbling louder. In the flickering glow of candles, as the rain rattled above our heads, the sense of a gathering concentration of energy was tremendous. Music filled the air: a woman's voice singing sweetly; notes from a flute; a strummed guitar; drums and a charango. A shy man I had briefly spoken to earlier began to dance. A woman shook a maraca of sea shells and joined in with Crispin's yagé chant.

The *pinta* was gaining force in symbiosis with the storm. I closed my eyes and visions rained down on me – a cascade of complex, beautiful, alien forms; figures reaching from afar with enigmatic smiles and long, spectral fingers; glimpses of unearthly landscapes. Language grew out of itself, bent and warped in rapid mutations, like passages from *Finnegans Wake* assuming synaesthesic presence. The storm raged now and it was clear to everyone that we were witnessing something majestic, abysmal. It felt as if we had summoned the storm, our frenzy dancing with its own. A boom of thunder exploded right above our heads. The music and dancing peaked, more ecstatic yet somehow solemn, sacrificial. Everything was shaking now, as if the house might be uprooted and hurled into the violence. Overwhelmed, I rushed into the bathroom to throw up. Afterwards I crouched over the bowl, stilled by the humming aliveness all around me, the bliss that follows the purge.

I went back outside. In the storm's fury it felt as if our survival depended on the continuation of our ecstasy, on not giving in to terror. The *taita* played a cheerful melody on his harmonica, the music rising and falling from the roar of the wind and the crash of thunder. I wondered at what I was seeing, these unassuming people from the cities and islands coming here to connect with something grand and ancient within themselves, communing with an alien superconsciousness that dwelled inside a jungle plant. There was all of Colombia here: the blood of Spain, Africa, the Caribbean and the tribal Amazon; *negro* and *blanco* and *moreno* and *mestizo*.

Then I looked at Consuelo and became afraid. She was sitting in her chair on the veranda, facing out at the booming night, lit up in flashes of lightning. She was jerking back and forth with unreal speed. Her face contorted in grimaces and her body spasmed violently. She clawed at the air and moaned. Dark-clothed, she appeared as a black hole about to swallow itself, or through which something terrible was struggling to be born – an uncanny form raging to break through to our world.

On the second night smoking DMT with Matt in Rosslare Harbour, when I worked up the courage for a breakthrough dose, this is what happened: I encountered a being so beyond my capacity to comprehend it, so dwarfing of my categories of thought and belief, that it may as well have been a god. Scepticism was no longer possible: I was flung into the presence of something whose very existence was an affront to all that my society believed in, all it didn't believe in. There was no message, no communication in the encounter beyond that which can be summed up in a single word: *Behold*. Intuitively I knew I was in a realm absolutely without morality, beyond good and evil, where my values, beliefs and concerns were terrifyingly insignificant. The encounter left me dumbfounded, aghast, and haunted by questions I suspected would never yield adequate answers.

It is an admission of failure when a writer calls something indescribable, yet there are limits to what can be performed by language, and categories of experience that can only be gestured towards, never conveyed in words. Describing psychedelic experiences to those who have never had them is as futile as describing music to someone who was born deaf. This is what makes DMT in particular so maddening: the inherent frustration of being unable to talk about it. Just as the encounter is ineffable, the implications of the experience can only be met with scepticism if one voices them in public, so fantastically at odds are they with the orthodox models by which we conceive of reality. I consider myself a sceptical person, allergic to deluded and wishful thinking, the saccharine credulities of the New Age and the self-serving beliefs of religion. Nevertheless, after smoking DMT, I found myself giving serious consideration to the most outré speculations: for instance, that the drug allows us to perceive dark matter or parallel universes; that it is a technology, perhaps put on earth by extraterrestrial or interdimensional beings, or sent from the future, that causes hidden realms to become visible; that what we call reality is merely one small pocket of a much vaster, teeming multiverse that we will continue to inhabit after physical death. In the wake of my experiences, I became newly interested in the cosmologies of Buddhism and other ancient belief systems, for the first time wondering if such multidimensional universes and their inhabitants were not metaphorical supplements to the core philosophies but attempts at literal truth. I wondered if yogis and Buddhist monks in states of deep meditation perhaps flooded their brains with a superabundance of DMT, allowing them to perceive the astonishing realms glimpsed by smokers of the drug.

From the perspective of the scientific, materialist paradigm that has prevailed in the Western world for three hundred years, no such phenomena are possible. All that can happen through the use of psychedelic drugs, we are told, is agitations of brain chemistry, the production of mere hallucinations. If one remains within that paradigm, claims about the ontological implications of DMT are hokum. However, in a sort of gnostic double bind, it is extremely difficult to maintain faith in the validity of that paradigm after peering behind the veil. The DMT rush is a genuinely gnostic experience: it can only be known directly, and when known directly it cannot be denied. Lived experience indicates that the drug is not psychedelic, not 'mind-manifesting' at all: it opens on to an abyssal and disturbing beyond.

Certainly, the drug's appalling and inexplicable nature encourages obsession. After taking it, I found myself thinking about little else for weeks afterwards; trying to steer every conversation towards DMT; mentioning it in every email I sent; feeling exasperated with anyone who was incurious. I sent long emails to writers and artists I admired, urging them to try the drug; I fought the temptation to flood social media with similarly evangelical appeals. It was the same for Matt and other friends of mine. A group of us would text and email each other late into the night, sharing theories, speculations and experiences, linking to articles or YouTube videos, quoting books on DMT, comparing Buddhist mandalas and hieroglyphic imagery. We set up an email forum to share this stuff. It began to feel like the inauguration of a cult.

On a Friday afternoon towards the end of May, I met Matt and our friends Fran and Paul on a cafe terrace on South William Street. Dublin was lit up with bare arms, bright dresses, the colour and Eros of imminent summer. We took a LUAS to Stoneybatter and walked up Parkgate Street, into Phoenix Park.

Paul would not be smoking DMT, but he wanted to show us the megalithic tomb nestled away in a corner of the park. Paul was a long-term mental-health patient who resided in St Mary's Hospital on the park's inner fringe. He had been diagnosed with paranoid psychosis two decades earlier, initiating a total exclusion from the official world of jobs, relationships, property and communal engagement. For all his life he had heard voices, seen spirits and entities, roamed invisible landscapes. In other cultures he would have been a shaman, living with dignity and experimental curiosity on the edge of a society that respected him; here in the Irish twenty-first century he was a nobody – medicated, pitied and marginalised, his lived truth explained away as developmental pathology and aberrant brain function. His life was a case study in hellish unhappiness. Once he had figuratively described his status in the universe: he was, he told me, the worst knacker's one-eyed donkey. He wandered in the Phoenix Park most days, drinking cans and smoking the odd joint, and spent his mornings painting. Fran, his oldest friend, had recently developed a website to display and sell the work. A few days earlier, Paul had sent me a text:

Hi RoB fran was tellin me aBout yeR dmt BReak thRU i have Books Coming out my eaRs on this occult stuff and a lot to say too plus some pRaCiCal adviCe on the pitfalls of having a mystic expeRienCe so you

dont end up like me mistakes Cost a lot at this point so
Be CaReful fuCk nietzsChe

As we descended into a glen, Fran pointed towards a copse through which the sun was dancing: it was the park's herd of deer, migrating slowly to the forested areas.

'Knockmaroon, the tomb place is called,' said Paul as we walked on. He was interested in our experiences on DMT and reckoned it would be a good spot at which to smoke it. He told us that the tomb dated back to some three thousand years BC, and suggested that it was an 'energy point'. I liked the sound of it, but really I was happy just to be back in the Phoenix Park, in the afternoon sunshine, with the sounds of the city in the distance.

The tomb was a thick, raised slab of rock, fringed by a low fence, unseen from the footpaths that wound through the hills in that part of the park. Before turning off my phone, I opened a news app and saw that an airliner had just gone down over the Mediterranean, killing everyone on board.

'I'm getting that dread,' I said.

'It's normal,' said Matt.

'It's bad,' I said. 'I always imagine the worst.'

'Breathe,' he said.

'There are things in my mind I probably shouldn't see.'

'It's not about your mind.'

We sat down in a sunlit clearing, strewing our briefcases and bags around us. Fran had got off early from his 'soul-destroying' job maintaining surveillance systems, and was relaxed and eager. He had smoked DMT for the first time a week earlier with Matt: the experience, he said, had been 'metaphysically shocking'. He wanted to try it again and not be so dazzled this time, so he could observe more. After his first experience he had texted me:

> *My impression: 100% there is categorically another consciousness present AND they have better computers than we do.*

None of us would bother with lower doses this time: 70 mg was what Matt measured out on the DIGI scales. Fran went first. We sat in silence as he closed his eyes and commenced his trip. Afterwards, he shook his head. 'Wow,' he kept saying. He laughed, frowned, laughed again. He spoke about bodhisattvas, negative space, Quetzalcóatl, tokamak machines, quantum computing, the dance of Shiva, the gods of ancient Egypt, game theory, Heidegger's nightmares, the eternal return, CERN and the God particle, war machines, the *Red Book* that Carl Jung composed in secret, glossolalia, strange loops and tangled hierarchies, the Rig Veda, the rose and the fire.

He said, 'Tell me this: what the hell would Richard Dawkins say if he smoked that?'

Matt laughed.

'Seriously,' said Fran.

'You can still be an atheist up to forty milligrams,' Matt said.

'The world in its nakedness is vast, vivid and shocking,' said Paul.

Matt went next. Upon smoking the DMT, he was taken yet again to what he now called 'the Machine' – a realm of code, unfathomable technology, and busy, whirring worker entities who, he had come to believe, were exerting themselves in the construction of reality – our reality and perhaps many others too. The world we inhabited was a kind of simulation, Matt concluded. He speculated that when we died we would go straight there, to the Machine, and learn what happened next. At one point he mentioned being shown the 'source code'.

'This world seems to be only some sort of minor realm,' he said. 'Like a suburb. The Kilnamanagh of the megaverse.'

'People are still bleeding, though,' said Paul. 'There's still responsibility.'

'That doesn't mean the game's not rigged.'

'It makes it more sinister,' said Fran.

Paul said, 'Each of us is guilty before the others, and I more so than the rest of them.'

Matt thought for a moment. He said, 'There's no comfort in all this. It was reassuring when I still believed that this material world was all there is, and we're annihilated at death. There was an ease in thinking nothing matters, the whole Western nihilism rap. Which is the fucking orthodoxy, the basic view, even if they dress it up as humanist progressivism. It's so much scarier to think that *everything* matters, every little thing is of the utmost consequence. That's the shocker. Now there's, yeah, responsibility, and no escape.'

All was quiet in the park. It was my turn. I am a fearful person. I imagine the worst, anticipate abysmal horrors and fates worse than death. DMT was the most bizarre phenomenon I had confronted in my life, eerier than the life forms lurking in the deepest ocean trenches, weirder than the recesses of space or the unconscious mind. I wanted everyone to try it, and then have a global conversation, the human race applying its brightest minds to the mystery. Everything would change, it seemed to me then: the science books would demand drastic revisions; even the religions would appear simplistic and naive in the cosmologies they posited. It wasn't that Nietzsche, Sartre and Descartes had been wrong about everything: they'd simply lacked the technology we had now. I took a deep breath. Matt tapped the pale-orange powder into the pipe bowl. He held the lighter as I drew on the translucent pipe and watched the bowl clouding up, then took all the smoke into my lungs, tasting plastic. Matt withdrew and I lay back on the ground. The afternoon sun was high above, the sky clear and bright. When I couldn't hold it any longer I let the smoke plume from my nostrils, out into the blue. I recalled what a white-haired San Diego hippy had told me once in Dharamsala – unless you're worried you've taken too much, you haven't taken enough. There was no point being afraid – it was too late. My palms dampened and my heart rate accelerated. The blue sky above me began to dissolve, and as it filled with something ancient and nameless the quickening came on – a sense of imminent and awesome power. I knew it was going to be overwhelming like never before. And then I began to be pulled out past it all, into the unfathomable, with the sense, euphoric and terrifying, that everything was possible again.

Acknowledgements

I am grateful to everyone who helped or supported me in writing this book, not least my editor Alexa von Hirschberg for her faith, passion and encouragement, and Alexandra Pringle, Marigold Atkey, Callie Garnett and all the team at Bloomsbury. Thank you to my agent Sam Copeland, and to Silvia Crompton for copyediting. Thank you to Brendan Barrington for consistently superb editorial input when parts of the book were published in *The Dublin Review*. *Herzlichen Dank* to Róisín Kiberd for friendship, love, mutation and support, along with continuous intellectual and comedic stimulation. Special thanks to Simon Kelly, Andy West and Phil Kelly for generously reading and commenting on the book as I wrote it, often chapter by chapter. Thank you to Alice Zeniter for advocacy of my work, even before I'd ever published anything. Thank you as ever to my parents, Jimmy and Antoinette. For inspiration and support of various kinds, thank you to Katie Standen, John Holten, Liam Cagney, Geoff Dyer, Ángela Rivera Izquierdo, Mike McCormack,

Simon Brennan, Joanna Walsh, Dave Banim, Arnold Thomas Fanning, Cormac O'Síocháin, Lisa McInerney, Teddy Wayne, Alex Donald, and Joseph O'Connor. I am grateful to the Arts Council of Ireland for their generous financial assistance, and to Sinéad Mac Aodha, Oona Frawley, Literature Ireland, and everyone who was involved in the residencies I availed of while writing the book: at the University of Maynooth; the Museum of Contemporary Art in Zagreb; the Centre Culturel Irlandais and Les Récollets in Paris; and the Literarische Colloquium Berlin.

Note on the Author

Rob Doyle was born in Dublin. His first novel, *Here Are the Young Men*, was published in 2014. It was chosen as a book of the year by the *Sunday Times, Irish Times* and *Independent*, and was among *Hot Press* magazine's '20 Greatest Irish Novels 1916–2016'. Doyle has adapted it for film with director Eoin Macken. Doyle's collection of short stories, *This is the Ritual*, was published by Bloomsbury in 2016. Doyle is the editor of the anthology *The Other Irish Tradition* (Dalkey Archive Press), and *In This Skull Hotel Where I Never Sleep* (Broken Dimanche Press). His writing has appeared in the *Guardian, Vice, TLS, Dublin Review*, and many other publications, and he writes a weekly books column for the *Irish Times*. He lives in Berlin.

robdoyle.net
@RobDoyle1

Note on the Type

The text of this book is set Adobe Garamond. It is one of several versions of Garamond based on the designs of Claude Garamond. It is thought that Garamond based his font on Bembo, cut in 1495 by Francesco Griffo in collaboration with the Italian printer Aldus Manutius. Garamond types were first used in books printed in Paris around 1532. Many of the present-day versions of this type are based on the *Typi Academiae* of Jean Jannon cut in Sedan in 1615.

Claude Garamond was born in Paris in 1480. He learned how to cut type from his father and by the age of fifteen he was able to fashion steel punches the size of a pica with great precision. At the age of sixty he was commissioned by King Francis I to design a Greek alphabet, and for this he was given the honourable title of royal type founder. He died in 1561.